"Claudia Whitsitt spins a suspense-filled nail biter that won't let go. Readers will hunger for the next in the series. Bravo, Claudia!"

~ Michael Thompkins
Author of *Gun Play*

"Disaster magnet Samantha Stitsill returns in INTERNAL ISSUES, author Claudia Whitsitt's 3rd offering in The Samantha Series. As she copes with one crisis too many, Samantha races against the clock to protect those she loves from a lethal adversary. A 5-star achievement."

~ Laura Taylor
Author, Romantic Times and MAGGIE Award Winner

D1569043

BOOKS BY CLAUDIA WHITSITT

Blue Jay Media
IDENTITY ISSUES
INTIMACY ISSUES
INTERNAL ISSUES

Echelon Press
THE WRONG GUY

INTERNAL ISSUES

Claudia Whitsitt

A SAMANTHA SERIES NOVEL BY

CLAUDIA WHITSITT

PLEASE VISIT MS. WHITSITT AT:

Website: www.ClaudiaWhitsitt.com
Facebook: www.facebook.com/claudia.whitsitt
Twitter: twitter.com/claudiawhitsitt

ACKNOWLEDGEMENTS

It's impossible to express my deep appreciation for the love, support, and expertise of so many. To Laura Taylor, my expert editor and dear friend, thank you. To Don Whitsitt, my husband, listener extraordinaire, and questioning developmental critic, a big sloppy kiss. To Lori LaBoe, my treasured BFF and biggest cheerleader, I owe you big time!

To all the rest… the Southern California Writers Conference and all of my dear friends from my writing community, including but certainly not limited to Patty Hoffman, Kathy York, Barb Stark-Nemon, Robert Yehling, Jean Jenkins, Jennifer Silva Redmond, and Jeremy Lee James, thanks for letting me bend your ear and standing by me through thick and thin.

This book is dedicated to my parents, Pat and Larry Teal, for instilling in me the idea that I could reach the stars if I just stretched my arms high enough!

CHAPTER ONE

THE ANSWERING MACHINE nagged at me for two days. Everyone I needed to speak with could reach me through my cell. At this juncture of my life, it would be best if the rest of the world faded away. *Tug, tug, tug.* I poised to press delete, but I didn't. I pressed play.

"Sam... it's Lisa Macchione. I need your help. Call me, please."

Damn it.

But I was done! Done with danger. Done with mystery. Done with business not my own. D.O.N.E.

Her voice sounded, what, anxious? No, more than that. Desperate. *Shit.* Lisa was more than the mother of a former student; she was a friend. Her message challenged my newly adopted "stay-out-of-it mantra". Good Sam repeated: *I will not call her back. I will not call her back. I will not...* Bad Sam argued: *She's a good friend. I don't ignore friends. Something's wrong. I can help.*

As I leaned down to press redial, I heard the tires of McGrath's Jeep hum on the driveway. I peeked through the slats of the blinds and watched him step out of the car. The mere sight of him caused my heartbeat to quicken, even after two tumultuous months fending off my dead husband's assassin. The bag at his side made me smile. He intended to stay the night. My pulse raced into overdrive.

Was it his square shoulders, befitting of a cop? His height and purposeful stride? Or his equipment and skills I knew so well?

I rushed back to the phone and hit redial, needing to tie up this loose end before my delicious evening began. I left Lisa a quick and succinct message, "I'm here for you. Whatever you need, just let me know." In a flash, I replaced the receiver, ran to greet McGrath with a warm smile, and pulled him inside. He placed his hands on my waist and drew me close, pressing his body to mine. I backed away after a tender and tempting kiss and refined my assessment. It was his dimple-bracketed smile and the twinkle in his eyes that did me in.

He squeezed my shoulder. "I'll take my bag upstairs."

"Meet you on the porch in ten?"

"Nine," he said, and placed a bottle of wine in my hands.

Six minutes later I stepped outside with a tray. (I have this thing about being early). It was our last night alone together before my five kids returned from their summer at the lake with Grandpa Ed. We toasted to our health and incredible luck as I sat down beside him.

Worry lines furrowed his brow. "How are you?"

"I'm fine." *I'm lying.*

He laughed his deep, hearty, you're-full-of-shit laugh. "We travel 6,500 miles to Japan, meet your husband's possible mistress, confront his killer, narrowly escape death, and you're fine…" He shifted in his chair. "I'm still a wreck."

I sighed and narrowed my eyes. "I have no choice. The kids are coming home. I have most of the house cleaned: washed floors, dusted, finished five loads of laundry. But I still have to put fresh sheets on the beds, mow the lawn—it's autopilot time and I'd appreciate it if you didn't disrupt my trusted coping mechanism—there's hardly a minute to fall apart."

"What are you feeling?"

My stomach flipped and churned. There was no way I

would allow myself to go there. "Is this part of the in-service you attended today? Sensitivity training?"

A troubled look shrouded him. "Skipped training today. New case."

Perfect. I was off the hook! "Already?"

He sipped his wine and nodded. "Missing person case. It's sticky."

"Missing person? Why are you involved? I thought you were working on a hush-hush fraud and corruption case."

McGrath fell into cop mode and explained. "Once the Feds took over that case, I was out of it. That's how it goes; when they come in, all goes quiet. Now, I'm back in. The cases actually cross paths. A guy claims he woke up to find his wife vanished overnight. She took nothing with her... not her purse, not her cell phone, not her car... not her two daughters. I've only had the chance to interview three of her friends, but their accounts indicate she would never have left her girls behind. Plus, the husband waited twenty-four hours to call."

"Isn't that the requirement?"

"Family members never follow that rule. They're too frantic to wait."

Visions of another *Dateline* episode danced in my head: *Tragedy Strikes A Quaint Midwestern Town.* "You think there's more to it."

"It's still early, but yes, my instinct tells me something is very wrong."

I waited.

"This couple separated for two months, then reconciled two weeks ago. During the separation, the woman and kids stayed with her sister— "

"Why would she keep the kids with her during their separation, yet leave them behind when she decided to walk away for good?" I paused to reflect. "Did she leave a note?"

McGrath scratched his head and chuckled. "Like what? 'Sick of your sorry ass. See you later?'"

"It's what *my* goodbye note would have said."

"The husband's well-connected. His brother is the mayor, Vincent Macchione. Have you turned on the television since we've been back?"

I shook my head.

"He's about to be indicted on charges of corruption, fraud, tax evasion... the grand jury found a preponderance of evidence... the dots and dashes are in all the right places."

My heart arrested. "Wait. Who's missing?"

"Tony Macchione's wife, Lisa."

"Oh my God, no!"

"Sam, you're pale as paste. What is it?"

I swallowed over the knot in my throat. "She called me... maybe two days ago. After you dropped me off from the airport, I believe I checked the answering machine. I can't recall, but I don't think there were any messages. I was exhausted, and it's all pretty fuzzy with the jet lag, but I went straight to the shower and then to bed. She must have called when I was in the shower, because I noticed the light blinking the next morning. But I needed a time out; I couldn't face talking to anyone, so I ignored it." I shivered. "Why didn't I listen to her message? She must have called right before she disappeared. Think about the timing. I returned her call as you pulled in, but she didn't pick up. I left her a message. If something's happened to her, I'll never forgive myself."

McGrath gripped my arm. "Did I just hear you right?"

Tears welled in my eyes. "Yes. Lisa Macchione. My friend."

McGrath's voice softened. "How is she your friend?"

"From work."

"I don't recall you mentioning her."

I swallowed hard. "We've been busy. There hasn't been time to talk about work."

He stroked my hand. "Relax. It's not an accusation. I'm just looking for information."

I inhaled and nodded. "Ten years ago, I was an Early Intervention specialist." My airway constricted, and I searched McGrath's face for encouragement. *She couldn't be...*

He looked confused. "What does that mean?"

I closed my eyes and exhaled in mild frustration. *Had I not told him about my career?* "It's a teaching position, but working with families of children from birth to age three who were born with an impairment. I visited their homes twice each week for an hour, providing support and therapies to use with their children. Adrianna, the Macchione's daughter, was born with aniridia."

"Their daughter was born with a disability."

"I'll spare you the gory details, but yes, she was born with a degenerative condition, limited vision that leads to eventual blindness. This little girl was a whippersnapper, though, and it didn't slow her down, not one little bit."

"And you were in their home for three years?"

"They were my first case when I returned from maternity leave after Lizzie's birth. Monday and Wednesday mornings."

McGrath's cop mode kicked in. "Tell me about the parents."

"Tony's a lot like his brother, the mayor—an ass. He's a pompous control freak who treats women as if they're his personal servants. He thinks he..."

"He's not one of your favorites."

I rolled my eyes.

"Give me an example."

"He refused to believe Adrianna would lose her vision. It's normal for parents to experience denial, even blatant refusal, but at the end of my three years with a family, it was quite unusual for them not to have come to some kind of acceptance or at least acknowledgement of the facts. Adrianna's impairment made her sensitive to light, yet he wouldn't allow her to wear sunglasses as an infant, or anything else that would draw attention to her.

"He claimed we would be giving in if we read her large print books, or introduced any beginning Braille activities..."

"And Lisa?"

"Tenacious. Realistic. A real go-getter. She implemented every suggestion I made and worked tirelessly with Adrianna. That little girl wouldn't be where she is today without her mother."

"And you," McGrath said.

"Promise me you'll find her."

He rubbed my knee. "That's the plan."

My head spun. As hard as I tried, I couldn't rid myself of the sinking feeling that Lisa's life was in danger. The thought of her...

McGrath pulled his pad from his pocket and began to take notes. "How did Lisa manage her husband's resistance?"

"She fumed and waited until he was out of the house to work with Adrianna on vision-related exercises. Funny thing about it, Adrianna's sight remained stable until this spring. A miracle, really. She has very little vision now... light perception, but that's about it." I forced my next breath.

McGrath peered at me, trying to suck information from me without putting me through the agony of reliving it, kind of like a human straw. "You *are* close to them."

I shivered in spite of the August heat. "Very."

"What else can you tell me?"

"Tony treated me as if I were the help. Ordered me around, barely said hello; he was rude. He treated Lisa the same way, but she juggled him. Put out the sparks before they caught fire. She talked to me about him, but with a great deal of hesitation. She seemed conflicted when she complained about him, like it was against the rules to voice her frustration. Maybe it was how she was raised, I don't know. I couldn't have been married to him for three minutes." I paused for a long moment. "We have to do something. Lisa. Those poor girls."

What a nightmare!

McGrath met my eyes. "At the risk of ordering you around like your friend, Tony, the controlling asshole, I'm going to ask you to listen to me. You are NOT to become involved with this case. Under any circumstances. Do you understand? You've been through hell these past two years. Be a mom and teacher. Get your life back."

I frowned. "Trust me, I have no desire to get involved, but she is my friend, and it's going to be beyond difficult to sit back and watch the news. Plus, I'm fine. Why do you think I need taking care of? I'm not some fractured individual... just because I lost my dog and my husband... just because I stared death in the freaking face..."

Suddenly, I remembered something: the mail. I sprung from my chair and darted into the house. Where had I piled it? The counter. I leafed through the envelopes, found the invitation and read it this time, rather than scan it like I had yesterday.

Annual Alumni Reunion Picnic
for former students of the Teach Our Tots Early Program
August 23, 2013
12-4PM
Lexington Park Pavilion
(bring a dish to pass)
Beverages and paper supplies will be provided

Tomorrow. Thank God I hadn't missed it.

I looked up. McGrath, who had followed me inside, wore a puzzled yet suspicious expression. "What are you doing?"

I averted my eyes. "Nothing. Just checking on an appointment." I wouldn't get involved. I'd just check on Adrianna and make sure she was okay. Not that she would be there... shit, her mother was missing. I would check in with her teachers. Just put out my sticky fingers and gather information.

He grimaced. "You forget that I'm a detective."

"I certainly try."

McGrath inserted himself at my side, his eyes boring into the paper I clutched in my hands.

This required quick thinking. I waved the invitation like it was nothing. "There's a picnic tomorrow. I promised I'd go."

He persisted. "You are *not* getting involved."

McGrath was not pretty when disgusted.

"It's work related." I blew him off with a shrug. "There is no danger here. None. We eradicated all possibilities of threats to my life in Japan."

McGrath's jaw clenched. "You go ahead and live in that cloud. You are the single-most headstrong woman I have ever met. You insist on screwing up your life."

An opportunity for diversion. I smiled sweetly. "Screwing up?" I raised my eyebrows and stepped a little closer. "I invite you to screw up my life."

"You are not going to distract me with your feminine wiles."

I pushed him into a chair, slid onto his lap, ran my hand along his thigh, and dipped my tongue into his mouth. McGrath moaned and wrapped his arms around my waist.

I disentangled myself, laced my fingers through his, and led him up the stairs.

"You are *NOT* getting involved," he repeated as I undid his belt and unleashed it from his waistband. "Promise me, or I swear on my mother's grave, I'll leave... You know what? No sex. Not until you promise."

I ran my pinkie along the cleft of his dimple. "You can't be serious."

"Do you have any idea what you're about to stumble into? The Macchione brothers are going down. Both of them. Not just the mayor. Tony, too. They are being charged on about five hundred seventy-four counts."

"Five hundred seventy-four? Surely, you're exaggerating." *Make it fun, Sam. Keep it light.*

Fire blazed in his eyes. "I'm making a point." He fastened his pants and weaved his belt through the loops. "Listen to me. These guys are mob. Italian mob. The real deal. Not like on TV. They kill people. Remember Hoffa? Almost forty years now... and still no body. We can't prove it, but make no mistake, the family did Jimmy. They're cold-blooded killers.

"We've been working on this with the Feds for ten years. It's taken forever for the indictment to come down because we have to make sure the case is locked up tight. Lisa's disappearance is a separate police matter, not your concern. You go looking for trouble, Sam, you're going to find it."

He lifted his cell phone, pocketed his change, and turned away.

"McGrath, you can't be serious. You're leaving? We only have tonight. The kids are due home by dinnertime tomorrow! C'mon."

He turned to me, his face carved with anger. I looked closer. Concern, too. "No slack. No compromise. This is my job. I'm the cop. This isn't your husband, and we're not in Japan. Do you not remember the terror we faced?" His eyes misted with tears. "Well, I do, and thought of losing you... this is deadly business. Once you've decided to stay out of it, give me a call. Until then, I won't stand witness to your death wish. I love you too much to let you do this just because you think you should. I understand you have a strong stomach. I do too, but not for this. And I'm taking the answering machine with me. It's evidence."

I stood frozen. Shocked. "McGrath!"

Instead of answering me, he slammed the door.

CHAPTER TWO

SHIT. DID MCGRATH not understand? Lisa was my *friend.* I don't let friends go missing and fall asleep at night and dream sweet dreams. I take action. Safe and controlled action like attending the picnic, talking to Adrianna's teachers, and gathering information on Lisa's life over the summer. This was not just McGrath's problem, it was mine, too. We could be working together on this. I could aid in the investigation *and* remain safe.

Something all too familiar about this scenario played in my head. Disturbing. Wasn't this what I told myself when I became involved with Jon's impostor and his wife, Rosita Stitsill, and was nearly killed on two separate occasions? *Back away, Sam.*

A door lock beeped in the driveway. Hallelujah, McGrath had come to his senses. If I hurried, I could throw on a teddy and meet him at the door. *Did I own a teddy?* The doorbell rang before I reached my closet, so I tucked in my shirt and ran downstairs, my pulse rate quickening.

I threw open the door, prepared to beg forgiveness and promise to stay out of the Macchione mess so McGrath could do his job.

It wasn't him.

"Jack? What are you doing here?"

"Good to see you, too, Stitsill. Are you gonna invite me

in, or just leave me standing on the stoop like a door-to-door salesman?"

I gestured for him to come inside. "Sorry, surprised to see you is all. I thought you were someone else. Can I pour you a glass of wine? I was just going to have a glass myself."

Jack scowled. "You know I don't drink wine. By the way, your wine is sitting on the porch along with a second full glass. I guess you *were* expecting someone else."

I grabbed a beer from the fridge and handed it to him, pressed my palm to my forehead, and regretted mucking up the evening with McGrath. "We might as well sit on the porch; I'll drink the wine if the gnats haven't partied in my glass."

Jack slapped me on the back as we headed outside. After we sat down, he turned to face me. "How was Japan?"

I inhaled a deep breath and let it out very slowly. "It was fine."

"I hate it when you lie to me and think I'm gonna swallow it."

"Dammit, Jack, I hate it that you know me so well."

"It's what makes us such great teaching partners. C'mon, let me have it."

I paused to take inventory. He looked better than ever, his robin's egg blues alight with humor, tanned from a steady diet of golf and baseball, and toned from hours in the gym. No wonder all the girls adored him. Not only was he handsome, but he also had this way about him, almost as if truth serum flowed from his eyes to my heart. I told him my innermost secrets; things I hardly admitted to myself spilled out when I was in his company. It's one of the reasons I could never be involved with him. He read me like the alphabet.

"We killed the guy."

Jack's head fell and he palmed his face. "You killed someone else?"

"No, I didn't do it. McGrath did. He shot Stitsill or Drummond or whoever he called himself... Jon's impostor.

It's a helluva long story, but the trailer would read something like this: 'Woman faces husband's killer in a remote Japanese village. Will her detective boyfriend rescue her at the last minute?'"

"But Stitsill was already dead," Jack said. "You killed him on your basement steps. What are you talking about?"

"Turns out he wasn't dead. He infiltrated the U.S. Embassy in Japan, and positioned himself in the perfect spot to come after me when I sought information about Jon's death. I don't know who I shot on my basement stairs, but it wasn't him. The good news is, he's gone now and won't ever come back."

"Are you sure this time?"

"Oh, yeah."

"This is way better than another *As the Stitsill's Turns* episode. It's more like..."

I nodded. "*Dateline*. I know."

Jack chugged a healthy sip of beer. "Are you sure you're safe? You scare the shit out of me. You dive into these messes and land on your feet like a cat with nine lives, but you're ticking those lives away. How many do you have left?"

"I know, I know. McGrath said the same thing to me tonight. He's a tad frustrated with me right now."

Jack glanced at McGrath's unattended glass and nodded, then scrubbed his face with his hand, and shook his head. "Good Lord, Sam. I can't blame the guy. What are you into now?"

"Nothing."

"Stop lying to me, and tell me what's going on."

I locked eyes with him and the serum worked its magic. "Ten years back, I had a student in the Early Intervention program."

Jack sighed. "Go on."

"Her mother is missing and McGrath's been assigned to the case."

"Shit. The Macchione woman. It's all over the news."

Jack shook his head and sighed. "Of course you know her. You're lucky that way. Stay out of it. Those guys are dangerous!"

"That's my intention, but there's this picnic tomorrow, and I thought I'd attend... and chat with people. You never know, I may discover something useful."

Jack surveyed the table. "Is this why McGrath left so abruptly?"

"He didn't even listen to me... I need a cigarette."

He rolled his eyes. "We've been through this before. You don't smoke."

"I know, but if I did, this would be a good time."

"Good Lord, woman."

"I want him to understand that Lisa is my friend, and I don't sit home and knit socks when a good friend of mine has disappeared. I do something."

"Here's a thought," Jack said. "The guy loves you and cares about your well-being. I know you're unfamiliar with a significant other who is home full-time and *connected*, but this is how they treat their loved ones. They're honest when their partner is about to do something *STUPID*. They share their worry and concern in hope they serve as the voice of reason."

"But he said he wouldn't have anything to do with me unless I dropped the idea of getting involved. How am I a good friend to Lisa if I abandon her when she needs me most?"

Jack shook his head and scoffed at me. "You're a maniac. This is a police matter. McGrath's a good cop. Let him do his job and offer him support. Cook him a nice dinner, make him smile at night, pump him up. We need that, you know? A little pat on the back now and then."

"Right. That totally fits my personality. I'll turn into a *hausfrau* whose goal is to keep her man happy."

Jack sighed and set his empty beer bottle on the table. "That didn't come out quite right, but you know what I mean."

I sank back in my rocker and sipped my wine. A gentle breeze blew through the leaves and a squirrel skittered up the tall oak. Another peaceful night on the porch should calm me, but it did nothing to soothe my angst. Instead, my blood pressure rose as I remembered...

How could McGrath treat me like Donna Reed? It chewed at my gut. How simple for him to tell me to stay home, take care of my kids, teach school, correct papers. On the heels of seeing the barrel of a gun on my nose. I'd faced down death twice. While I didn't want to risk my life again, my past made me stronger: Jon's murder, Rex's death, facing Jon's possible mistress...

"Oh yeah, I met the woman who pretended to be Jon's mistress, too. And she has a baby. Not Jon's, but I didn't know that until the faux Stitsill pointed a gun at me and talked about how he had set it all up to mess with my brain. Great guy."

"Take a very deep breath, Sam. Please, I'm begging you. I've never seen you like this. You're derailing and you can't even see it. You're acting like one of our crazy ass students who has lost the ability for rational thought. Do you get some kind of sick adrenalin high from putting your life in danger? You're scaring me. No one can deal with this kind of real-life drama and be fine. The past two years will catch up with you when you least suspect it, and I'll be visiting you in a padded room for 30 minutes every other Wednesday."

I leaned back and sighed. Jack was right. McGrath was right. I needed a normal life. It would serve me well to stay out of other people's drama. This time, when I inhaled a measured breath and let it out slowly, my pulse returned to normal, and a welcome calm enveloped me. "Thanks, Jack. You're a good friend."

"I try." He patted my knee. "Normal isn't so bad, really. My life has purpose without facing demons. Playing golf every day suits me just fine. Think about it, you could teach the kids to play golf, sign up for a league yourself. You love to be outdoors. Golf, drink a cold one, then grill outside and have dinner with the kids. Play games with them. How simple a life it would be. Be honest: it has appeal, doesn't it?"

I tried on his idea. It felt like a trophy wife life, and I wasn't married to a millionaire. I was a widow with five kids and a full-time job teaching special education. But he had a point; I could envision spending more time with my kids during the summer. Heck, I could stay up north with them, swim the lake for an hour each day, fish for perch, fry them up in a pan. Now I felt like that '80s perfume commercial. Still... it could work.

Jack's voice broke my thoughts. "You should talk Di into golf. She'd love the break from the kids. You know she was awarded custody of the Stitsill boys this summer, right? I think the adoption process will be finalized a year from now."

"I haven't had time to call her yet, but I knew it was in the works. How's it going?"

Jack laughed. "You know Di. She had to adopt them because she related to their loss, but in the meantime she's on the verge of a nervous breakdown, barely dealing. Joey's doing well, but Emilio is suspicious of her even though she was his teacher."

"You can't blame him, considering his history. He's lost his mom and step-dad, and never knew his biological father. His foster mother died, and his foster dad is an alcoholic. More than a thirteen-year-old should have to handle. Chris will win him over with the man cave he created for them and his love of sports. It will all work out.

"Kind of ironic, isn't it? Stitsill killed his wife, Rosie, my dog, and my husband, and my best girlfriend is adopting Rosie's kids."

Another thought popped into my head. What about the money their mother had me put into trust for them? Would Di and Chris have access to the funds to assist in raising them? *Stay out of it, Sam.*

Jack changed the subject. "Class lists will be in the office tomorrow."

I groaned. "It's not that I'm unhappy to go back to school, it's just coming up way too soon."

Jack rested a basketball-sized palm on my back. "We can meet to send out parent letters on Monday."

I nodded, listening to him, but distracted by my other musings. "This is going to be a lot harder than I anticipated."

"What's that?"

"Staying out of other people's business."

CHAPTER THREE

I NOTICED DEEP grooves accentuating the dark circles under my eyes. Rough night. Hell, rough couple of years. I eased into a pair of khaki Capri's and a sleeveless top, then tucked my hair into a ponytail. My constant companions, the voices in my head, were arguing again.

Good Sam: *Stay home and mind your own business.*

Bad Sam: *She's your friend. You can't back out on Lisa at a time like this.*

Bad Sam won. Teaching provided me with life-giving medication, and I needed to hug those little people who loved me so unconditionally. I stopped at the store and purchased two packages of cookies, then drove to the park. I slid into a spot at the edge of the lot, for ease of early access should I come to my senses. A rustic pavilion blocked the noonday sun and held two dozen picnic tables; it was lunchtime. About fifty students lined the tables, and a group of parents stood behind the food stand, chatting and munching on snacks. I spotted a group of former students seated at a nearby picnic table.

To my surprise, Adrianna stood at the far end of the table; her delicate chocolate curls, trademark ball cap, and pink sunglasses gave her away. My heartbeat zipped as I exited the car, cookies in hand, and trotted over to the gathering while repeating Good Sam's mantra: *Just say hello, gather a few facts, then step away.*

Bad Sam knew better.

Ten-year old Tonya, self-proclaimed leader of the pack, stepped towards me, her crutches carving a path in the sand. "I hoped you would come! We were just talking about you."

"Oh boy, that can't be good! Let's talk about something exciting instead. How's summer?"

As they chattered, I half-listened, too focused on Adrianna to pay full attention. I made my way down the line of students on the bench, squeezing their shoulders in greeting. When I reached Adrianna, I laid my hand on her arm. She wrapped her arms around me and gripped me tight. I'd been her life-preserver before; it felt natural. If I did nothing more than offer her support, then that would be enough.

She clung to me. "I always recognize you by your perfume."

"It's my moniker," I joked.

"Last week, Mom played the DVD of you and me when I was little. She loves to watch that."

"I bet you love hearing your sweet little voice, too."

"I was cute." Adrianna became thoughtful. "My mom loves you."

"I love her too. She didn't come today?" *Evil, but I needed a clue if I was going to help, even if just to hand that clue to McGrath.*

Adrianna turned and walked a few feet away, as if she didn't want her classmates to overhear her. Her anxiety was palpable. I eased my arm around her shoulder and walked her even further from the crowd. "What's wrong, sweetie?"

A single tear slipped down her cheek. "She left without saying goodbye. She's never done that before."

"Your mom told me that you stayed with your Aunt Lori this summer. How was that?"

"Okay. Just mom and dad were fighting a lot."

"When you were at Aunt Lori's?" *If I ask the questions, the kids answer them.*

"Mom stayed in the bedroom next to mine. I heard her on the phone at night when I tried to fall asleep. I could tell she was crying."

"You've always been an adept eavesdropper."

"That's how I see." She giggled and added, "I get in trouble for that."

"I know it's tough when your parents aren't getting along, but since you moved back home, aren't things better?"

"I guess, but I can tell mom is still sad."

I hesitated. I could proceed with caution and ask a few more questions, but I wanted Adrianna to feel as if she could confide in me. Pumping her for information would do just the opposite. I decided to let her take the lead. We reached the game pavilion and Adrianna became distracted by the noise. "Can I play now?"

I gave her a quick squeeze. "Sure, sweetie. I hope everything settles down at home. Try not to worry." I wondered who accompanied Adrianna to the picnic. Had she ridden with a friend? Had Tony dropped her off, or her Aunt Lori?

I deposited the cookies at the food table and turned to see Carol Marsh, Adrianna's vision consultant, standing beneath an old oak tree, sopping up the shade. A tall, angular woman whose soft smile belied her tough exterior, she waved at me, and I joined her. "How do you think Adrianna's doing?"

Carol frowned. "Who can say? The poor girl. Can you believe Tony let her come?"

I adopted the high road. "Maybe he thought a distraction was in order."

She scoffed. "He killed Lisa."

My heart arrested. "What? There's news?" I practically screamed, then dropped my voice, checking to be sure Adrianna hadn't heard me.

"No," Carol hissed, "but if she's dead, he's responsible."

I thought for a long moment about Carol's words and shuddered. "You really believe he's capable of killing his own wife?" She looked at me as if I sucked a stupid lozenge. I remembered McGrath and Jack's words about the Mafia connection. When last in their home seven years ago, I saw no evidence of violence on his part, but that didn't mean there was none. "You're right."

"She moved home a couple of weeks ago. I was shocked and called her when I heard the news. She was evasive when we talked — not the norm. I asked her if Tony was close by, trying to figure out why she wouldn't confide in me, but she said no. Tony must have threatened to sue for custody, or frightened her in some other way. It's the only explanation."

I nodded and waited for her to continue.

"Dave and I separated in June, so Lisa and I shared many conversations."

"I'm sorry to hear about you and Dave."

Carol shook her head. "Don't be. It's the healthiest decision I've made in years. The kids are struggling, but mostly it's a relief."

I nodded as I recalled the relief I felt after escaping from Annie and Nick's dad. For the first time in forever, I slept free of the worry he'd make it up the stairs after ingesting a fifth of whiskey; and the guilt of wishing that he wouldn't. The mere thought of his abuse caused me to cringe. I extinguished the unnerving flashback and turned back to Carol. "I haven't talked to Lisa since she told me she decided to leave Tony."

"Something went wrong. I spoke to her several times after they separated. She seemed strong and confident in her decision to divorce. Her moving home… it doesn't make sense."

I hesitated, unsure whether to pursue her further or not. "Have the police spoken with you yet?"

"They asked me to stop at the precinct to speak to a

detective on my way home. I don't know how I can help, but I'll do what I can."

"We all will."

I had to face the very real possibility that Lisa was dead. Bile rose in my throat, and I glanced at my watch. "I need to head home. My kids return from the lake today."

Carol smiled. "You lucked out in the father-in-law department."

"You got that right!"

"Enjoy your kids," Carol called to me as I walked away.

Her message replayed as I headed for my car. *Enjoy your kids.* I heard those words wherever I went. *Get back to normal.* I scrambled to switch gears and forced myself to focus on my grocery list and my kids. *Why was this so damned difficult?*

I noticed a Lincoln Town Car parked two spaces from mine. It was nothing I would normally pay attention to, and at first I couldn't determine what made the hair prickle on my arms. Probably the dude sitting inside the car. Italian-looking with slicked back hair, a muscle shirt, and a powerful upper body, he seemed out of place at a park where throngs of kids had gathered for an afternoon of fun and games. I might be overreacting, considering my life was on the line a few weeks ago. But I had learned some time ago, out of some very real and horribly frightening circumstances, to respect my gut feelings. It seemed wrong to ignore my spiked antenna now. I quickened my pace, trying to sneak an unobtrusive glance at the guy as I zipped inside my vehicle. I cast my eyes over my shoulder as I backed out of the parking spot. Definitely Italian. Definitely creepy. Was he there to watch me? Or was he keeping an eye on Adrianna?

Stop being paranoid, Sam.

I rifled inside my purse for my cell. No texts. No voice messages. No missed calls. McGrath meant business. How could I reassure him that attending the picnic was the end of my involvement? I'd call him later, after I settled in with the kids.

I glanced in my rearview mirror. The Lincoln followed two car lengths behind me, keeping a safe but steady distance. I swallowed hard. Why trail me? I hadn't done anything out of the ordinary. Did Tony know that Lisa had tried to reach me before her disappearance? Did he think she would show up at my place?

I sped up. So did the town car driver. I veered from my standard route, and watched him cross lanes and pursue me as I exited the freeway. Five miles down the road, I swerved into the parking lot of the grocery and parked near the door. I felt safer when I stepped inside. Thirty minutes later my heart rate steadied, and I tossed an extra bag of chips into the cart, my reward for keeping my head attached.

I peered from the checkout line to the parking lot and searched for the town car. Gone. *Whew.* I thought about calling McGrath and filling him in, but considered how angry he would be about the fact that I had put myself in a precarious position; I decided against it. For now, the emergency had passed.

I drove home, vigilant to spot a tail, but there was none. It must have been a coincidence. Maybe I had a touch of post traumatic distress disorder from Japan; maybe I was imagining things. It didn't make sense for anyone to be interested in me when it came to the Macchione's. I needed to listen to Jack and turn my eyes toward home, my kids, and the start of the new school year.

I shelved the groceries, turned on my iPod, and listened to Sara Bareille's *1000 Times* while marinating the chicken. The lyrics caused a pang in my heart. I missed McGrath. I wanted to call him, but my indignation wouldn't allow it. Not ten minutes later, Ed's Suburban pulled into the drive and I rushed to greet my crew.

Nick climbed out of the front seat and lumbered over to me. I read the excitement in his sparkling eyes, but his puberty hormones raged too much for him to run up to me. When he finally reached me, I cupped his face in my hands for a long moment, then planted a kiss on his freckled cheek and held him close. Whether he liked it or not.

McGrath was right. I had lost sight; I could have been killed. *Get a grip, Sam. Appreciate what you have. Stay grounded.*

Lizzie raced to me next, squealing, "Mommy! Mommy!"

How had I managed these final days, waiting for them to come home? We were together again and out of harm's way. *A miracle.* Lizzie's arms encircled my waist and she cuddled into me.

I stepped back, amazed at how the past two months had changed Marie and Annie. Their new-found maturity was stunning; they'd left little girls and returned as young women. Will approached, followed his siblings' lead, and jumped into the action. We joined in a group hug.

I swallowed hard. My armored heart burst open to let them in, and I blinked back tears.

Ed sauntered behind them, sporting his usual warm-hearted grin. He appeared intact, save for deeper creases in his smile lines. He hugged me close as the kids broke away to explore our newly remodeled kitchen and family room, courtesy of last spring's house fire.

"Hi Dad. You alright?"

He laughed. "Just fine, young lady. Glad to be home, but don't think the kids are responsible for that."

"They're each a head taller than they were in June. Can I pour you an iced tea?"

He ambled toward a wicker rocker. "Beer'd be better."

I ran inside to snatch a cold one. Nick wasted no time sprawling in the recliner of the sectional. His legs stretched out over the edge, and he caressed the remote with a gentle touch normally reserved for his guitar strings. The sight of him made me chuckle.

I met Ed on the porch and sat next to him.

"How are you, Sam? Tell me about the trip."

Goosebumps rose on my arms. "It was good for the heart, Dad, making some peace with Jon's death. It helped more than you can imagine. I'm forever in your debt."

"Don't be silly. Having the kids was exactly what the doctor ordered. I had no idea how much I'd been grieving for Betty. You should be very proud of them. They are growing up great."

I nodded, my eyes brimming with tears. I was the lucky one, not Ed. Then, my prying ways took over. "What's this secret the kids tell me? There's a lady in your life?"

He nodded. "You remember Helen Williams? She lives just down the beach. Lost her husband to cancer two years back."

"I do remember. Petite, blonde, baker extraordinaire. Betty would be happy for you, Dad. She wouldn't have wanted you to be alone."

"I'm taking it slow. My girl was one of a kind. I'm ready for companionship, but not in a rush to make anything permanent. You?"

His candor surprised me, although it shouldn't have. I hesitated for a brief moment, weighing my options, but quickly forged ahead, hoping McGrath would be back in my life soon. "There is someone, Dad, but I want to do this right. I don't want to step on your toes, or the kids. I'm guessing it won't be easy for anyone to accept a new man into the family, but I'd like to introduce the two of you when the time is right, whenever you feel ready."

"It's your life, Sam. Stop worrying about everyone else. If you're confident, we'll all follow happily along. Don't waste time fretting, just get on with it. If problems arise, we'll do what we always do, deal with them and move on."

"Wow." What else could I say?

A hesitant grin enveloped me. Before now, I hadn't allowed myself to picture the two most important men in my life meeting. My stomach knotted. "He's a detective in Lexington Heights." The words rushed out of me and

my heart beat wildly against my ribs. "He helped me…"
I stammered for a moment. *What could I tell him? He knew
nothing of Jon's impostor, the circumstances of Rex's death, or the
true events surrounding Jon's death.* "I… uh, met him…"

Ed looked puzzled. "Calm down, girl."

I inhaled deeply. "How we met isn't all that important.
You'll like him, Dad. I know you will. He's a man with
strong values, easygoing, and smart."

Ed must have sensed my anxiety. "Can't wait to meet
him, honey. Set up a dinner, alright?"

A shiver raced down my spine and I nodded. "I will.
Soon. I'm barbecuing tonight. Stay for dinner?"

"Think I'll head for the ranch, if you don't mind. Been
away all summer… I'm anxious to get home and check on
the house. Bill Jones has been keeping an eye on things, but
I need to lay eyes on the place and putz around."

"I understand."

Ed hugged me, and then squared his shoulders. "Set up
that meeting, okay? Don't wait. Let life take you places. If
we've learned nothing else in the past year, it's that life is
short." He gave me a nod, turned, and walked inside to say
goodbye to the kids.

I gazed around. Sunny skies, green grass, birds flitting
though the branches, squirrels chirping and chasing each
other up the oaks. Sixty seconds of nirvana. I savored it.
Home. Family.

Ed waved as he backed out of the drive, and I headed
inside. The girls made short work of toting their bags
upstairs and organizing their lives. They lay parked on their
beds, laptops lit up and chatting online with friends. Lizzie
curled up in the recliner with Nick, watching television, and
Will sprawled on the floor.

I announced dinner within the hour; once at the table,
we shared summer tales. Only two and a half weeks
remained until the start of school. Sports practices began
the following Monday, and there was school shopping to

accomplish; they would all need new jeans. I set a shopping date and they disbursed to their own pursuits... trying out the new furniture in the adjoining family room.

Nick stayed back and started in on me. "You look different."

"My hair's longer."

He grinned sheepishly. "No, it's not that. You're happier."

I tousled his hair. "I'm glad to see all of you. Overjoyed, really."

Nick began whistling. Damn him. He made up songs whenever the girls were interested in new boys. A flush rose up my neck and onto my cheeks. "Mom's got a boyfriend," he teased. He sang at the top of his lungs as he drummed out the beat on the tabletop. "Love is a marvelous thing..."

I shot him my fiercest behave yourself look. "Stop it right now."

Annie shot a curious look in my direction. "You have a boyfriend?"

Marie asked, "Are you getting married?"

"No to both questions," came my firm retort. I couldn't believe I lied to them. *What the hell is wrong with me?*

Nick continued, "Mom, you've taught us that honesty is the best policy, remember? Are you sure you wouldn't like to change your answer?"

I cleared my throat. "It's my business. If and when I'm ready, I'll share what I feel you need to know."

Nick shot the girls a knowing glance. "She's got a boyfriend. Just look at her. That's guilt in the flush of her neck." He laughed full and deep.

I could have flogged him.

The girls giggled.

"Who is he?" Annie asked.

"Is he cute?" Marie added.

Nick winked at me. "Better question, does he drive a sweet car?"

"Jeep," I answered simply.

"Not bad, not bad." He bounced around the kitchen, snapping his fingers, humming his rendition of a love song. "When do we get to meet him?"

As soon as he forgives me. "You'll frighten the poor man to death."

Nick winked at his sisters and bobbed his head up and down a least a dozen times. "We can arrange for that."

"Out," I ordered. "Or I'll make you do the dishes."

Nick kissed my cheek. "C'mon Lizzie," he called. "I'll get our bikes down." To me, he added, "Going to take a ride and let my peeps know I'm back in the hood."

I rolled my eyes. "Shoo." The girls sat with their elbows glued to the kitchen table, their eyes glued to me. "Shoo," I repeated.

"Come on, Mom," they chorused. "Tell us."

"Not now. Not today. Now, go."

They sighed heavily before leaving me to my own devices.

After I cleaned up the kitchen, I joined the girls upstairs, laying across their bed as they pulled out clothing and decided what to keep and what to pack for donations. They passed a knowing look between them, but had obviously decided that I'd fill them in on matters of the heart in my own good time. Despite not being biological sisters, Marie and Annie were cut from a similar cloth. I noticed it in their hunger for organization, which had increased tenfold since Jon's death. I translated it into their need for control on the heels of losing their dad and their dog.

An hour passed. I watched them and marveled. Soon, they'd be grown and off to college. If only I could stack bricks on their heads to slow down the process.

The doorbell interrupted my reverie. I listened to see if Will would answer it, knowing better, and heard it ring again. I hopped up and ran downstairs.

McGrath stood on my doorstep, hands driven deeply

into his pockets, a serious look on his face. My eyes narrowed. Not part of the plan. Something was wrong. *Lisa?*

I hesitated. Should I ask him in? I walked onto the porch and closed the door behind me. "Hi," I said.

He took my arm, led me over to a rocker, and instructed me to sit.

Nerves bubbled inside me. Something *was* wrong. McGrath wouldn't show up unannounced without good reason. Especially after we fought. I glanced toward the driveway. The blue bubble sat atop his Jeep, which he'd parked on the apron of the asphalt. "I'm surprised to see you."

He looked disturbed. "Where's your phone?"

"I don't know. What's the matter? Just tell me."

He paced a few steps, and returned to my side. "It's going to be alright."

"Is it Lisa? Is she... dead?"

"There's been an accident. Nick was struck by a hit and run driver."

I broke into a sweat and my heart slammed against my ribs. Hit and run? Nick? I peered at McGrath. *How? When? Why McGrath? This wasn't even his jurisdiction. There was no possible way this could be happening. Nick? My boy?*

Tears welled in my eyes. My throat clogged. "Tell me he's okay, please! Where is he?"

"Your firefighter friend, Marty Jaeger, was first on the scene. He called it in. When I heard Nick's name... we should head to the hospital."

No, damn it. I shook my head, attempting to will away the terror sinking its claws into me. "Please. Tell me he's alive."

McGrath drew me up from my chair. "As far as I know, he's alive. Now, grab your purse. Hurry."

I bolted inside. "Girls, come here!"

Marie and Annie raced downstairs, sensing the urgency

in my voice. McGrath stood in the foyer with me. The girls eyed him while I recited firm and direct instructions. "Keep an eye on Lizzie and Will. Nick took a spill on his bike. This kind policeman, Detective McGrath, offered to drive me to the hospital. I'll let you know what's going on as soon as I know. In the meantime, hold down the fort. Lizzie is across the street at Katie's. Go and get her. Everyone stays home. Wait here until you hear from me. I paused and then spat out, "No candles!"

"Should we call Grandpa?" Annie asked.

"Not yet. We don't want to bother him for a minor injury."

In robot mode, with leaden legs, I followed McGrath to the car and somehow hoisted myself inside. Prayers formed on my lips. After several long minutes, I summoned the energy to speak. "Damn it. Not Nick." I swallowed hard. "It's serious, isn't it?"

"Yes, it's serious. Very serious."

CHAPTER FOUR

MCGRATH PARKED HIS Jeep in the ambulance drop-off lane of The University Children's Hospital Emergency Room. I dashed out of the car and into the hospital, rushing to the reception desk.

"My name is Samantha Stitsill. My son, Nick, was brought in by ambulance. Where is he?" I swiped away the tears as I felt McGrath come up behind me and place a steadying hand around my middle.

The receptionist nodded at me. "Your son is being triaged right now. Please be patient. I'll let the doctor know you've arrived. Someone will be out to speak with you as soon as they know something."

Bile filled my throat. I'm not good at waiting. I'm not patient. I fought for breath. No dice. McGrath led me to a vinyl couch in the crowded waiting room and sat next to me. He massaged my knee as I began to mouth the *Our Father*.

"I'll move the Jeep and find you some water."

I nodded mechanically, wrung my hands, and continued to pray. Marty Jaeger appeared at my side. "Sam."

"How is he? What happened?"

Marty squeezed in next to me and enclosed my hand in his. "From what we can tell, Nick was riding his bike along Main Street. First reports suggest someone veered into his path, then sped away. It may have been a distracted driver who got scared and took off. Maybe a teen who was texting. They're stabilizing Nick, then they'll run tests."

"But he's okay?" *He has to be.*

Marty gazed at me with compassion. He coached Nick's basketball team. He knew my story, and he knew how much I loved my kids.

"Nick's tough," he said. "We'll just have to wait and see."

That was not good news.

I thanked Marty, then marched up to the reception desk after I checked my watch for the fiftieth time. "I've been waiting for thirty minutes. I'm happy to let the doctors do whatever they need to do to help my son, but I insist on seeing him."

The nurse nodded toward the automatic door and pushed a button. The heavy door swung open, and I darted inside. McGrath, just reentering the ER, spotted me and followed quickly. We made it inside just before the door closed. I peered down the long corridor and located the Emergency Room nurse's station, strode up to the counter, and cleared my throat. The nurse, whose eyes remained firmly planted on her computer screen, finally looked up at me.

"I'm Nick Stitsill's mom. Where is he, please?"

"Upstairs. ICU. Bed 4," she said, and pointed to the elevator.

"This way." McGrath led me to a staircase. We raced to the fourth floor, then down the hall.

I steeled myself before pulling back the curtain. Nick always wore his helmet, didn't he? No, that was Will, my rule follower. Nick was the boundary pusher. I uttered another prayer and stepped inside the stall. My precious Nick lay there, motionless. I noticed the tubes first. Too many tubes. Monitors blinking and beeping. An IV drip led to the vein in his right arm. A machine breathed for my son; oxygen was being delivered to him via a clear flex hose. Whooshing. In. Out. Nick's eerie quiet caught me off guard. Suddenly, I felt woozy. The room began to spin.

McGrath ushered me to a chair. "Sit down," he instructed. "Head between your knees."

I'd been through this before. By now, I should have mastered the art of having the wits scared out of me and still standing, but I hadn't. I swallowed dinner for the second time and struggled to regain my bearings. *Shit.*

McGrath tried to sooth me. "Take a second. Nick's right here beside you. He's breathing. You do the same."

Something snapped inside me when McGrath said Nick was breathing. With the aid of a machine. I broke through the shock and looked at my son. Even though he required assistance, he *was* breathing. I stood at his bedside, leaned over, and kissed his cheek.

"Nick, honey, it's Mom. I'm here, sweetie."

Nick didn't move. I turned to McGrath, panicked.

"They may have given him a sedative or pain medication. Don't worry. I'm sure someone will be in soon."

"How can they just leave him here... alone?" I knew better. It was just my anxiety kicking up. I forced a breath through my lungs. "Sorry. I need a minute."

McGrath wrapped his arms around me and held on tight. "Sit down, Sam. Hold Nick's hand and breathe."

I nodded.

No sooner had I taken my seat than Nick's monitor began to beep. "Call a nurse," I ordered McGrath. "We need a nurse."

McGrath opened the curtain and disappeared. Seconds later Nick began to seize. Just like Rex had done. Stricken with fear, I froze. I refused to lose another member of my family. I would not lose Nick. Instinct kicked in, and I rolled him onto his side.

"Hurry," I shouted. "Someone hurry."

A nurse strode purposefully into the room and viewed

Nick and his monitors. He glanced at me and turned his attention to Nick, who had calmed. "It's not abnormal to seize after a head injury," he said. "Probable concussion. The doctor ordered a CT scan and some x-rays. As soon as the techs are free, they'll run the tests." He looked at me with compassion. "As you know, it will take some time."

"So… he's okay?" Annie had suffered a concussion after a fall down a flight of stairs at age three. I rushed her to the doctor's office after she began vomiting. Hauling Nick and his car seat under one arm and Annie in the other. Annie had come out all right. Certainly, Nick would, too. He had a thick skull. Maybe this time it would do him some good.

"We won't know his condition for a while," he restated patiently, kindly. "We're still evaluating him."

Obviously, I wasn't thinking clearly. I shook my head, clearing the fog. "What do you know? Was he conscious when he was brought in?"

I hated the thought of Nick being scared or alone, but took solace in the fact that Marty, my high school friend, had been at the scene.

"He lost consciousness after the accident."

"And? Has he been awake since?"

The nurse shook his head. "No."

I beckoned a calm I did not feel. "Please arrange for a doctor to speak to me as soon as possible."

Beads of perspiration formed on Nick's brow. His thick head of strawberry-blonde hair always caused him to sweat profusely. I ran cold water in the sink, moistened a washcloth, and placed it on his forehead. Once his body cooled, I tucked his sheets loosely around him. He seemed peaceful now, and the numbers on his monitors no longer alarmed me. His blood pressure remained high, which I imagined was expected, but his oxygen level seemed normal. I willed myself to think. *One rational thought after another.*

"Stay with him so I can call home?" I asked McGrath.

His quick grin soothed my nerves. "Absolutely."

I left the two of them and walked outside into a steamy August afternoon. I hated calling Ed, but I did so. I filled him in on as much as I knew. He assured me he would stay with the kids for as long as needed.

"I'm praying, Sam. Anything you need, just let me know."

Then I called home. Will answered in an absolute state of panic. He and Nick were only ten weeks apart, and had adopted each other as twins more than ten years ago. I reassured him.

"Nick's alright. We don't know much yet, but the doctors gave him some pain medication. He's sleeping." It was a stretch, but calming Will took priority in that moment. "ER's take forever, remember? Even for simple stuff."

Will's breathing was ragged.

"Remember when you broke your collar bone?" I asked.

"We were at the hospital all day."

"Precisely. The doctors are going to want to run a lot of tests. X-rays and all. Grandpa Ed is coming to the house to stay with you guys."

I ended the call as I headed back to Nick's room. I heard McGrath's voice as I approached.

"I'm a friend of your mom's, Nick. My name is Jim McGrath. She's told me a lot about you. From what she says, you're of strong stock and as stubborn as she is. You're gonna be fine, son. Just hang in there."

I immediately teared up. Had Nick awakened? I eased back the curtain and swallowed the scene. McGrath sat perched on the side of Nick's bed. He rested his hand on a sleeping Nick's arm.

As I walked in, McGrath gestured for me to take his spot. Before he moved out of the way, he leaned down, planted a kiss on Nick's forehead, then locked eyes with me. "I'm fully aware of how strong you are. I'm also well aware that even the strongest of women can only handle so much.

Lean on me. I'll be here with you every step of the way. You don't have to handle this alone."

"Thank you," I said. "I can't imagine doing any of this without you."

McGrath squeezed my hand. I choked back a sob and rested my head on his chest. He wrapped a comforting arm around my shoulder. "He's going to be okay."

That moment, McGrath sealed the permanent place he'd taken in my heart.

CHAPTER FIVE

THE NEXT TIME I glanced at the clock it read 6:00 p.m.
Twice now, Nick had been wheeled down the hall for
tests. I had recited Nick's uncomplicated medical history
the same number of times. Normal pregnancy and birth.
Developmental milestones achieved ahead of schedule.
While docile until the age of two, his strong personality
surfaced soon after his second birthday. He turned out to be
headstrong, friendly, extremely bright, musically talented,
and incredibly intuitive. His health had been excellent, other
than a couple of broken bones and a slightly off kilter nose
as the result of a few crashes into inanimate objects. Nick
tackled life with an abundance of enthusiasm. Although
sentimental and detailed, he was a rough and tumble boy
through and through.

Still, he slept.

McGrath stepped out and returned a short time later
with coffee. I couldn't take a single sip.

The doctor finally arrived two hours later. A tall,
thin man with a direct manner, he shook my hand as he
introduced himself and delivered the news.

"I'm the neurologist, Dr. Stern. There is evidence of
intracranial hemorrhage and cerebral edema in your son.
With children, we find it best to take a wait-and-see approach
rather than rush into the OR. Research shows that surgical

intervention is sometimes more harmful than corrective in youth. We'll place your son on anti-seizure medications, a corticosteroid to reduce swelling, and keep him sedated. With your permission, we'll try to cool his body. That will help decrease the edema. Also, we'd like to give him an intravenous drug called Mannitol. It helps to reduce the amount of water in the brain as well as swelling."

My head throbbed. "Of course."

The doctor continued, "If that doesn't work, I'd like to induce a coma."

I nodded, stunned. The news began to sink in. In inches. *Brain bleed. Swelling. Coma.* "Why?" I asked as soon as my own brain began to function again.

"A medically induced coma will allow his brain a chance to heal. The key is to protect the brain from secondary injury. Increased pressure and swelling can cause damage to the healthy parts of the brain. We don't want that."

"But he's stable. That's a good sign, correct?"

The doctor paused for a long moment, deciding what to say.

I tried to lock eyes with him. "He's strong. He's healthy. His outlook is good, right?"

McGrath stood behind me and massaged my shoulder.

The doctor looked at me with sympathetic eyes. "I'm sorry. We'll do everything we can, but I can't make any promises. We just don't know enough yet. We're going to keep him here in the ICU so we can monitor him closely over night. Will you allow us to proceed?"

My head fell into my hands. I choked back a sob. *Was my life really falling apart? Again?*

I pulled myself together and nodded. "Of course. If I need to sign anything, let me know. The sooner we get started, the better."

"The anesthesiologist will try the Mannitol first. If that doesn't work, he'll give Nick some Phenobarbital. During this time, your son's EEG will remain flat. He'll remain unresponsive. He won't feel pain. We will also put him on a ventilator so that we can control his respiratory rate mechanically. Again, we do this in order to rest his brain, and give it a chance to heal."

Medical jargon. Phrases like "control his respiratory rate mechanically" must have been used for a purpose. Sorting through the words, their mere interpretation, slowed down *my* brain, and allowed ample time for the severity of the situation to sink in.

"Is he going to die?"

"We've had a great deal of success with this procedure. Our goal is to decrease the swelling and intracranial pressure. Your son's situation is very serious, but know that we will do everything we can." He stood, shook hands with McGrath, then me, and left.

McGrath offered to spend the night with Nick so I could return home and get some rest, but I couldn't envision leaving Nick's side for a single moment.

"He's sleeping. This is your kids' first night home. I don't mean to sound cold, but spend time with them. They need you as much as Nick does right now. You need them. I'll stay right here. I promise to call if anything happens. Please go home."

I recognized the need for a sensible decision. McGrath was right. Will, Marie, Annie, and Lizzie needed my reassurance now, and being with them would ease my numbness. I'd do everyone a service if I managed to get some rest. This could be a long haul. I kissed Nick's forehead and then his cheek. One, two, three times. Then, I told him that I loved him all the way to the moon. McGrath handed me his car keys and ushered me out the door to a spot in the 'Emergency Vehicles Only' lot.

I texted Annie and let her know I was on my way.

I drove home in a stupor. After I pulled into the driveway and parked, I rested my head on the steering wheel for a long moment. *Our Father*, I began again. Then, I took a measured breath and entered my home. The kids were huddled on the floor, watching a movie. Ed sat on the couch, his head tilted back against its cushion. He opened his eyes when he heard the kids begin to chatter.

I sat down next to Ed and gathered the kids around me. As Nick had reminded me earlier that day, honesty is our family mantra. I explained Nick's condition in as much detail as I knew, but tried not to alarm them at the same time.

Lizzie climbed into my lap and consoled me. "Don't worry, Mom. Nick will wake up."

I nodded. I was supposed to be comforting her, not the other way around. All the same, I took solace in her words.

Will fidgeted with one of Nick's guitar picks, and prompted a brainstorm. "In the morning, let's gather a few of Nick's favorite things."

Will piped up first. "His guitar!"

"And his music," Annie suggested. "In Science, I learned that people in comas can still hear. He loves his music. It'll cheer him up."

I didn't have the heart to tell her that Nick probably wouldn't be at all responsive during this time. I'd save that information for tomorrow.

Lizzie plopped herself in my lap. "I'll sing him a song and you can record me."

Marie hopped up and pulled out colored pencils and recent photographs. "I'll make him a collage."

"When can he have visitors?" Will asked.

I kissed them and urged them to hit the sack. "It's late. Let's get some rest, and we'll sort out the details in the morning."

Ed reached for his keys as I ushered the kids upstairs. "I'll head to the hospital right now."

"No. Wait until morning. You're tired, too. Get some rest. We can take turns tomorrow. McGrath is with him tonight."

Ed halted in his tracks. "McGrath?"

"Detective Jim McGrath." I realized that I'd never shared his name with Ed. "He's the man I'm seeing. He overheard the news at the precinct and then delivered me to the hospital. He offered to stay the night with Nick so that we could get some rest. It could be a while, Dad."

"Don't worry. That Nick of yours has an iron will. He's going to be fine."

"I appreciate the reassurance. And I believe you're right. Now, let's get some sleep."

Ed kissed me on the cheek before he left.

I brewed a cup of tea and curled up in the only remaining remnant of our old family room, an overstuffed chair that I'd insisted on reupholstering. It had been Jon's chair, and it brought me comfort in the days after his death. Before long, Lizzie padded downstairs and climbed in beside me. I rested my cheek on her silky head, and we both fell asleep.

CHAPTER SIX

THE FOLLOWING MORNING, a few minutes after 5 a.m., I ushered a sleeping Lizzie up to bed. When I phoned, McGrath assured me that Nick had made it through the night without any significant or alarming changes. Nick remained unconscious, but the doctors had not been forced to induce a medical coma. I counted that as a good sign.

I sat at the kitchen table, making a list as I sipped my coffee. It was important that my kids have school clothes, that they were fed each day, and, if it became imperative for me to take a leave from my teaching position in order to care for Nick, I jotted down a list of capable substitutes.

As a special education consultant, I knew all about traumatic brain injuries. Maybe too much. Over the years, I'd taught many children who'd suffered TBIs. If my son needed a caretaker, there was no doubt in my mind who that person would be. *Me.*

My concern now was to keep my wits about me, and not let the shock overwhelm or immobilize me. Rather than call Di and Jack, I sent them emails. That way, I held my emotions in check and avoided a major break down. The kids would likely sleep late, so I donned some exercise clothing and went for a quick run. When I returned home, I showered and called Ed.

He insisted on stopping by the hospital before heading

over to stay with the children, so I spent the next two hours preparing soups and casseroles which I could freeze and reheat later. By the time Lizzie awoke, I had accomplished a day's worth of tasks.

She insisted on practicing a song for Nick while I prepared her favorite breakfast, chocolate chip pancakes. My little girl had perfect pitch. She chose to sing *Somewhere Over the Rainbow*. I used my smart phone to record her performance. And I wept.

After we finished her recording, I hurried her off to dress and busied myself cleaning the dishes. *Do it mode.* Ed arrived a few moments later. I ran upstairs to kiss the kids goodbye, packed Nick's favorite stuffed dog, Bingo, the sweats he preferred, and a family photo, then grabbed the gear the kids had gathered for him. I fought off tears as I drove to the hospital, and prayed for good news. Time alone would not be my friend right now, and I discovered my foot pressed too firmly to the accelerator. I slowed my speed and exited the freeway, a series of knots gripping my stomach as I reached the children's hospital, pulled a ticket from the parking kiosk, and drove up the concrete ramp. *Lord, give me strength.*

Somehow, I powered through my trepidation, made it upstairs, and entered Nick's room. McGrath's five o'clock shadow brushed my cheek when I hugged him. I held onto him for a full minute before turning my eyes to Nick.

The tubes and monitors choked me up, and I had to sit down to avoid a fainting spell.

I cleared my throat and swallowed, reduced to a puddle of emotion. "I'm sorry. Head home and get some rest."

McGrath held me in his gaze. "I called off work. I'll stay here with you. You don't look so hot."

I held my head in my hands and murmured, "I have to get it together. I have to be strong."

McGrath rested a gentle hand on my shoulder. "You are strong. And I'm right here with you."

I sighed. "Thank you."

"A nurse checked in a while ago. I asked her when the doctor would be in. She guessed he would arrive for rounds about 10 a.m." McGrath glanced at his watch. "Anytime now."

I offered him a weak grin. "Really, go home, grab a shower and get some sleep. I'm going to need you later, once I've been here for a few hours and reality sets in. Please."

"Are you sure?"

I nodded. "Absolutely sure."

Doctor Stern entered Nick's room as McGrath prepared to leave. "We ran another EEG this morning. Your son has some brain activity."

A tear spilled down my cheek. "That's my boy."

"Children's EEGs can be deceiving. But for the time being, we're optimistic."

"So," I asked, "what's next?"

"We will continue to monitor Nick and conduct further neurological testing. His responses to simple reflex testing didn't yield results. Still, all in all, I believe there's reason to be hopeful."

"When will he wake up? Has the intracranial swelling receded?" Like the parents I dealt with when I taught infants and toddlers, my nerves got the better of me. I reminded myself to stay in the moment. The more important concern was how much blood had been prevented from flowing to Nick's brain due to the increased intracranial pressure. While it was true that his waking up was essential, the lasting damage wouldn't be clear for quite some time.

Stern smiled weakly, looking as uncomfortable as a caged animal. And this was his line of work. "We're continuing to monitor the pressure. It seems to be somewhat relieved, so we'll stay the current treatment course. As I mentioned last night, it's wait and see."

"May I begin some stimulation therapy? Music? Tactile input?"

The doctor glanced at Nick's chart and scribbled some brief notes. "Brief snatches."

I stepped back. He was trying to tell me that Nick remained in danger, yet allowing me to feel in control of contributing to a possible recovery. I nodded my understanding and appreciation. As soon as he left the room, I felt a compelling urge to be alone with my son; if it were just the two of us, I could will him back to consciousness.

McGrath narrowed his eyes at me, his understanding of my needs evident. He rose, and planted a firm kiss on my lips. "I'll be back. I love you."

"I love you, too."

McGrath leaned over Nick and kissed his cheek before turning to leave.

"By the way," he said. "I like your father-in-law. He's a straight shooter, and it's evident how much he loves you guys."

"Oh my gosh! I completely forgot that you and Ed would have met this morning. He didn't mention it."

"You both have a lot on your mind right now," McGrath advised. "Not a problem."

I reached for him. "Tell me."

McGrath smiled, proud that he'd succeeded in distracting me.

"I was dozing when he arrived. He came in quietly, walked directly over to Nick, and began speaking to him. His words were totally encouraging."

"What did he say?"

"Called him 'Bud'. Told him what a trooper he was. Told him that he was tougher than any superhero out there. Offered him a trip to the Rock and Roll Hall of Fame as soon as he made it out of this godforsaken place."

"Sounds just like Ed."

"When he noticed I was awake, he stuck out his hand, introduced himself, and thanked me."

I nodded. Ed was a stand up guy. I thanked God for placing him in my corner.

"We talked sports and weather. Guy speak."

I smiled and meant it for the first time in twenty-four hours. It was time to count my blessings and concentrate solely on Nick's recovery.

"I'm leaving. You need some time with your boy."

I squeezed McGrath's wrist and kissed his hand. After he left, I washed Nick's face and brushed his hair. Then, I arranged the family photo on the windowsill and tucked his furry stuffed dog onto his shoulder. Sense of smell remained acute even in times of coma. While I didn't want to over-stimulate him when his intracranial pressure was increased, I couldn't resist urging him to wakefulness with a familiar scent.

I kept the conversation short and sweet. "Here's Bingo, Bud. I love you."

I clutched my phone, plugged in the headphones, and located Lizzie's song. After I situated an earpiece near Nick's ear, I turned on the music so that it played softly next to him.

I sat on the edge of the bed, my gaze locked on Nick's face. No reaction. I told myself it didn't matter if there was no noticeable response. He could still be listening. Still feel the comfort of Lizzie's sweet voice and the soothing companionship of Bingo, whom he'd dragged around like a third thumb during his toddlerhood.

I checked the time. Five minutes had passed. It was best to keep the stimulation sessions short, so I turned off the music. I decided to leave Bingo atop Nick's shoulder. As I ran a fingertip along his arm, I filled him in.

"You're in the hospital, Bud. You had an accident while you were riding your bike. You were lucky. Because you were wearing your helmet, your skull is in one piece and none of your bones are broken. You're just scraped and bruised. I know how you love photos of your injuries, and

I'll take some pictures soon, but right now I want to you rest. Sleep as long as you like. I'll be right here."

I patted his hand and closed my eyes. Before too long, I had to make some extremely important decisions.

CHAPTER SEVEN

M Y PHONE VIBRATED. Di. I stepped outside Nick's room and down the hallway.

"Hello?"

"Oh my Lord, Sam. How are you? How's Nick? What can I do?"

I inhaled a measured breath. The last thing I needed right now was Di on high anxiety, but that's Di's MO. "I'm fine. Nick is still asleep. Ed's with the kids. We're playing a waiting game right now. The doctors are cautiously optimistic, and Nick's vital signs are stable."

"I can't believe it. You've been through so much. It doesn't seem fair."

"It's not fair. But I have tons of support. Right now, I'm just praying for a quick and full recovery. If anyone can weather an injury, it's Nick."

Di chuckled. "He's certainly had enough experience."

I recalled the three times Nick had broken his nose before he turned four—jumping off his sister's bunk bed as he pretended to be Batman, slamming into the swivel stool at McDonald's, and crashing into a tree while he learned to ride a two wheeler. He also burned his forearm when he attempted ironing after watching me press one of Jon's shirts, except he was trying to iron one of his Halloween costumes, which promptly melted. In his rush to rescue the disappearing fabric, he leaned directly onto the edge of the iron. Nick always insisted on photos. He'd be miffed if I didn't capture his coma as well.

"You're absolutely right. Thanks for making me laugh."

"You're welcome. I'll deliver a meal later. And I'm happy to spell Ed so he can rest. You and the kids barely had time to settle back in before this happened."

I sighed. "You're right. We didn't. And thanks, Di. I'm sure Ed will appreciate the respite."

"I'll call the house after Ava wakes from her afternoon nap. She'll love visiting with the kids, and the boys can get acquainted with your crew."

"That would be wonderful."

"Take all the time you need, Sam. Chris can pick up the kids on his way home from work. I'll stay as long as you need me."

I thanked her again and ended the call. I had all the help I would need for the next week or so. It would get tricky when I had to return to work. Should I plan on taking a leave? I called Jack.

He answered on the third ring. "Stitsill, what's up?"

"You haven't read your email, have you?"

He heaved a sigh. "Not yet, but is this another episode of *As the Stitsill's Turn*?"

This wasn't the time for Jack's teasing. Once I explained Nick's situation, he backed off.

"Shit," he mumbled. "What can I do?"

"We're handling it. Don't worry."

"When did this happen?"

I paced the long hallway. "The day after I saw you."

"Hell, you're not even past the jet lag."

"Adrenalin kicked in," I retorted. "Jet lag takes a back seat to disaster every time."

"I'll be right over. University Children's?"

"Jim will be back. Not to worry."

"Jim? You're calling him Jim? This is serious."

I laughed. Jack had a valid point; I never called McGrath by his first name. It felt good to have a normal moment. I'd better savor it. Normal was a long way off.

"What's the prognosis?"

Until he asked the question, I'd only allowed myself glimpses of the possibilities. Tears slipped down my cheeks. "They don't know. I can't think about it, Jack. I only know that the longer Nick stays asleep, the worse the expected outcome."

I choked back a sob.

Jack barked, "Stop. He's gonna wake up, Sam!"

My conviction wavered. "I hope you're right."

"You better believe I'm right."

I retraced my steps to Nick's room, speeding up as I got closer, a sudden panic overwhelming me. I shouldn't leave him alone. What if he took a turn for the worse and I wasn't there? "I'll call you when I know more."

I returned to my son's bedside. Somehow, someway, I would make him well. Nick still slept, and I felt desperate for a distraction. I rifled my laptop from my backpack and typed a search into Google: Ways to kill people without leaving evidence behind. *It's scary what I do for entertainment. And the fact that I'd created this story about Lisa and Tony? Further proof of my insanity.*

I laughed aloud as I read the results. Poison dart frogs were suggested, along with beating a person with another person, so that it appeared to be a pedestrian accident. Mostly, I discovered advice on destroying evidence. I kicked up my feet on Nick's bedrails. This search would keep me busy for some time.

Ever since childhood, I've enjoyed reading mysteries. As an adult, I became hooked on true crime television. Perhaps that penchant led me to the desire to solve my own conundrums. What can I say? It's a bit of an addiction, and a powerful diversion.

I Googled a different phrase: how to kill someone and

hide the body. Injections of potassium chloride stopped the heart. Translation: the drug used in lethal injections. Air could be injected by hypodermic needle. The air bubble would be drawn into the heart, giving the appearance of a heart attack.

What to do with the body, though. Hmmm. My search lacked those pertinent details.

I discovered Ricin, part of the waste "mash" of castor beans, was a poison injected into a Bulgarian writer, Georgi Markov, by way of a rigged umbrella. He died three weeks after the attack. The bubbles in my stomach transformed themselves into willies.

Next, I read that adrenaline, calcium, and bicarbonate could be injected. Had McGrath investigated those possibilities? Would he have had any reason to? *Probably needs a body, Sam.*

Upon further investigation, I discovered that potassium chloride could be detected during an autopsy, but not directly linked to murder. So, even if they found Lisa's body, Tony could claim she was deranged, left home, and then died in the wilderness. Were the cops searching for a body? If so, where?

Chemicals could also be sprayed into a person's face, causing an immediate heart attack. I'd experienced enough of people taking each other's lives lately. The thought of Lisa's disappearance becoming the case of another good person at the mercy of some unhinged individual was more than I could bear in the face of my current situation.

I reminded myself to concentrate on Nick, shut the lid of my laptop, and went about performing his second stimulation session of the day. I spoke to him in simple sentences, keeping a lilt to my voice that I no longer felt. When he showed no reaction to my intervention, I offered up another prayer, then headed downstairs for some fresh air.

I spotted McGrath waiting for the elevator as I stepped

off. I fell into his arms and my legs turned boneless. He held me until I could stand on my own, then eased me back, and gazed into my eyes for what seemed like a full minute before pulling me close again.

"Is Nick alright?" he asked.

I could only nod.

"Let's get you some food. You look as though you've seen a ghost. What's wrong?"

"I'm crazy," I simply said.

He narrowed his eyes. "Crazy? What makes you say that?" I half-suspected he believed me.

"I've been Googling again."

McGrath chuckled. "Never a good choice."

"I thought it would keep my mind off my troubles."

"What this time?"

"Ways to kill people and dispose of a dead body."

He kissed my cheek and smiled. "I thought you decided to leave this to me."

"In spite of all that's happened to Nick, I can't shake the notion that Tony killed Lisa. I keep thinking that her body will be found, but it will look like an accident."

He guided me toward the cafeteria, steering me directly into the line and handing me a tray. Since I was too numb to choose an item, he reached behind the protective glass and decided for me. A turkey sandwich, orange, and package of baked chips soon filled my tray, along with bottled water. Smart man.

He led me to a table, pulled out a chair, and ordered me to sit. I obeyed and lifted the sandwich to my mouth. The first bite proved tasteless, the next a little better. By the time I peeled the orange, and the juice squirted over my tongue, I came alive again.

"Thank you," I mumbled to McGrath.

He passed me a sympathetic gaze. I hate sympathetic gazes. I'm the strong one. I don't require support, I offer it. "At least the color's back in your cheeks."

Admitting that I loved him taking care of me proved to be a mounting challenge. I fought the urge to fall completely apart in his presence, and leaned on him in baby steps. Even that felt unnerving.

One truth remained. I needed McGrath now more than ever.

CHAPTER EIGHT

MCGRATH'S VOICE BROKE my thoughts, but not my anxiety. "Sam, you've been through an incredible shock. You're attempting to carry on business as usual, but I'm sure this is eating you up."

I jumped up from the table. "Let's go outside."

McGrath left our trays on the table and followed me. When we exited the building, I located a bench and sank onto it. He sat beside me.

"I need a cigarette."

McGrath patted my knee. "You don't smoke."

"But if I did…"

"Let it out, Sam."

The floodgates burst open. I hated it, but I knew McGrath was right. He'd leveled all of my defenses.

He drew me into his chest, and I wept. For all the pain I'd been through the past year and a half, but mostly for my boy. I desperately wanted him back. Intact. No brain or physical injuries. I wanted my loving, joking, intuitive, talented boy back. Whole again. Aggravating the hell out of me. Forever and always, so that he could grow into the man God intended.

McGrath tipped up my chin. "Talk to me."

"I want it all to stop. I want Nick to leap out of that damn hospital bed. I want to rewind and erase the lot of it. Rex's death, Jon's death, Rosie's death. Now this. What does God have in mind for me? Does He really believe I'm the toughest girl on the planet? Is this a test? Because if it is, I'm prepared to fail."

"What you're doing right now is exactly what's required."

I stood and fisted my arms. "What I need to do is hightail it back inside and care for my son."

"Please, sit back down."

I looked at him through eyes veiled with tears. "I can't."

He reached out. I couldn't accept his extended hand. A war raged inside me. How could I turn to him now, have a relationship, when my son lay upstairs in a coma? What had I been thinking? I didn't have time for a man.

I turned away and then back toward him. "I can't do this."

His brow furrowed. "Can't do what?"

"Any of this. You. Me. I don't have time for this."

"You're upset. Understandable. Take a breath."

I followed his advice, inhaled deeply, and regained my composure. We sat back down and he swaddled me in his embrace.

"Meltdown," I simply mumbled into his chest.

"It's okay."

"I want Nick to wake up," I whispered.

He rubbed my back. "I know. Me, too."

I nodded and attempted to squirm free. "Shall we go inside?"

He strengthened his grip. "In a minute."

I allowed myself to truly relax this time. I rested my head in the curve of his shoulder, and the sun shone on us like a beacon. I accepted its warmth and healing rays. Oddly enough, in that moment, I sensed everything would turn out all right. False hope or not, I accepted the peace I experienced. I lifted my head to the sky, inhaled again, and let my shoulders fall. McGrath kissed my cheek and smelled my hair.

"Have I mentioned how good you smell?"

I chuckled. "Maybe once or twice. You're skilled at the art of the compliment. You're also quite good at distracting me."

His dimples deepened. "Just doing my job!"

One look at those dimples and I felt restored and ready to face my life. "Shall we go back inside?"

He stood and offered me his hand. "Sure."

Fingers entwined, we strode through the long hallway. The brightly colored murals stood in dark contrast to the crisis I faced, but I decided in that moment that I would allow myself to feel, at least in stages, some of the angst I experienced—and share it with McGrath. I'd been alone with so much for so long. Even this past summer, I'd been with him but had been enduring so much personal strife; I'd only allowed myself to be with him in stops and starts. Maybe I could take something larger than baby steps now. Perhaps I could truly allow this man into my life. Fully. Completely. From all appearances, he'd signed up for the long haul.

Once McGrath and I settled back inside Nick's room, he gestured toward the TV remote. I nodded and he turned on the set, muting the volume. A special news flash illuminated the screen. Mayor Macchione had been indicted on an assortment of charges, including tax evasion, fraud, and extortion. The U.S. Attorney, Beverly Johnson, issued a statement declaring an end to the city's "culture of corruption" and vowed to close in on anyone who had been a part of the years of dishonesty that accompanied Macchione's time at the helm of the city administration. Our eyebrows arched as the close-captioned words filled the monitor. What would this mean for Tony? When would his indictment come down? Who else would be named?

A sudden chill sliced my spine and I shivered. McGrath paced a path on the floor. It couldn't be easy for him to stay with me when the walls were closing in on Macchione. He wanted to be a part of the take-down and time proved of the essence. If he suspected Lisa's husband of a role in his wife's disappearance, there'd be little time to waste.

I touched his arm and whispered, "I'm fine. Go."

"I want to be here for you."

"Really, I'm fine. Nick's resting comfortably. Di is scheduled to be with the kids later so Ed can visit the hospital and I can get some rest. We'll be fine until your return."

McGrath kissed me before he left.

The next two hours passed without note. I closed my eyes and napped. Nick's room remained quiet with only the occasional check-in from his nurse. Unnerved by her sympathetic gaze, I strolled the halls for a bit, and busied myself musing about the ties that would bind Tony Macchione to his brother.

McGrath mentioned that no charges had been made on Lisa's credit cards since her disappearance. He also confided that Lisa had no known enemies. No surprise there, but not good news either. There must be a link between the brothers and Lisa's disappearance. What?

I entered Nick's room, kissed his cheek, and flipped on the television. The media would be in a constant frenzy as they attempted to unearth any and all information they could to bring Machionne to social justice. News flashes crammed the television screen. The indictment documented numerous schemes in which the mayor awarded millions of dollars in contracts to Tony's company, Macchione Enterprises. Macchione's business was not the low bidder in any of the deals. These guys were crooks, pure and simple. Vincent had evidently pressured development officials to award contracts to his brother's subsidiaries, as well. Indictment allegations suggested bribes had been received by the mayor in the form of cash, luxury vacations on private jets, and female entertainment in exchange for city business and city fund investments. Macchione allegedly used both campaign funds and non-profits. A News Flash filled the screen—Tony Macchione was being indicted as well. What a mess.

Media was the trial of choice these days and I wasn't at all surprised to see Vincent's wife, Trudy, positioned in his shadow as he held a press conference. Stand by your man had been popular for decades, Anthony Weiner's hijinx most recently, prompting me to wonder if a wronged woman would ever be ballsy enough to say, "You're on your own, dickhead."

Mrs. Macchione issued a short statement. She was certain that her husband and his brother would be cleared of all charges. She also defended the Mayor as a public servant who'd done great things for the city. Their three young sons sat in the first row of the attendees. Nice touch.

The Macchione lawyers vowed an energetic fight against the charges.

As I peered at the screen, I prayed McGrath was entertaining some success this afternoon. Once Nick recovered, I'd do my part in helping him to bring Tony to justice.

CHAPTER NINE

SITTING AND WAITING has never been my style, so I planned out my next intervention with Nick. The neurologist assigned Nick a score of "1" on the Rancho Los Amigos Scale. The short list determined that he wasn't responding to sound, sights, touch or movement.

Yet.

I always taught my kids there was nothing they couldn't accomplish with the right amount of practice and determination. Of all of my kids, Nick's fortitude had been evident from the time he entered the terrible twos a year too early. He'd kick this coma in the butt. Instead of waiting around for him to wake up, I reminded him of this. Maybe it was even more important that I reminded myself that Nick could do anything he set his mind to. His sleeping mind was far more active than most fully awake intellects.

I inched the vinyl chair closer to his hospital bed. I stroked his hand and spoke to him in a soothing tone. "Listen carefully. You're injured, but you can fight through this just as you've fought through other obstacles in your life. When you broke your hand two years ago, you were determined to play the guitar, so you wrote music and had your sister strum for you while you fingered the chords. This is the same thing, honey. I'll strum; you position yourself on the strings for me, okay?"

While I Googled the Rancho Los Amigos Scale on my Smartphone with one hand, I set an earpiece near to his ear with the other. I read that a person at the next level on the scale, which was called the Generalized Response Stage, will begin to respond to sounds, sights, touch or movement. Initial responses will be slow, inconsistent, or occur after a delay. The patient may respond in the same way to a variety to auditory, visual, or kinesthetic stimulation and those responses might include chewing, sweating, breathing faster, moaning, movement, or increased blood pressure.

I would settle for a response to any item on the list, but knew where the most likely avenue of connection would occur. Nick loved music like an ant loves watermelon. It nourished him. I connected the earphones to my phone and played one of his favorite tunes. My goal? A response, even if delayed. He needed to climb the scale. *We* needed to climb the scale.

My gaze remained focused on him. I kept my eyes peeled for any and all signs. Within this next generalized response stage, it was important for me to watch him *after* the music stopped. The doctors suggested only brief interventions. I didn't want to usurp their expertise or authority, and I wouldn't. But in the meantime, I could sure as hell find out as much as possible about what I needed to do and how to do it. *What the hell had been wrong with me the past two days?* I'd kept my head down, praying for a miracle and beginning some simple exercises with Nick, but hadn't set up a plan.

Now that I'd mapped out my course, I felt more confident of my son's recovery. Damn me for losing the past two days. I vowed not to let another day go by in that fashion. No more wallowing.

I coached him. "C'mon, Nick. C'mon."

When the song finished, I removed the ear bud and waited. Careful to keep additional stimulation at bay, I held my breath and sat absolutely still. I fought the urge to panic, which was made more difficult by my own lack of oxygen. Well aware of the source of Nick's strong stock, I powered through. My eyes flickered briefly to the wall clock. I remained motionless for a good five minutes. Then, another five.

Nothing.

With nothing to lose, I added a bit of massage to my grasp, applying gentle pressure to his palm with my thumb. Just a slow, simple pulse.

From McGrath I had learned the power of massage to get blood flowing in the right direction. I also remembered the Brain Gym activities I employed in the classroom with my students. The exercises increased the brain's ability to filter messages between the two hemispheres of the brain. I made a mental note to utilize those techniques with Nick as soon as he was more responsive. Even if I only put him through the motions, I remained confident that the movements would aid his recovery.

My mind raced a four minute mile. Nick was one lucky kid to have me as his mom. There was not one single thing that my son and I couldn't accomplish together.

My thoughts were interrupted by an ever so slight squeeze. Almost like the flickering I'd felt when my babies moved inside me for the first time. A quickening. Nearly imperceptible at first, but then, the dawning realization; my son had just pressed his fingers to my hand.

Had I imagined it?

In the depths of my being, I knew this was not the case. My son was coming back to me. It was important not to let my excitement get the better of me, or to scare him back into the deepest recesses of repression. I squelched the urge to shriek with excitement. A single tear slid down my cheek.

We were on our way.

I debated. Should I text McGrath and share the news? Should I call the nurse? The doctor? Would they believe me? After holding Nick's hand for another fifteen minutes without daring to move, I released him from my gentle grasp. I smiled at him, told him how proud I was, and how anxious I was to lock eyes with his pale blue ones. I bent over the bed, kissed his freckled cheek, and strode quietly from the room, heading toward the nurse's station.

Not one soul looked up as I stood front and center at the desk. I tapped my foot, then decided to play it cool. Curb my impulsivity for a change. I cautioned myself to speak calmly with the nurse, relay a simple report of what had occurred, and ask her to document Nick's reaction for the doctors. To expect the hospital staff to be as thrilled by this news as I was seemed silly; a recipe for disappointment. I'd save my renewed sense of hope for McGrath. He'd understand without my having to explain a thing.

The expected happened. The nurse played skeptic as I reported Nick's response to my massage. Arched her eyebrows like she thought I'd announced a three-legged donkey in the waiting room. But she dutifully wrote down my account and promised she would inform the doctors.

I wasn't at all sure what protocol had been set by staff for these sorts of first sightings by families. My guess? They took as guarded an approach with other parents as Nurse Morrison took with me. A faint smile graced her lips, but one of cynicism rather than warmth and compassion.

Good thing I had geared up for exactly this reaction in advance. Otherwise, she might have shredded my hope.

As I turned to leave the desk, I noticed McGrath's easy stride heading down the hall. His dimples, made deeper by the broad smile that covered his face and his sparkling eyes, set my heart into overdrive.

This had been a very good day.

CHAPTER TEN

MCGRATH HUGGED ME close for a moment, then held me at arm's length. "You're radiant. Tell me." He led me into a sun-streaked waiting room, and we sat next to each other on the upholstered sofa. The light reflected my mood, and I chattered about Nick's recent developments.

When I told him about the nurse's reaction, his lips curved into a gentle grin. "It's her job to be doubtful. Can you imagine how many times she's heard the same thing and then doesn't see evidence herself?"

"Resembles your job, I guess — and mine. I wanted them to be excited for me."

McGrath squeezed my hand, leaned over, and kissed me. "That's why you have me."

I nodded.

"Hey, you might think I'm crazy, but I have an idea."

If he were willing to admit an idea was crazy, he meant business. I steeled myself for a shock. "Well?"

"How about calling the kids? Let them know I'm coming to get them. I'll bring them back here for a visit with Nick. It'll give them a chance to get to know me, they'll appreciate seeing their brother with their own eyes, and you'll see how great I am with them."

"Schemer."

He shrugged. "Can you blame me?"

I rested my head on his shoulder and thought. It was three o'clock. If McGrath picked up the kids around four, they could visit with Nick and then we could grab a pizza. The idea of spending time with them comforted me, and I imagined their presence would speed Nick's recovery.

I agreed.

McGrath looked surprised. "Really? I figured I was shooting a three pointer from the nosebleed section of the coliseum."

"I'm stretching my comfort zone, but it makes perfect sense."

He looked a bit sheepish. "I admit, I have ulterior motives. I don't want to put *us* off. Nick's accident threatens to do that. I know you, Sam. You're devoted to your kids and you put yourself aside far too quickly when disaster strikes. Don't get me wrong, I get it, but I'm crazy about you, and can't wait to get to know the kids. I want to be a family."

He did know me too well. I had threatened to abandon *us* in order to care for Nick. There existed a litany of reasons not to pursue a permanent relationship with McGrath. In reality, life was short. If I hadn't learned that by now, I hadn't learned a goddamned thing. I wasn't sure how we'd make all this work, especially now, but I was determined to see if we could pull it off. Plus, the idea of having this man in my bed sooner, rather than later, held great appeal.

"You're on." I rifled my cell phone from my purse and called home. Di picked up, and I explained the situation.

"Perfect," she said. "I'll get to meet him."

"You caught a glimpse of him that day we fell in the river," I reminded her.

"From a distance. This is going to be amazing."

Leave it to Di to get excited in the midst of a crisis. I pictured her rubbing her hands together like a pirate who had just discovered the booty.

Truth? The idea energized me, too.

"Don't worry about a thing," she added. "I'll finesse it and tell the kids he's the cop who's investigating Nick's accident. They'll be ready at four. Do you want them to bring anything?"

"No. We'll take them to dinner afterward."

She giggled. "Dinner? Sam, I'm so proud of you. How unlike you to go for it. Especially now."

My stomach lurched. "Stop, or I'll change my mind."

"Don't," she ordered.

I thought briefly about reporting Nick's recent responsiveness with her, but decided to wait. I didn't want to jinx his progress, and I wanted to share the news with the kids first. It was family news.

"Thanks, Di. You're the best."

"I'll be on standby for a full report."

I smiled as I ended the call.

"You're on."

McGrath planted his lips on mine. My body went limp in his arms and I whispered, "I wish they had conjugal visit rooms here."

"No joke. We're going to have to get creative in the meantime. Got any ideas? How about a janitorial closet like the ones on those hospital TV shows? It's kinda kinky, don't you think? I'm up for it if you are."

I laughed as a shiver passed down my spine. "God, you're good."

McGrath kissed me again before he stood.

"What about Lisa Macchione? Any news?"

His demeanor became professional. "We entered the home today and completed an additional search. I had the photographer take detailed photographs, but we're at a disadvantage. Tony's had plenty of time to move things. I swear, the house is off-the-charts tidy. Too tidy."

"It was like that when I made home visits, too. The guy's a control freak. Lisa always kept things white-glove clean. I suspected she might be obsessive-compulsive, but it was

Tony's preoccupation with control that ruled that roost."

McGrath nodded. "Interesting. And useful. But, I've got it from here."

"I'm glad I could help. Have you checked the safe houses in the area?"

McGrath rolled his eyes with affection. "Yes, ma'am. Now, you stick to your business, and I'll stick to mine." He leaned over and kissed me again.

I grabbed him around the neck and pulled him back down onto the couch.

He stifled a laugh. "Nick's a good boy."

"Huh?"

"I'm reaping the benefits of his good deeds."

McGrath winked and departed. I returned to Nick's room, kissed his cheek, and sat at his bedside. I inhaled a measured breath, warning myself not to get ahead of the game. Even if Nick awakened soon, we'd most likely have a long road ahead of us. One filled with physical, occupational, and speech therapists. Would he be able to walk? Talk? Eat by himself? Live at home? Reality crept in. *Damn reality.*

I pulled out my laptop and typed a request for a three month leave from my teaching position. It seemed like the next logical step.

By the time I edited the email and pressed the SEND button, I heard familiar hushed voices in the hall. I stepped out of Nick's room, shushed the kids, and ushered them down the corridor to the lounge where I sat them at the round table in the center of the room. The room was painted with bright colors and murals decorated the walls, less scary for kids.

I attempted to make light of the situation. "Nick's still sleeping. We can't rile him up too much. His brain needs time to heal. One of the ways in which that happens is in silence. When you go in to see him, don't talk. You can give him a kiss, but then we have to be careful not to overstimulate him."

I looked from Annie to Marie, from Lizzie to Will. They looked frightened. I sought to reassure them, but Lizzie saw through my bravado. "Mom, aren't you scared?"

"You know your brother. He's one tough nut." I handed them each a sheet of the notepaper that I'd placed on the table, along with colored pencils. "Write him a note. Let him know you were here. Tell him you're rooting for him. That's what he needs from you."

Four sets of fearful, wide eyes met my instructions.

Suddenly, their visit seemed like a very bad idea. I glanced at McGrath. He nodded encouragement my way, and I drew in a deep breath.

"One at a time. Let's go see your brother."

McGrath stooped in front of the low bookshelf next to the vinyl sofa, and pulled a deck of cards from the shelf. "Who's up for a game of Crazy Eights?"

They were silent.

"Lizzie," he said. "Let's set up teams. The winners can play each other and then the losers. Any ideas for the grand prize winner?"

The mood began to soften.

I extended my hand to Annie, and we strode down the hall.

CHAPTER ELEVEN

IN SPITE OF WAKING to a threatening sky, I texted Di. It was still early enough that Chris would be home and we could squeeze in a power walk before he had to head to work and the rain descended upon us. Not ten seconds later, my cell screen read, "Come now."

I threw on a pair of shorts, a sleeveless tee, and my athletic shoes. Then, I left a quick note on the counter. The kids were bound to sleep at least three more hours, soaking up the last drowsy August mornings before school began.

Di waited on the sidewalk in front of her house. She hopped from one foot to the other as I slid out of the van and joined her. We sliced through the humid air as we began our trek into town.

"He's gorgeous," she started. "And seriously sexy. Great dimples."

I smiled, unsurprised by the fact that McGrath held the number one spot on her agenda. "My favorite thing about him."

"Really?"

"Okay," I admitted. "One of my favorite things."

"Spill. How were the kids?"

My thoughts fell back to the previous evening. I closed my eyes for a moment, making a conscious decision to focus on McGrath and the kids, rather than the agony of watching each of them with Nick.

"McGrath was masterful. I totally expected them to buck at his mere presence. Secretly, I think Annie and Marie were a bit captivated by his easy charm. I don't think they associated him as anything more than my friend."

Di laughed. "Go ahead and lie to yourself all you want, silly. Those girls of yours are over the top savvy. Check with McGrath and see if they pumped him for information. They probably schemed ahead of time to check him out without letting you know they were on to him. I listened to the two of them all afternoon yesterday. Trust me, they are totally fixated on relationships right now."

I remembered Nick's teasing on the day of the accident. Of course, they knew. "Shit. I hate it when you're right."

"I know how the teenage mind works. I was fifteen once. And my dad was single. Each of his girlfriends became a prospective step-mother."

I nodded. "You're right, but I guessed I thought, or hoped they'd be preoccupied with Nick's coma."

"They're a lot like you right now, Sam. They can't afford to think about it 24/7, so thinking and talking about boys is the perfect distraction."

I sighed. *Diversion. Paramount right now.*

"What do you think of McGrath? Did you find time to talk?"

"He's a sweetheart. Made a point to ask about Ava and Chris. He even asked about the status of Joey and Emilio's adoption."

"I feel horrible. I've been so wrapped up with Nick, I haven't even asked you how things are going."

"It's all good. Thankfully, we finished the bedroom before they arrived. Fresh paint, matching comforters for the beds, sports posters on the walls. Emilio is hesitant, Joey's bouncing with excitement. It's perfectly normal. There's bound to be an adjustment period, but I'm guessing it will be short once they bond with Chris. Remember how Emilio loved being in Jack's class? Clearly, they'll appreciate having a stable man in their life."

"They must be taken with Ava, too. Most importantly, they're together. They have two loving parents. It can't be anything but good for them."

"I can't tell you how blessed I feel," Di admitted. "I'm giving them what my childhood lacked."

"The fact that you lost your mom helps you relate to them, for sure."

Her eyes shone with joy. "Who would have guessed that I'd have three kids so close together?"

I nodded. Di felt she was doomed to all things broken and lonely for many of the early years of our friendship. In the final analysis, she proved to be a testament to the adage, 'good things come to those who wait'.

"How did the kids do with Nick?"

Her question caught me off guard.

I couldn't allow myself to journey to that hopeless place. I'd ventured there once or twice myself over the past hours. *Disastrous.* I functioned far better when I stayed out of my head.

"Great," I lied.

Di leaned closer and studied my expression.

"I'm worried about you. I understand that it's important not to allow yourself to get too down about Nick, but really, Sam, you need to talk to someone. I'm sure you're scared to death. You don't need to be Joan of Arc all the time."

Mostly, talking backfired, leaving me feeling weak and vulnerable. I functioned much better when I kept my head down. Focused on doing rather than feeling.

I lifted my gaze from the sidewalk. A beam of sun sifted through the clouds. Its warmth hit my face like a ray of truth. It had taken a great deal of courage for me to let in McGrath, but I'd done it. With incredible results. *Could I do the same with Di and share my fears?* The mere thought paralyzed me.

"I hear what you're saying, Di, but I can't go there. Not now, anyway."

"I'm here for you. At some point, the world will come crashing down on you. You're not going to know what hit you."

My feathers ruffled. "I've weathered my fair share of losses. I think I've done pretty damned well."

"You know I love you. You're the toughest woman I know. Just be careful. Don't forget *you* in all of this. You need to experience your emotions, not file them away for future inspection. You're treating Nick's coma like a case of strep throat. A quick dose of antibiotics and he'll be good as new."

Tears clogged my throat. I swallowed hard and choked out, "I'm doing the best I can." Then I reassembled my armor.

Di stopped, rested her hand on my arm, and squeezed until I stopped walking. She drew me into a hug. I closed off. Stiffened. I couldn't let her hold me. *Too dangerous. Five kids to care for. One to guide back from the depths of a coma. No time for me.*

"C'mon," I said, conjuring a chuckle. "You're way more upset about this than I am."

Thunder clapped and the skies opened. Half-dollar sized raindrops plopped on our heads. The storm allowed me a quick exit from a far too heavy conversation. I dashed the last half-mile straight to my van, waving goodbye to Di.

"Call you later," I yelled.

I trembled on the short ride home, hating that I let her get to me. She needed to leave me the hell alone. I operated just fine without her cockamamie advice, thank you very much. I parked, ran inside, and grabbed a thick towel from the laundry room inside the back door. I dried off, slipped out of my wet clothes, and into a hot shower. I long believed that water could wash away all of my troubles. I recognized the metaphor, and surmised it was a metaphor for a very good reason.

I stood under the hot, pelting spray for a good fifteen minutes. I scrubbed my hair until it squeaked, then stepped out. I wrapped a dry towel around myself and wandered into my closet. After I dressed in a skirt and top, I applied some make-up and dried my hair. My reflection agreed with me. *I'm fine.*

I headed downstairs. Coffee. Bacon. Pancakes.

Ready.

CHAPTER TWELVE

ED PROMISED TO arrive by 9 a.m. By fifteen minutes of, I had downed a full pot of coffee, several pancakes, and too much bacon. The kids still slept soundly. I considered waking them. Instead, I climbed the stairs, and kissed each one of them on the cheek.

When Ed arrived, he smiled at me, sympathy etched into his eyes. "What's up?"

"I'm fine," I grumbled.

He hugged me.

I softened in his embrace. "Really," I promised.

"Good girl."

Thank you, God. No pressure from Ed today.

He pulled out a ladder back chair from the table, eased himself down and slung his arm over the top spindle. "What's on your agenda?"

I turned and reached inside the cupboard for a man-sized mug, then filled it with hot, black, very strong coffee as I filled him in on Nick's progress. "I recognize it's a small sign, minute probably."

"Special education teachers are accustomed to noticing and acknowledging small signs. There's wisdom in that."

He understood me as well as McGrath. "People have accused me of being naïve and foolish because I believe in the little things." I placed the mug in front of him, then sat down across from him, frowning.

Ed reached over and patted my arm. "They're too quick to give up. You have patience. And you believe that everyone has a gift to share. There's no shame in that."

I stood and refilled my mug, my gaze still fixed on him. "Sometimes I wonder."

"Well, I don't." Ed looked definite in his assessment of my abilities.

I laughed, twisting away for a moment, and then cocked my head in his direction.

"What's so funny?"

"I'm not sure exactly what I did to deserve you, but I'm sure glad you're here."

Ed grinned. "I've got your back."

I nodded and took comfort in his support. Someone on my side. *Pity party over.*

The short twenty minute drive to the hospital brought clear blue skies along with it. Most rainy August days were socked in. Lucky for me, the clouds parted today. It would mean an easier day for Ed if the kids could get outside and hang with their friends, and sunshine always lightened my mood.

I rode the elevator to the fourth floor amidst a crowd of smile-less parents, stopping off at the nurse's station to inquire about Nick's night.

"No change." The nurse's perfunctory report threatened a dampening of my sunny disposition, but I refused to allow it.

Like it or not, I again faced the lack of progress as I entered Nick's room. For the fourth straight day, my son lay motionless in his bed.

Between Di's remarks and Nick's continued unconsciousness, I threatened to unravel. My confidence wavered. Still, giving into my feelings translated into giving up. I had a serious and somewhat laborious conversation with myself. Soon enough, I knocked myself back into shape. It's what worked for me. *Pity party number two. Over.*

I drew my cell and headphones from my bag, repeating the routine I performed yesterday. I opted for the recording of Lizzie's song again today, hoping the familiarity of her voice would spur a reaction from Nick.

Truth was, I couldn't bear the thought of him not reacting. At the same time, I steeled myself to the possibility. The music played for several minutes; the faint, sweet strains of my baby's beautiful voice singing to her brother. I fixed my gaze on Nick and held his hand. When the song finished, I closed my eyes to pray. I shook my head and refocused on Nick's slack form, but was soon distracted by his neurologist's entrance. Dr. Stern laid a gentle hand on my shoulder.

"How are you, Mrs. Stitsill?" His soft, brown eyes bespoke kindness and compassion. Two more things that scared the shit out of me. *Stop it, people.* I couldn't allow myself to admit my greatest fears to him or anyone else. I spun away from those thoughts and took an objective look at the doctor. He appeared about fifty years old, tall and lean, but with a baby face that seemed out of place atop his athletic form. The contradiction struck me as odd. If I'd seen him on the street and guessed his occupation, a game my late husband and I played in our early years of marriage, I'd have said he resembled Mr. Magoo.

After a moment spent chastising myself for entertaining such catty thoughts, it occurred to me that I hadn't previously addressed him by name. I hadn't allowed myself to let him in. I hadn't let anyone in. Not really. I sighed and nodded.

"Please, call me Sam."

"Wait and see is never fun. I wish I had more definitive answers for you. The CT scan indicates that your son's intracranial pressure has decreased, which gives us reason for optimism." He pressed his hands together and focused on the ear buds still in Nick's ears. "I see you're trying to stimulate him. Keep up the good work."

I fixed my eyes on the clock, neither noting the time nor the tick of the second hand as it circled its face. "The nurse told you what happened, didn't she? Nick squeezed my hand."

"If he responded," Dr. Stern conjectured, "that provides another encouraging sign. Once Nick is fully awake, we'll be better able to assess the damage and prognosticate his recovery."

If. Stern doubted me. That pissed me off. I fought the urge to criticize him, and reminded myself that it was his job to play Doubting Thomas. Still...

"You're a neurologist. You have no idea? None at all?" The words spilled past my lips before I could stop or filter them. An embarrassing loss of control.

Dr. Stern locked eyes with me. He looked sad and considerate. "I'm sorry. No."

I swallowed hard. "How about Brain Gym?"

Stern looked puzzled.

I explained the exercises to him. "Crossing midline, one hand touching the opposite knee, for example, encourages interaction between the two hemispheres of the brain. May I run Nick through the paces?"

Dr. Stern spent a moment in thought. "Can't hurt. Just allow him plenty of rest in between your interactions. His brain needs time to rest and heal."

I nodded, feeling somewhat encouraged. Then, I smiled. "Thank you."

"You're welcome," he said, before turning and leaving the room.

I glanced at the clock again, this time reading it. Only 10:00 a.m. Already, I felt as if I'd been riding a terrorizing roller coaster for a small eternity. I grasped Nick's hand, recognizing that I'd probably missed his response window. I held his slender, freckled fingers, and stroked a large speckle on the top of his hand.

The door creaked again and an older, portly nurse, Sue,

her name tag read, entered the room. I hadn't met her before, so I introduced myself. She leaned against the counter, making small talk before informing me that Nick would have some tests and she'd prefer it if I skedaddled. That's what she said. Skedaddled. Her sweetness encouraged my compliance. I had to give her that. I wondered if she'd been a teacher in a former life.

"Take a few hours to yourself," she advised.

After kissing Nick on the cheek and gathering my belongings, I headed downstairs. I had no idea how to occupy myself.

School would begin in nine days, the day after Labor Day, and I was expected the week before then. My leave. I'd only sent my email request yesterday, but I suddenly panicked. What if administration failed to approve my request? I decided to place a call to the superintendent. I needed fresh air, and a personal call might assist my case. If I knew more about the status of my leave request, I'd have one less thing to fret about.

I chose an isolated park bench in the shade of a stout oak from which to make the call. I spoke briefly to the secretary and then my boss came on the line. Anita Tompkins assured me that my leave would be approved, offered me her best wishes, and asked me to keep in touch. She'd already connected with the teacher that I'd recommended as a substitute, and she felt certain that I'd return to my position soon.

I appreciated her kindness, feeling a tad less bi-polar now that I'd spoken with her. A warm breeze gusted, and I brushed a lock of hair from my eyes. As I turned away from the gathering wind, I caught McGrath's familiar stride in my peripheral vision. I sprinted to his side. He pulled me into his embrace, and I inhaled his intoxicating spicy scent.

"Fancy meeting you here," he whispered.

"I missed you." I focused on his turquoise eyes and the smile lines encasing them.

He cupped a handful of my derriere and knocked me

slightly off kilter. "I have a thought."

"Really? Now? My kid's in a coma. Have you forgotten?"

McGrath laughed. "You can't blame a guy for trying. You have to understand something about me. I know things about people. I know you. You dare your demons, which is admirable, and don't get me wrong, I respect you for it, but taking a break and doing something for yourself is essential to your survival. Consider the idea. It would do you a helluva lot of good."

"This is about you, not me."

His dimples deepened. "It's true, I love making love to you. I'd like to think it's as important a part of our relationship to you as it is to me. Right now, you're in crisis. Doing something for yourself would fuel your soul."

I shook my head. Was he crazy? Did he know me at all? How could I be a woman when I was busy being a mom?

"I know this is outside the box of 16. We can stay right here if you'd like. It's your call."

"The nurse said it would be two to three hours."

"And there's nothing for you to do during that time."

I nodded, the thought of entertaining my womanhood enticing. On the other hand, could I forgive myself for an act of selfishness when my kid was unconscious? God help me, Good Sam and Bad Sam began to argue. *You still need to make up with McGrath... you have responsibilities.* "Let's go."

McGrath's mouth dropped open. "This isn't like you, Sam. Are you sure?"

"Take me, now. Before I have a chance to change my mind."

He smiled, relieved me of my backpack and tossed it over his shoulder before he guided me toward his Jeep. After loading me inside, he rubbed my shoulder. "I'm so proud of you."

We arrived at his place thirty minutes later. Within seconds, he drew the blinds in his bedroom, turned back the bed linens, lit a candle, and played soft music. I stripped off my clothes and placed them in a neat pile on the chair next to his bed. By the time I turned around, he was lying naked on his back, his arms folded over his head. His grin, as well as his other parts, indicated that he was happy to see me.

I took shelter in his very masculine embrace and when that little voice chastised me: *you're a bad mom*, I told her to *SHUT UP*.

God, he was sexy. He smelled of cedar and musk; inhaling his scent kicked my heart into overdrive. I kissed him, toying with his tongue and teeth, and pressed my breasts against his chest. His skin was warm and smooth. "You are amazing."

He nuzzled his head on top of mine. "Go on."

I rested my head on his chest and toyed with his nipple. "It's your skin. I could spend the rest of my life touching you. I feel safe with you. It sounds silly, embarrassing really..." I ran my fingers over his muscled shoulder. "But I melt when you touch me."

He lifted my hand to his mouth, and sucked on my fingers, one at a time. Then he gripped my arm and massaged it with a gentle pulse.

A frission of sensation ran through me. How could I have considered turning him down? I should allow him to coach me in the art of living more often. "I get away from you and forget how good you are for me."

He kissed my neck and mumbled, "The mistress of denial."

His words hit me with a thud. I'd called Jon 'the master of denial'.

McGrath's continued murmurings brought me back to him. "I love you. Every blessed inch of your skin, every rational word that comes out of your mouth." He laughed gently. "And every crazy word, too."

"I need to feel you."

His fingers inched down my spine and pressed into the small of my back. I arched my body into his, begging him to make me whole. His heartbeat raced; his breathing quickened. I lost all sense of time and place as my body melded with his in thrusts, shudders, and throaty exclamations... one euphoric earthquake. His body fell atop mine and we twisted into a mess of tangled limbs and chuckles. He locked eyes with me and smiled. "Wow."

"At least."

We snuggled into each other, our breathing evening out, gazing into each other's eyes and laughing. I felt happy and complete for 12 whole seconds before real life sunk its hooks into my chest. "I should to get back to the hospital."

He glanced at the clock. "We've only been away for an hour. Put your head on my shoulder. Another five minutes won't hurt, I promise."

I felt torn, but took his words to heart. He was right. I hated how well he knew me and loved it at the same time. Another few minutes wouldn't hurt. I settled against his chest and closed my eyes. "I struggle slowing down the train. Thank you for being patient with me."

"It's my pleasure."

I took a long moment. I'd spent so much time and energy denying myself; I fought the compulsion to mount the mommy horse, the work horse, the solve-the-next-crisis horse. Making love with McGrath? My heart and soul elixir. Yet, I struggled with self-reproach. *You have responsibilities. Your child could die. You're shameless.* I fought to stay in the moment and deal with one damn problem at a time. I needed to be sure McGrath and I were on solid ground, I needed this fortification, to build up my walls in order to handle the onslaught of jackhammers that waited outside of these four walls. "I hated our fight. I hated being without you. But I did what I always do, and blamed you. I was wrong and you were right. I have no business involving myself with Lisa's disappearance. I promise I'll stick to worrying, and nothing more."

He rubbed my arm and nodded.

I smiled. "Does this mean we're over our stupid fight?"

"As long as you promise to take care of yourself and the kids, all is forgiven. I thought you understood the parameters."

"I love you." I gave his cheek a peck and jumped up to grab a quick shower. He pulled me back down and kissed me, long and hard.

"Okay," he said. "Now you can go."

I glanced at him as I padded out of the room. He looked happier than I felt. I could have imagined it, but he looked... unencumbered. I, on the other hand, couldn't allow myself to feel that free. Not under the circumstances. *Would I ever feel free? Happy? Probably not. Pity party, Sam. Knock. It. Off.*

As we drove back to the hospital, the second storm of the day brewed. The earlier sunshine had been a temporary reprieve after all. As hard as I tried to quell it, guilt reared its ghastly head, and I prayed Nick had remained stable during my absence. Shit, I felt like a kid who'd snuck out of the house, ready to face dire consequences for her dastardly deed, self-recrimination far worse than any sentence imposed from an honorable court. Menacing skies matched my sour mood, and I needed to get out of my head. I decided to change the focus. I could have talked about the weather. I could have talked about Nick. But I didn't. *Distraction and curiosity are my friends.* Now that McGrath and I had made up and I had reassured him that I would stay out of it, I figured I could ask him about the current status of the case. *I'm Lisa's concerned friend.* At least that's what I told myself.

"Nothing new," he said. "Lisa testified before the Grand Jury several months ago. I can't obtain a transcript of the testimony yet, but between you and me, her husband made millions from the corruption schemes he and his brother orchestrated. That guy's going away for a very long time."

My motherhood gene popped to the forefront. "What happens to the kids if Tony goes to prison?"

"Your guess is as good as mine."

"I met Lisa's sister, Lori, once at the house. Maybe she'd talk to me."

McGrath laughed and squeezed my knee. "Your hands are full right now. Leave the detective work to me."

"I know. I will." A thought suddenly occurred to me. "What about Hammer?"

"Hammer?"

"Sorry." I squeezed my eyes shut. Shook my head. "I'm an idiot. I should have remembered this sooner. Right before Adrianna turned three, Lisa bought a German Shepherd. Hammer. She thought it would be good for Adrianna and Lauren to have a pet."

"Not sure I'm following."

I felt an adrenalin release. "What happened to the dog? Was he there? You never mentioned the dog."

"Never saw a dog."

I mentally added the numbers. "Seven years," I said. "It's a long time, I know, but dogs are usually around for longer than that. I don't know if it means anything or not. Probably not. But it's worth asking about. Just thinking."

I recognized McGrath's pensive expression. The one that shrouded his face when he questioned himself about how he'd put the facts together.

His concentration finally broke. He winked at me. "Thanks, Sam. You're awesome."

CHAPTER THIRTEEN

PERSONALLY, I DIDN'T consider remembering the Macchione dog to be much of a lead. I speculated that once I had Nick home and settled, I could be much more helpful to McGrath and Lisa's 'missing person' case. On one hand he said he didn't want my help, but he sure perked up when I mentioned Hammer. Besides, what good detective turns down a valid clue, no matter how small? While I sat with Nick that afternoon, I scribbled a list of questions I had about Lisa and her disappearance. Lists helped me to feel in command during the times in which I actually had no control—not one smidge.

McGrath had mentioned that Lisa's sister, Lori Woodruff, had been extremely cooperative. She'd spoken freely of her dislike for her brother-in-law, Tony. No surprise there. Indicated that she wouldn't put acts of violence past him. She had denied speaking with Lisa since the day of her disappearance. I questioned that.

Probably my own desperate need to keep Lisa alive. I let those thoughts float around in my brain for a bit. If Lisa were alive and interested in returning at some point to claim her children, it made sense for her to hide out. Tony's indictment could have placed her in extreme danger. I could certainly imagine him threatening her about her testimony. He wouldn't have been allowed in the Grand

Jury while she was testifying, but he could have pointed out her vulnerabilities if she were to slant things in a harmful direction for either his brother or him. I ventured it wouldn't have been the first time. Maybe she'd run away before the charges were filed in order to protect herself. Still, I couldn't reason, try as I might, why she would have left her children behind. There must be a better explanation. I just hadn't thought of it yet.

If she had simply fled, had she had help? Was she having an affair? If so, her lover might have aided her getaway. I discounted that possibility. If she'd been having an affair, Tony would have known. He'd have hired a private investigator the moment she separated from him in June. He'd have killed her if she'd become involved with another man. They were Mafia, for goodness sake. These guys knew how to get rid of people. In light of the indictment, I wondered if the threat of murder had been bandied about during the Grand Jury investigation. Mob ties and all that.

Within an instant of that thought, I realized Lisa's sister would have lied for her. If Lisa had been my sister, I would have done the same. I needed to speak with Lori Woodruff. I made a note on my pad.

What about Tony? He'd always considered himself God's gift to women. Guys like that are rarely faithful. Did he have a mistress? If so, had McGrath found the woman and interrogated her? Had Tony been unfaithful with more than one woman during their marriage?

Part of me felt like McGrath would have shared information like this with me, had it come to light. Another part of me knew that he'd been careful not to overburden me since Nick's accident. I made another note to ask him.

What if Lisa had left as Tony reported? Wouldn't he have put someone on her tail? He possessed as many resources as the authorities. Maybe more.

Where would Lisa have gone? Where could she have remained safe? Her photo had been plastered over the news for five days now. Although the frequency of the news reports had dwindled as the week passed, her disappearance was still considered a big deal. People loved scandals. Lived for them.

My mind wandered to the Bourne movies. Jason's girlfriend, Marie Creutz, had chopped off her hair, dyed it, disguised herself. Changed her identity. I pictured Lisa's shoulder length mahogany colored hair. Bleached and trimmed, she'd look completely different. She could gain weight, wear glasses. Frump up her normally polished attire.

What if she'd entered the Witness Protection Program? *Getting carried away now, Sam.* I inhaled. Long and deep. If she'd done that, she'd have taken her girls with her. Duh. And McGrath would have known.

Think, Stitsill, think.

My head slumped back against the chair. Famished and exhausted, I squinted at the clock and realized I'd been engrossed in my thoughts for the past hour. I'd blocked out the rumbling thunder and the crackles of lightning. I walked to the window, and lifted the slatted blinds. Slanted rain slapped the window, car tops, and pavement. Black as night, the storm dampened my already somber mood.

After I kissed Nick's cheek and checked his monitors, I entered the ICU hallway. The ward was quiet. One o'clock. Everyone must have headed to the cafeteria for lunch. I didn't feel like mixing in a crowd, or sharing war stories with another parent of sick kid, so I purchased a turkey and Swiss cheese sandwich and a bottle of water from a nearby vending machine. I scrounged around the visitor's lounges, located a conference room with an empty table, and ate there. The walls were stark, the only bare ones I'd seen in the cheery-muraled hospital. The bleak white walls met my needs. I required time with my emotions. To clean them up and cast them out.

I finished eating. Called home. Lizzie answered. My throat clogged with tears. The seriousness of the past few days caught up with me. Between my conversations with Jack, Di, Ed, and Dr. Stern, then my love-making session with McGrath and losing myself in thoughts of Lisa's disappearance, the ups and downs were taking their toll. I craved normal. Too bad normal had departed for a better climate. Would it return? Who knew!

I pulled a chair over to the window in the tiny room, gripping a box of hospital issued tissues. I gazed out at the rain, fought not to jump as thunder boomed, and then opened the faucets. Had a cleansing cry. More like major weeping and despair. Only in the shadows would I allow myself this treat. Not that it felt like much of a luxury. Suffering and crisis had been a moniker in my life. For a long time now. While I never realized it in the middle of a crisis, I recognized that the heartaches had made me stronger. I couldn't imagine what good would come out of Nick's coma, what I would learn or how it would make me better. I knew that it opened my heart and validated the importance of love in my life. In that moment, I asked God to help me weather the unknown.

Control the things you can, give up the rest. Serenity. Courage. Wisdom.

A good while later, calm took hold. I rejoined Nick in his room, opened the blinds, and took a chair at his side. Warm rays of sunshine poured through the window. The monitors kept track of his vitals, the ventilator continued to push oxygen into his lungs. I reached into my bag and retrieved my notepad. I'd write to pass the time. I'd simply sit with my son.

I glanced up as Nick's eyes opened. Someone had heard my plea, and answered my prayer.

He appeared to focus on me. I cautioned myself to remain still and peaceful, but I couldn't contain myself. I smiled at him, and whispered, "Good boy. That's the Nick I know and love."

Big news. Gigantic. The coma scale described eye

opening on the generalized response level. Level II. My thoughts raced. I should do something. I should let someone know. Instead, I did what all proud mothers do in a moment of sheer delight. I retrieved my cell phone and snapped his picture. It would be time-stamped, right? No one could ignore me now.

My brain finally kicked in, and I pressed the call button for the nurse. Her voice sounded over the speaker.

"Yes, may I help you?"

Seriously? Her booming voice would have awakened the dead.

I stammered, "My son. Nick Stitsill. His eyes are open."

"I'll be right there."

Here I sat, holding my proverbial breath, a smile frozen on my face, not taking my eyes off my son for a second, and she comes barging in the room like he'd gone into cardiac arrest.

She peered at him, assessing him, no doubt.

"Go ahead," she directed. "Talk to him."

I fought to hold back tears. Not the first thing I wanted him to see, his mother burbling and carrying on. I willed a smile to remain on my face and spoke to him again. "Hey, kiddo. You're in the Children's Hospital at the U. I know you like to keep memories of your injuries, so I clicked a photograph for posterity." I appealed to the nurse for encouragement. I felt uneasy. Didn't want to screw up anything. Make anything worse. She nodded.

"You were hit by a car when you were riding your bike in town. Do you remember?"

Nick stared at me. I hadn't expected an additional response. I struggled to remember what I'd witnessed in the movies. "Squeeze my hand if you can hear me." Cheesy, I know. But moments after I spoke, his hand moved in mine. Ever so slightly. Not a grip or a grasp, but the pressure of his thumb against my palm.

I glanced toward the nurse and nodded that he had

responded. She rearranged one of the lines from his IV. As she did, her pants made a rustling sound. She moved about the room. Nick's eyes moved ever so slightly, almost as if he was trying to track her. She hadn't made additional noise, so I guessed he had seen her. Hoped he had seen her.

Thank you, God.

CHAPTER FOURTEEN

I EXPECTED THE nurse to alert the doctor instantly. She
did not. She just stayed close by, watching. She didn't utter
a sound, simply continued to observe Nick. She stepped
behind me and laid a reassuring hand on my shoulder. I felt
like turning cartwheels. I longed to share the news with Ed,
the kids, and McGrath, but I sat perfectly still.

Could Nick be this lucky? Would he return to us so
quickly? I wasn't accustomed to good things happening.
I knew better than to count on one good thing happening
right after another. McGrath and I were on solid ground.
The rest of my children were healthy. Enough? No. Nick
was too important.

I glanced back at the nurse. Her name tag read 'Melissa'.
She wore pink scrubs decorated with smiling pets, her long,
dark brown hair piled atop of her head. Like an angel sent
by God, she laid a healing hand on my shoulder. Her smile
reflected my joy.

I'd never forget her, or that moment.

Pinpricks of anxiety raced through my arms. What if
Nick's alertness proved temporary? What if he fell back to
sleep and didn't wake up again?

Melissa whispered, "It's good. He's going to require a
good deal sleep after this, I suspect. It's a lot for him to sort
out. He'll have challenges ahead, but the fact that he's only

been comatose for a few days and is now awake is a very good sign. Try not to worry."

When I glanced back at Nick, his eyes were closed. Blissful tears streaked my cheeks. Melissa gestured for me to step outside, and her gentle gaze rested on my face. She took me in her arms and held me; I shed tears of relief. After a long moment, I wiped my eyes and thanked her.

"Why don't you go home and get some rest?" she suggested.

"I can't leave now."

"He'll sleep if you allow him to rest. Go home, catch your breath, and spend time with your family. I'll keep a close eye on him. I promise." Her smile spoke volumes.

"Only if you're sure. I would like to at least make a phone call or two."

"Go."

I glanced at my watch. 3 p.m. The sun still shone. There was time enough to drag the kids shopping for school clothes. Renewed energy surged through me. I labeled it: hope.

I nodded at Melissa and slipped into Nick's room. He slept soundly. I kissed his cheek. "I'm so very proud of you." I stepped back in to the hall, located Melissa, and pressed a note with my cell number into her hand before heading home.

The usual claustrophobia I felt upon entering the parking garage disappeared. I phoned McGrath as soon as I reached daylight and concrete-free air. He picked up on the first ring. Nice to know I held a top spot on his priority list.

"Guess what?" I said.

"You sound happy. I'm guessing it's good news."

"Today has been a very good day. Alone time with you, then my boy woke up and looked at me. He squeezed my hand, too."

I heard the rush of his breath through the phone. "Wow. Great news!"

"I'm running home to school shop with the kids for a bit. Want to come over after that?"

"You're ready for that?"

"Totally."

We agreed on six o'clock. McGrath offered to deliver pizza.

When I arrived home, I discovered Ed and the kids tossing the Frisbee in the backyard. He walked up the drive to greet me.

My grin must have said it all, because his face lit up. "News?"

"Nick opened his eyes today, and he squeezed my hand."

Ed gathered me into his arms. When we looked at each other, tears streamed down both of our faces. "Thank God," he said.

I nodded. "I've decided not to mention it to the kids yet. If things spin in another direction, I don't want them to suffer a let-down."

Ed turned and studied the kids. "Makes sense."

My eyes followed. They were still lobbing the Frisbee, laughing and chasing the disc. "What?"

He choked up as he swiped away a tear and shook his head. "Just hate this for all of you. Too hard."

"Hard on all of us," I said softly. "You, too."

"I'm a tough old bird. Don't worry about me. Just take care of yourself and the kids, honey."

I sighed. Felt the energy whoosh out of me. "I'm going to load them up and chauffeur them to the mall."

Ed nodded. "I'll mow the lawn before I head home."

Nick's job since Jon's death. I swallowed hard. We were inching closer to normal, just not there quite yet.

"C'mon, guys," I called. "Get ready to pick out some new duds."

Annie, Marie, and Will ran into the house. Lizzie dashed to me and threw her arms around my waist. "How's Nick?"

I smiled, hoping that she'd sense my optimism and not

press for further details. "He's sleeping right now, sweetie. Now, get ready to go."

She skipped inside. Ed nodded and trod to the shed to pull out the mower.

I felt blessed. "Thanks, Dad."

We spent the afternoon gathering school supplies, backpacks, jeans, tees, and new shoes, then stopped for ice cream before returning home. I ached for Nick the entire afternoon. We'd never school-shopped without him. Hopefully, it wouldn't be much longer until he joined us at home.

My breathing became ragged as the six o'clock hour approached. Maybe I was asking too much of the kids. If I lacked confidence, they would catch on in an instant. I gathered a deep breath and called them to the kitchen table. "My policeman friend is bringing pizza for dinner."

They stared at me. Awkward silence.

Annie finally spoke. "Your boyfriend."

Accusation. Ouch! The lump in my throat grew. What had I been thinking? *Too much. Too soon.* "He's a good friend."

"If Nick were here, he wouldn't let you get away with this," Annie muttered.

I locked eyes with her. "Get away with what?"

Annie pursed her lips and shook her head, disgusted. "Not being honest."

I found myself struggling with the word boyfriend. Was he my boyfriend? Boyfriends were for teenagers, not mothers. My stomach knotted.

"As I said, he's a good friend. I'm not going to marry him."

Damn. I did want to marry this man. Someday. Not right now. For some time, it had been my intention to marry him. But the reality of admitting that desire aloud eluded me. Was I doubting myself? Holy hell. *Yes.*

Annie lurched up, shoved in her chair, and stomped out of the room.

"Annie, please come back."

She turned and glared at me, tears rimming her eyes.

"It's just dinner," I said, reminded of my words to Di when she hesitated to meet Chris for coffee. *Shallow. Lame. Excuse.*

Annie sneered and planted her hands on her hips. "I'm not hungry."

I scanned the table's filled chairs. Marie, Will, and Lizzie's eyes rested on me. They appeared suspended, as if hanging in midair as they awaited my response. Annie, always the most outspoken of the crew, tested me in different ways than Nick. My ire spiked. *Not now,* I cautioned myself.

"Maybe you could give him a chance. He's not arriving until six. Think about it," I said calmly.

"I'm not changing my mind, Mom." Annie's voice rose as she spoke. "Go ahead. Have him over if you want. I'll stay in my room."

I tried to reassure her. I could only imagine how threatened she felt. "He'll never replace Daddy. Come here. Please." I patted my knee.

Like boxers in the ring, we stood in opposite corners. I wanted to be in *her* corner. A long moment of silence ensued. I locked eyes with her and extended my hand. When Annie arrived in this place, stomping her feet and planting them so firmly that she became unmovable, the ground beneath us became precarious. I had been in this face-off position with her many times.

She needed me right now. Whether she could allow me in through her pain remained the question.

In my peripheral vision, I saw the other's gazes travel back and forth from Annie to me. They'd likely follow the winner's lead on this. Sticking together remained key for them.

Lizzie reached out for Annie, bridging the chasm between us. Such a young soul, but wise beyond her years. "Daddy will always be with us, remember?" Her soft voice soothed. "He's watching right now. He wants Mom to be happy."

Annie looked shocked. As if Lizzie had joined me in enemy camp. Then her gaze traveled from Will to Marie. Jon had been their biological father. If anyone should have had a problem with me being involved with McGrath, it should have been them.

"No man will ever take your dad's place," I said. "We will always keep him alive in our hearts. Try to think of…" My voice trailed off. I had no idea what to call McGrath with the kids. I hardly ever called him Jim.

I located my voice and my wits. "Detective McGrath is a good man. I'd like for all of you to get to know each other. Let's not make this a bigger deal than it needs to be, okay?" My eyes traveled from kid to kid.

Will, Lizzie, and Marie nodded agreement, anxious to relieve the tension. Our eyes settled on Annie. We waited an interminably long moment. Finally, she nodded, blinking away her tears. I patted my knee. She drew nearer, settled on my lap, and rested her head on my shoulder.

I wrapped my arms around her. "It's going to be alright, sweetie. I promise."

Fifteen minutes later, McGrath rang the doorbell. I opened the screen door and smiled at him, retrieving the three large pizza boxes from his grasp. "Come in," I said, stifling the urge to kiss him. "Everyone's starved."

CHAPTER FIFTEEN

THE HOUSE FELL quiet when I climbed into bed a little after midnight. I folded my arms over my head, stared at the ceiling, and took stock. We'd all been on edge. Me, McGrath, the kids. Perfectly understandable. Periods of awkward silence preceded artificial small talk. If McGrath and I hadn't indulged in a beer with our pizza, I guessed that the evening would have been a total cluster of nerves.

When I'd pulled out the game of Clue and given McGrath the detective plug again, things lightened up a bit. While things had gone swimmingly when they had ridden with him to the hospital and spent time with him there, it was entirely different having him as a guest in our home. We'd crossed a serious boundary, a double line. Their discomfort with him eased long enough to ask him a few questions about solving crimes, but those had been the only easy moments of the evening.

In the end, McGrath, wise man that he is, did not reach for my hand or kiss me goodbye. He headed for home before the kids trotted off to bed, after we agreed that we'd speak in the morning.

I rolled over, closed my eyes, and recited the promise I'd made to Annie earlier that evening. "It'll be alright." A few minutes afterward, I drifted off to sleep.

A while later, I sensed someone standing at the side of my bed. I opened my eyes to see Lizzie staring at me.

"I can't sleep," she whined.

I opened the covers and she scrambled into bed with me, curling her tiny frame next to mine. "What's the matter?"

"I can't stop thinking about Daddy."

Made sense to me. "You were so brave tonight. You convinced your sister to welcome my friend into our home." Way more than our home, I thought. More like our lives. "I'm sure having a man besides Grandpa here made you think of Daddy, just like it made Annie think of him. It's hard because no one wants to let go of Daddy, and Mommy having a new friend makes everyone afraid." I should have said nervous. Or worried. Fear seemed too strong a feeling to interject into the mix of emotions going on inside her head. "But Daddy will always be with us. We carry him in our hearts. Every day. Every night."

I had handled McGrath's visit all wrong. The kids needed time to adjust to being home. When they'd left in June, our house had been in complete and total disarray from the fire. On the heels of arriving back home, Nick had been injured. I forced a new man into their lives before they had time to adjust. *Slow down, Samantha.* Why did I always have to be in such a goddamned hurry?

I vowed to phone McGrath in the morning and explain my thinking. He'd understand, wouldn't he?

"I know Daddy wants us all to be happy, Mom. Especially you. Annie's just nervous. Not afraid really. She doesn't want to forget Dad."

"It's normal to worry about forgetting him, but none of us will ever forget Dad, kiddo. We'll keep him alive by talking about him, watching videos, all of it." We locked eyes in the soft moonlit room and smiled at each other. "It's not your job to worry about Annie. It's my job, alright?" I gave her a gentle squeeze. "Let's try to get some rest."

I cuddled her close and evened out my breathing,

hoping she would match it and doze off to sleep. Before long, I heard her soft snores.

Calming Lizzie had been easy. Now I needed to unravel my own nerves.

I tossed and turned until dawn. Nothing would be right until I spoke to McGrath. I brewed a pot of coffee, poured a cup, and carried it and my cell phone onto the front porch. I rocked in my chair and waited until 7 a.m. to call, when I knew he'd be up and running.

It seemed best to use straightforward approach, but I was nervous, nonetheless.

"Hi." My nerves jangled when he answered.

"You don't sound so good," he said. "Is something wrong?"

"We're rushing things. Not we, but me. *I'm* rushing things."

He tried to reassure me. "What do you mean? Things went well last night. Did something happen after I left?"

I'd never lied to McGrath before. Didn't seem like a good time to start. Instead I told him a half-truth. "I'm feeling overwhelmed. I need to spend more time at the hospital with Nick and the start of the school year is right around the corner. I don't want Nick to wake up and see me with you before he's had a chance to acclimate to the world again."

His regret pulsed through the connection. "I thought we were on solid ground. Do you really want to sneak around?"

"I'm not talking about sneaking around. I'm talking about taking a break."

A long, cold, silent moment filled the air. I shivered in spite of the sun's warm rays.

I sipped my lukewarm coffee. It left a bad taste in my mouth.

"I'm sorry."

He sighed. "Are you sure this is what you want?"

"I hoped you'd understand."

"It's not that I don't understand, but I don't have to like your decision or agree with it. If anything, I thought Nick's accident would persuade you to speed things up, not slow them down. Life's short. You've had plenty of examples of that over the past two years. I gave you space when you needed it after Jon died. We're a couple, aren't we? Why put things off?"

"It's a temporary hiatus. I promise."

McGrath cleared his throat. "I let you go once, I'm not about to do it again."

"You're not making this easy."

"This shouldn't be easy," he said flatly.

Anger bubbled inside me. "Do you have any idea how difficult this is for me? I don't want to hurt or disappoint you. I have five kids, one who's hopefully on the verge of awakening from a coma. I'm all my kids have. It's a steep mountain I have to climb."

"Let me help you."

"Not yet. I don't want to argue about this. I respect and appreciate your opinion, but I've made up my mind."

"Okay, then I guess I'll talk to you later."

"Jim, please. Don't be angry with me."

"It's not anger."

"Then what?"

"Disappointment. I love you. I want to spend the rest of my life with you. I'm willing to do whatever it takes. Be with your kids. Help raise them. But if you shut me out, I can't do any of those things, and I think you need and want me to be a part of your life."

A ragged breath escaped me. "Just give me some time."

"I've gotta get to work."

I tried to reassure him. "I'll be in touch."

"Yep."

And with that, he was gone.

CHAPTER SIXTEEN

I SHUFFLED INSIDE and poured another cup of coffee. If only I had a cigarette. It would calm me. Since I didn't smoke, I'd have to stew for a while. Damn it. Why did McGrath have to be so difficult? I tromped upstairs to take a shower. After I dressed, I woke Marie and Annie and asked them to hold down the fort until Grandpa Ed arrived. Staying away from the hospital had been a mistake. I needed to be with Nick. The more time I spent coaching and reassuring him, the sooner he'd recover. I left a note on the counter for Ed, and marched out the door.

I remembered a quote my mother shared with me when my first boyfriend broke my heart. *Hell hath no fury like a woman's scorn.* Yep. I was pissed. How dare McGrath hold Nick's illness over my head!

The concrete jungle had no effect on me this morning. I dove into the elevator and rode in blind anger to Nick's floor. Was it time for the doctors to remove the ventilator and reduce the medication so that he could be more awake? After a stop at the nurse's station to ask about his night, I took a steadying lungful of air. No news. He'd slept through the night.

Carrying my stress into Nick's room would accomplish nothing, so I took several cleansing breaths and shook off my inner tension. As soon as I entered Nick's room, I calmed. This was what I was meant to do. At least for the time being.

I kissed my sweet boy's freckled cheek and grasped his hand. "Hey, Nick, it's Mom. I love you, buddy."

I dragged a chair forward and sat down. "Can you open your eyes?"

I leaned back and waited. In those moments, I wondered what it was like for Nick. Did he hate the ventilator breathing for him? He had always been such a spitfire: independent, and headstrong. He couldn't have liked it. What if it didn't breathe in the same rhythm he did? That would stir his ire. Could he hear it? Did he compose songs in his head to its beat? I couldn't wait for him to awaken and tell me all about it.

I pulled my cell phone from my purse and played Lizzie's song for him. All the while, I stroked his hand and smoothed the fine silky hair on his forearm. I told him how hard Lizzie had practiced his song, and about Marie and Annie's driving. About how Will loped around the house like a lost puppy missing his best friend.

"We bought you some new jeans and t-shirts yesterday. Each of your sisters picked out shirts with guitars on them. Will found one with Led Zeppelin on the back. Of course, just to aggravate you, I bought you a nice button down for picture day." I chuckled and squeezed his hand. Nick hated it when I made him dress up on picture day. Will, too. It hit me then. If Nick woke up and could attend school by picture day, this would be the year I'd relent. He and Will could wear whatever the hell they pleased.

What other trivialities would I shed when Nick woke up? That would be when I would feel like speeding up my life, my dear, sweet, Detective McGrath. And not a minute before.

As I continued speaking to Nick, sharing neighborhood news and his upcoming class schedule, I noticed his increased heart rate. While he didn't open his eyes, I felt certain this indicated a response.

"Good job, Bud." I prattled on about this and that, pausing every now and then to coach him into opening his eyes.

The door creaked open behind me. It was Dr. Stern. I smiled and stood to shake his hand. "My boy's more responsive."

"I heard the news. It's a good sign, but we have to be patient and watchful. There's no way to tell how much damage he's suffered."

He must have read the discouraged look on my face, because he placed a gentle hand on my shoulder. "I'm not trying to dampen your mood, just want you to be realistic."

"I'm a special education teacher. I know all about patience and reality." I paused, embarrassed that I sounded so huffy. Dr. Stern had certainly witnessed worse reactions in his tenure as a neurologist. Apologies weren't on my agenda today.

I squared my shoulders. "When will you remove the ventilator? It can't be comfortable for him."

Dr. Stern tried his gentle smile with me again. "We'll gradually reduce the sedatives and see how he does. Once we determine his ability to breathe on his own, we'll let you know. We should be able to assess that within the next day or so."

"Thank you." I turned toward Nick.

His eyes were open. My face flushed. He'd witnessed the entire scene. One of these days, I'd learn to curb my impulsivity. I vowed, then and there, that would be another weakness I'd abandon once Nick made it back to normal. I chuckled to myself. Before too long, I'd be perfect.

"Hey, Bud. Welcome back." I again explained Nick's hospital stay to him. I asked him if the ventilator made him crazy. He didn't respond, but his eyes remained focused on me.

The doctor patted my shoulder before leaving. "I'll check back with you both after rounds."

I nodded, my eyes glued on Nick.

I had tucked his favorite childhood book in my bag. After I pulled it out and showed him the front cover, I read *Where the Wild Things Are*. Many a night, Nick had been sent to his room without supper. We had joked about it on occasions since. Somehow we had bonded over his childhood and knew each other as well as we knew this book. By heart. His watchful eyes remained locked on me the entire time I read. I held up the book before I turned the pages and showed him the pictures. I recalled his five year old self, thick strawberry-blonde hair, wide smiles dimpling his sprinkled face, dressed in some superhero costume, wearing his crown of power, conducting all manners of the universe while sequestered in that tiny room, standing on his bed and barking out orders. It made me smile.

"Find your inner Max, son. I've never seen you this quiet. Fight. Come back to me." *Damn it. Come back to me.*

Just like in the movies, he squeezed my hand. Or applied a bit of pressure. Reality. Not dreams. But he reacted. Damn the doctors. I knew my son. He had reacted. I picked up my cell phone and dialed Ed.

"Nick's awake," I said when he answered. "Can you bring the kids over? I think he needs to see them. And you."

"Give us an hour."

"Hurry. He's watchful, and he just responded by pressing his fingers to my palm. He needs us right now."

"As soon as we can." Ed signed off and I said a prayer.

"Thank you, God, for bringing my boy back to me. Thank you."

Ed must have had a police escort, because he arrived, kids in tow, less than thirty minutes later. He looked like a papa duck with his ducklings; they fell behind him in a single line. Their tenuous approach made me realize how frightened they felt. I'd rarely seen them like this. Nick's eyes remained open, and he seemed to narrow them as his family walked inside the tiny room. His siblings immediately shrouded his bed, speaking to him in low voices, all at the same time.

A single tear slipped down my face. Nick didn't move his head, but I could almost feel his heart swell as his sibs gathered around him. They each held onto one of his limbs. Lizzie gripped his foot and sidled up on the bed next to him. Marie grasped the hand opposite the one in my grasp, and Annie rested hers on his knee. Will stuck his face up to Nick's. Not ever had that boy been aware of personal space, and if ever I'd been glad for this anomaly of his, it was now. Nick saw him. I swear to God he did. Ed stood behind me, offering support with a tender touch on my back.

I could feel Jon. He was there with us. *God help me.* I'd made the right decision about McGrath.

Lizzie discovered *Where the Wild Things Are*, and insisted on reading it to Nick. Even though I explained that I'd just read it to him, she persisted. Then Marie and Annie decided that singing *Stairway to Heaven*, his favorite song, would be next on the agenda. My heart bulged with pride. I had the most amazing family.

I prayed to Jon that night: *watch over all of us, and if you have any direct connections, use them. Pull out all the stops, Jon. We need you.*

CHAPTER SEVENTEEN

THE DOCTORS REMOVED the ventilator the following day—a day of clear skies, bright sunshine, and loads of humidity. Nick remained awake and watchful for many hours. We flooded him with family, each taking turns spending time with him. Afterwards, we met in the lounge to compare notes.

Lizzie said, "I could tell he loved my song the most. Nick says I have perfect pitch."

Will reported, "He can't wait to get home and play his guitar. I can tell."

Marie said, "My brother's one tough linebacker. He's gonna kick some serious butt when he gets outta here."

And Annie, "I'll never forgive him for spitting in my hair."

Yep. That's my girl.

Patience and a firm grasp on reality, I cautioned myself. But I knew my boy would make it, and somehow be better than ever. *Screw the doctors. Screw McGrath.*

Each day, for the next eight days, we spent at Nick's side. Either Ed or I spent the night. Being with Nick was crucial right now. Day nine, school started. Ed stayed at the hospital later that morning, so I could attempt normalcy at home. Once the kids climbed onto their respective busses, I jumped into the van and headed to the hospital.

Overwhelmed, exhausted, and depressed, I longed for energy and a hopeful spirit.

Di called as I made the drive. I hesitated answering, but hadn't spoken with her in over a week. She'd been great about accepting my one line texts, which only apprised her of Nick's condition. By now, Joey and Emilio had to be blending members of her family. I owed her the courtesy of a conversation.

"Hey, you," I said. "How are you?"

"More importantly, how are you?"

In spite of my sour mood, I feigned optimism. "Better by the minute. Nick's off the ventilator now, and more wakeful every day. He's even hinting at a smile now and then. I'm certain he'll start talking soon. It's all good. Enough about me, how's the transition going for you?"

"It's a process, but you know all about that, having blended your own family. The boys are anxious about school, but since they are both playing soccer, making new friends hasn't been a problem."

"How's Ava adjusting? And Chris?"

"Ava loves them. But she loves everyone who showers her with attention. And Chris is in his glory, dragging them out after supper to toss the football."

"And you. How are you, my OCD friend?"

Di's laugh tugged at my heart. I missed her and our daily walks. "Honestly?"

"Always honestly," I said, smiling to myself.

"It's such a fucking lot of work. There are days I'm holding my breath, expecting a catastrophe; I'm exhausted with worry, and I'm sure I'm over-thinking every detail. Should I pack lunches or let them buy? Am I serving enough vegetables? Should I ask them to do chores? How the hell have you raised five kids on your own?"

I laughed. "One day at a time."

I struggled to make small talk with Di about school and sitters and such, and as good as it was to hear her voice, and as important as her concerns were, they seemed insignificant compared to shit pile which had become my life. I hated feeling sorry for myself, but in spite of the fact that I had tons to be grateful for, I didn't I feel it.

I pulled into the parking structure, again struck by how small it made me feel. So far, this was shaping up to be a day full of emotional hurdles. I prayed it wouldn't continue.

The elevator, crowded with somber parents, didn't nothing to lift my mood. By the time I reached Nick's room, I'd resigned myself to a disquieted day. When I opened his door and he gazed at me, my world righted again. We were so fortunate; Nick was awake, and breathing on his own. I sat by his side and chatted with him. His eyes remained fixed on me the entire time, so I decided to try some new exercises. I moved to his left and called his name. It took a while, but he turned his head. After I applauded his response, I moved to his opposite side. He looked in kind. Localizing sound, a developmental milestone of an infant, mastered. Yesterday, he had actually squeezed my hand with a bit of strength. Sweet progress.

I asked the doctors if I could attempt feeding him some soft foods. They said yes, so I dug inside my sack and pulled out some of Ed's homemade applesauce, which I kept in the freezer. One of Nick's favorite things, I dipped a tiny spoonful into his mouth. His tongue touched his lips to taste the sweet flavor. He seemed to enjoy it. I fed him half a cup, then he closed his eyes and fell asleep.

While Nick slept, I rested my head and dozed.

"More applesauce, please."

I heard the words in my dream.

Then again, "Applesauce, Mom."

I opened my eyes slowly, unsure of myself. Questioning.

But it *was* Nick. He'd spoken. And what he'd said made sense.

A wave of nausea overwhelmed me. Maybe because I had held hope hostage for so long. A lump grew in my throat. I swallowed hard and reached for Nick's hand. "Sure, honey." I rifled blindly inside my bag. I didn't want to take my eyes off of him for a second. "Tasted good, huh?"

Nick nodded. I shoveled applesauce into his mouth until I emptied the container. Almost a quart. I briefly wondered if I should have asked someone if Nick could eat that much at one sitting, but decided it didn't matter. He grinned at me now and then.

Dumbstruck while he ate, it took me a few minutes to click into gear.

"How are you feeling?"

He squeezed his eyes shut. "Headache."

"I'll call the nurse and ask for a pain reliever."

I pushed the call button. "My son is awake and complaining of a headache. Could he please have something for pain?"

I recognized Melissa's voice. "I'll be right there."

By this time, I had the shakes. When Melissa walked into the room, she did so with caution. I supposed she didn't know what to expect. Her face lit up when she saw Nick and I engaged in a conversation of sorts. I did most of the talking, asking questions.

"Does anything else hurt?"

"No, Mom. Just my head."

"We should be able to get you out of here before too long." I'd spoken out of turn. I had no business making promises I couldn't keep. I stood and stepped back so that Melissa could reach his IV and insert medication into the tube to ease his pain. She squeezed my shoulder as she moved past me.

"Hi, Nick, I'm Melissa. Glad to see you awake and chatting." She smiled at him.

"Hi," he said.

"I'll call the doctor," she said to us both.

"Where is everybody?" Nick asked.

"School started today, but your brother and sisters will

be here later. I know how crazy you are about school. Guess you're willing to go to any length to take a day off, huh?"

Nick's eyes sparkled. To that he could relate.

Dr. Stern strode through the door several minutes later. He extended his hand to Nick, who raised his arm and shook the doctor's hand. I reminded myself that these were proven signs of a sure recovery, but that there would be certain hurdles to jump.

Stern introduced himself to Nick, supplied him with a quick history of his accident and injuries. He informed us both that he would order physical and occupational therapy evaluations, as well as a speech assessment. Since Nick spoke with ease, I guessed that Stern's concerns rested in Nick's ability to process information and his memory.

Nick, in true Nick form, said, "Thanks, doc."

As soon as the doctor left the room, I telephoned Ed. He deserved to be one of the first to hear the news. I thought about handing the phone to Nick and telling him to announce his arrival back on planet Earth, but I didn't want Ed to have a heart attack, so I shared the news first, then put him on speaker phone.

"Welcome back, Nick," Ed said. "Can't wait to see you, boy. How about if I head over to the hospital?"

Nick lifted his head a titch, smiled, and then laid back. Exhaustion took over. "Sure, Grandpa, come see me."

"He's wearing out, Ed. I'll have him nap until you arrive."

"Great, Sam. Follow your mother's orders, Son." Ed signed off.

While Nick slept, I grabbed *The Lexington Examiner* from my backpack and caught up on the Macchione case.

> New state felony charges were filed on Wednesday against Lexington Mayor Vincent Macchione, even as a judge, ruling in a prior case, had previously allowed the

Mayor to leave jail with restrictions that included a GPS tracking device.

State officials charged Macchione with three counts of assaulting police officers, stemming from an August 31 incident.

Macchione, along with his brother, Anthony Macchione, is already facing charges of corruption, embezzlement, bribery, extortion, and tax crimes.

Macchione remains defiant, refusing pressure from critics to tender his resignation from public office, including pleas from the president of the Lexington City Council.

Governor Mary Cavanaugh, acting under a seldom-used state law allowing her to remove a city official, has set a September 15 hearing that could remove him from office, Cavanaugh spokeswoman Ivy Bowen said Tuesday.

Macchione, who appeared before Magistrate Ryan Moore, did not speak in court Wednesday. A not-guilty plea was entered on his behalf. Attorney General Mark Cole said the altercation took place when police officers attempted to serve a subpoena on friend of Macchione's who is a potential witness for the prosecution.

"In my twenty-five years as a prosecutor," Cole stated, "I cannot recall a single case of a police officer being assaulted when trying to serve a subpoena."

If convicted of assault, Macchione faces up to two years in prison. As a convicted felon, he could no longer serve as Lexington's mayor.

Macchione, who was free on $150,000

bond of previous charges, was jailed last week for attempting to leave the state without notifying the court in advance. The assault occurred the day before this incident.

Macchione's attorney, Howard Edmunds, promises to fight these trumped-up charges, and assured his client that he will be out on bond in a matter of days.

My eyes glazed over. Pure and simple, Macchione thought he was above the law.

I'd learned the hard way not to trust a single living soul. In my book, everyone was suspect.

In an article further down the page, I read:

Attorneys for Anthony Macchione, brother of Mayor Vincent Macchione, recently indicted on charges of embezzlement and corruption, have requested additional time in preparing his defense.

He is currently free on bond. It is anticipated that it will be six months before he appears in court.

Corruption and pay-offs afforded him the luxury of walking the streets. His power and position afforded him the country's finest attorneys. What a sham.

Lisa's disappearance weighed on me as I apprised myself of recent events. I searched for news, but there was nothing in the paper. Not a word. Since I hadn't spoken with McGrath, I had no idea if there were any leads. She'd vanished into thin air. No media reports. Nothing. Maybe Tony *had* killed her, but how could news of the investigation have disappeared? If she was dead, and I was holding out hope that she was not, where was her body? Had Tony paid off the press to let the story evaporate? Wishful thinking on my part, but I concocted a story in which Tony let her disappear. Beneath her fear of Tony lurked a tough, independent, and savvy woman. Maybe she had struck a deal with him. Then again, she left the kids behind. *Get a grip, Sam.* As soon as I had the chance, I promised myself that I'd get to the bottom of this.

I turned on the television, hoping there would be an update on the noon news. Sure enough, the news ticker read, "Mayor Vincent Macchione released from jail." What on earth? Why couldn't the authorities keep this guy locked up?

Disgusted, I flicked off the set. Ed walked into the room moments later, wearing an enormous grin. "Happy day. I knew our boy would come around."

"His spirit is invincible. My superhero reigns."

Ed kissed my cheek, then patted Nick on his shoulder. "Atta boy."

In an instant, I jolted back in time. Ed's cadence as he recited that line reminded me of Jon and the banter he and Nick had shared over Rex, who had a habit opening his jaws and ingesting Jon's breakfast off the kitchen counter most mornings. I swallowed hard, knowing that Jon would have been glued to Nick's side with me over the last eleven days had he still been alive. Then, reality stepped in to remind me that Jon would have been there if he hadn't had a business trip on his calendar. I'd clouded the truth since Jon's death. Probably natural.

Still, Ed's words tugged at my heart. I missed Jon.

I hadn't allowed myself to miss him, or McGrath, for that matter, in the days since my decision to focus solely on Nick. It had been the right choice. Centering my energies on Nick had paid off. I'd continue on this path until my boy was completely whole again.

Nick opened his eyes and looked at Ed. "Hi, Gramps."

Ed teared up and blinked. "How's my boy?"

"Better," Nick said.

I became weepy. No matter how sick or injured Nick was, when asked, he always claimed to be better. This boy was meant to recover and live life to the fullest. I rubbed his arm and smiled. Ed sat on the other side of the bed and rested his hand on Nick's leg. Neither one of us wanted to let go of our boy. "I'm so proud of you, Bud."

The door squeaked open and a short, squat young man entered. He offered his hand to me, and then to Ed, then stood and focused his gaze on Nick.

"Hi, Nick. I'm Scott, the occupational therapist. I'm going to assess your injuries and see where we stand. I parked your new wheels outside. Let's load you inside and we'll go down to the clinic and get started, alright?"

"Sure," Nick said.

I kissed Nick on the forehead. "Do your best work, Bud." Scott wheeled him out the door. Ed suggested a bite to eat and we headed down to the cafeteria. I didn't feel like I could eat a thing, but grabbed a yogurt nonetheless. Keeping up my strength seemed like a thing to do.

Like father, like son, Ed ordered a hearty breakfast. I couldn't for the life of me figure out why everything Ed did today reminded me so completely of Jon. But it sliced my heart like a carving knife. Even Nick reminded me of Jon today. Maybe because Nick and Jon had shared such a special bond, I imagined how overjoyed Jon would have been about Nick's recovery. *Damn it.*

Ed jolted me from my ruminations. "He's something, isn't he? I knew he'd come around. Now, think about getting back to work."

Again, reminders of Jon flooded me. He'd been the apple that had fallen off his father's tree. Jon would have said the same thing. Crisis averted. Get back to work and on with life. *Too soon for that, dear Ed.*

"Not yet, Dad. Let's wait and see what the evaluations show. My guess is Nick will suffer some residual effects from the coma. To say that he's completely well would be jumping to an early conclusion. Work will keep. Trust me. I need to be with my boy until I'm sure he's as fit as possible. We don't want to set up a relapse by rushing into normal life too quickly. Patience."

"You're good for me, Sam."

No kidding.

"As you are for me, Dad. Now, tell me about your girl."

"Think I'm going to marry her."

His revelation startled me.

Ed must have read my surprise, because he abruptly became a fast-talker. "I wasn't in a hurry two weeks ago, but Nick's accident brought a truth to my attention... grab life while you have the chance. Not going to waste it on technicalities like it hasn't been a year since Betty's death."

"When are you thinking?"

"Soon. Think we'll take off for Vegas some weekend."

"Vegas? Really?" There was a message in all of this for me. I couldn't decide if I was ready to listen to it yet.

"Neither of us wants anything fancy. Don't need or want a gaggle of onlookers. Once we found each other, I realized ceremony matters little to folks our age. What we share is ours alone. We don't require witnesses."

"I had no idea."

"I just decided, honey."

Ed's announcement pushed my thoughts to places I hadn't allowed myself to visit over the last week. Life is short. If anybody knows that, it's me. I avoided my feelings for McGrath. Put up barriers rather than boundaries. I couldn't permit myself to abandon them quite yet. Only after Nick's health returned to normal.

I laughed. "When do I get to meet her? Are you going to let us know when it's happening? Or is it going to be an elopement?"

"We'll probably just disappear for a weekend. Maybe even four or five days. Once Nick's home and I'm sure you're both okay."

"Helen sounds like a great gal. Will you live here? Move full-time to the cottage? Does she live at her cottage year round or somewhere else? Fill me in on the details."

"We'll keep my place here and her cottage up north. That way, we'll have the best of both worlds. Old folks like us don't like big changes. We'll both have the stability of a familiar place. Live here most of the time, but head north whenever we like. In fact, I thought you and the kids would like the cottage."

"Dad, that's too much. Sell it. Keep your money."

"It's a family place, Sam. I want to keep it that way. The kids love it there. It would mean the world to me if you'd accept the gift."

"I don't know what to say, Dad."

Ed pursed his lips and raised his brows. "Mind's made up."

I knew he meant business. "Let's talk more about this later."

"What about your guy?"

"McGrath?"

Ed nodded.

"Everything's great," I lied.

"Haven't seen him around lately."

"He's busy with the Macchione mess."

CHAPTER EIGHTEEN

"LET'S TAKE HIS guitar," Will suggested.
I avoided that idea with, "He'll be home soon. Let's not get carried away."

Our visit with Nick was nothing short of amazing. Exhaustion gripped him, but he rallied to visit with his sibs for an hour before shutting off like a light. I ushered the kids home, then waved them off to shower and hit the sack. As tired as Nick, I fell into bed and slept a dreamless sleep.

The next morning, after I fed everyone and ushered them out the door, I went for a quick run in the rain, then readied myself for another day at the hospital. Today would be the day I'd receive the news of Nick's PT evaluation, and the status on his homecoming, I hoped.

My windshield wipers flapped like an anxious bird, and I rounded the corner into the parking structure a little after 9:00 a.m. The elevator to the children's hospital, located adjacent to the main hospital, was crowded with parents and children making their way to early morning clinic appointments. I squeezed into the lift and turned to face the doors, unwilling to make small talk. But I felt a tug on the back of my shirt and heard a familiar voice.

"Mrs. Stitsill, is that you?"

I turned, startled to see Adrianna Macchione. Her aunt,

Lisa's sister, Lori, stood just behind her.

"Hi, sweetie."

Lori must have read my puzzled expression, because she offered me an explanation.

"Ophthalmology visit."

I'd met Lori many years ago during my Early Intervention visits to the Macchione's, and she hadn't changed a bit. She looked so much like her sister, it caught me off guard. I offered her my hand and re-introduced myself.

It seemed odd that Tony allowed Lori to accompany Adrianna to the doctor. He must have been desperate. Or too busy extorting money, arranging his defense, and sleeping with one of his bimbos to bring Adrianna himself. Far as I could remember, he openly despised Lori. Not that I ever heard him utter one nice word about anyone.

Had McGrath had a chance to investigate Tony's other women? There might have been a lead there. *Silly me.* Of course he would have gone there.

"How are things?" I asked Lori.

She looked pained, but nodded. Adrianna began to chatter about school. "I won't miss too much. It's just the second day."

"You'll be fine," I assured her. "You're a smart girl. You'll catch up tonight."

We stopped at the sixth floor, and Lori excused herself and Adrianna. Don't ask me why, but instead of riding up to Nick's room on the eighth floor, I stepped off the elevator with her.

As we exited, I rested my hand on Adrianna's shoulder. "Why don't we meet in the cafeteria when you're done with your clinic appointment? I'd love to hear what the doctor has to say and to catch up with your aunt a bit."

Lori piped up. "It takes forever at the clinic. You'll probably be done with your business here long before we finish. They have to dilate Adriana's eyes, then we sit. Then they move us to an exam room, then we sit."

I laughed. I'd accompanied many students to their doctor's visits. I knew the routine all too well. "Been there, done that."

I locked eyes with Lori. "I'll be here all day. Please, let me buy you coffee or lunch."

She wavered.

I dug deep in my bag for a business card. I scribbled my cell number on the bottom and pressed the card into her hand. "If today doesn't work out, just give me a call and let me know what Adrianna's doctor says, alright?"

Lori narrowed her eyes and focused on my card before she nodded. "Sure. I'll do that."

Running into Adrianna and Lori could have been a coincidence. But I knew better. *There's a reason for everything.*

The stairwell, located next to the elevator, supplied privacy. I dove inside and caught my breath. My heart raced and I inhaled a measured breath. By the time I climbed the two flights to Nick's floor, I still hadn't calmed down. This could be my big chance. Why I felt the need to involve myself in another mystery, I'll never know, but it gripped me like cocaine grips an addict. I couldn't wait to hear from Lori. *Please call.*

When I entered his room, Nick sat up in bed, awake and alert.

I kissed his cheek and rubbed his freckled hand. Blessed by his smiling face, I pulled up a chair next to his bed. "I hope we hear from the doctors soon."

"I want to go home."

"Sure you do. And we want you home ASAP. But the speech therapist still has to complete an evaluation and then I'm sure we'll have a meeting of some kind to establish your home care…"

"I'm better," Nick broadcast. "Let's get out of here."

I laughed, and Nick joined me. "That's my boy."

I pulled out a deck of cards and pushed the tray table between us. Unsure if Nick could hold a hand of playing cards, I suggested a game of war. It would be good practice for him, using his thumb and index finger to lift the individual cards.

Nick sneered. "I know what you're trying to do. God, Mom, can you drop the teacher, just for once?"

Nick called me on everything. Why, now that he'd awakened from his coma, I imagined things should be any different, I hadn't a clue. He was right. I had an agenda. Always. For myself. For my own children. For my students. One of these days, I'd be able to relax. When, I wasn't quite sure.

I smiled at him and winked. "Humor me."

Nick tried winking back. I witnessed his frustration and tried to soothe him. "You were never a good winker," I teased.

"That's Annie, Mom, not me." His memory appeared to be intact, too, damn it.

I dealt the cards. He couldn't hold them, but trooper nonetheless, he played by laying the cards across his lap and blocking my view of them with the tray table. Nick struggled to use his pincer grasp. I let him fight through it, watchful. Frustration could discourage my son, not necessarily push him to battle harder. If I wasn't careful, he'd shut down.

We were playing our second game of cards when someone rapped on the door. "Come in," I called.

It was Detective Stevenson, a local cop who I had met at the kid's sporting events. His son, Justin, was the boy's age. He shook my hand, then Nick's, smiled, and pulled up a chair.

"It's great to see you awake, Nick. How are you feeling?"

Nick half-smiled. "Better than I was, for sure."

Stevenson made small talk about a fast recovery and the advantages of extending summer vacation before he got down to business. "We're looking into your accident, Nick, and hoped you could provide some information about what happened."

Nick frowned. "I wish I could help. All I remember is riding on Main Street. Then, I woke up here. Mom said I was in a coma for over a week."

The detective nodded. "You're a lucky guy. Do me a favor. Try to remember."

Nick became pensive and we sat quiet for a full three minutes, waiting for his memory to engage. "I got Lizzie and my bikes down from the garage. I took off down the street, headed to Rob's house. I turned onto First Street and then onto Main. I was on the right side of the street. That's all I've got."

"Do you recall hearing a car approach, or looking over your shoulder to check traffic?"

"Um... no, I don't think so. I was pretty excited to see Rob. I hadn't seen him all summer. I guess I was thinking about what I'd tell him when I got to his house."

"No problem, Nick, but if you remember anything at all, give me a call." He handed Nick his card. "We don't want to let the person who hit you go free."

Nick shrugged. "It was an accident."

I smiled at him. Nick had always been easy to forgive.

The speech therapist arrived and interrupted our talk. We said goodbye to Stevenson and loaded Nick into his wheelchair. Destination: her office. I considered asking if I could accompany them for the assessment, but thought better of it. My anxiety would transfer to Nick, and he needed to be free of my wishful thinking and worries.

I kissed him and wished him luck.

"We'll be about an hour," the therapist indicated.

Now that the crisis had unofficially ended, I pulled out my cell and dialed my brother, Tom. He let me know right away that I was on his list for not having called him about Nick.

"Damn it, Sam. Do you have to handle everything on your own?"

Good question.

"I've been too busy to call in reinforcements. Plus, I have Ed."

"Nick's my nephew. I have a right to know what's going on."

"I haven't heard from you in three months. Really? This is my fault?"

Tom sighed. "You've got me there. Forgiven and forgotten. I'll be up to the hospital after work."

"No, come to the house after Nick comes home. Can you call Mark and let him know, too?"

Tom cleared his throat. "He's going to be pissed. You're pushing your luck, letting me do your dirty work."

"See you later." I twiddled my thumbs before deciding my next move. I still had fifty minutes to kill. My notepad surfaced first when I reached inside my backpack, so I wandered outside and jotted down some ideas about what I'd say to Lori and Adrianna when I met with them. Just a brief outline of the questions I wanted to ask. Then I thought through how to acquire the desired responses without letting my suspicions surface.

I raced upstairs, pausing on the sixth floor to peruse the clinic waiting area for Lori and Adrianna. There, at the check-out desk, they stood.

"Lori, Adrianna," I called.

Lori turned to face me. Adrianna smiled.

I approached, friendly and chatty, but restricted by Adrianna's presence. "I wanted to ask you and Adrianna something."

"What, Mrs. Stitsill?"

"I have an old Brailler. It's almost an antique. But I have no use for it. Would you like to keep it at your aunt's house and practice when you have the chance?"

Adrianna turned to her aunt and tugged on her shirt. "Can I Auntie, can I?"

It was an impulsive idea, but one that would leave a door open if I needed to speak to them later. And it would provide me the opportunity to glean more information from Lori without pumping her head on about Lisa.

"I can ask the secretary at school to leave it in the office for you, and you can pick it up at your convenience."

"Thank you," Lori said. "That's very kind of you."

Good enough. I laid a hand on Adrianna's shoulder. "You can call me if you have questions."

Lori offered a half-smile and patted her handbag. "I have your number."

"Great. I have to run, but it was so nice to see you both."

Adrianna wrapped her arms around me and I gave her a quick hug.

"See you!"

One mission accomplished.

I headed back to Nick's room. He hadn't returned yet, but his food tray had arrived. I inventoried the items on his tray: mashed potatoes, yogurt, jello, juice… and a blank 4x6 card. Odd. I flipped it over. A photograph… date and time stamped… Nick riding his bike on Main Street the day of the accident.

My throat clogged and my heart froze. I dashed into the hall, still holding the snapshot. Who left this? Why? Because I talked to Lori? I searched the long corridor. What did I expect? Whoever had been in Nick's room would have stuck around? I planted myself in front of the nurse's station.

"Excuse me."

An aide looked up from her desk.

"Did you see anyone in my son's room? Nick Stitsill. His room is there, two doors down, on the right."

"No. Are you looking for someone?"

"Yes… well, no." The blood drained from my face. My knees turned to rubber, I felt faint.

I tucked the photograph inside my back pocket, gripped the counter and willed myself to breathe.

"Ma'am, are you alright?"

"I need to sit down."

The aide rushed to my side and led me to a chair. I stuck my head between my knees and fought to stop the white noise from rushing between my ears.

"I'll call for help," she said.

I managed to shake my head. "That won't be necessary. Just a momentary drop in my blood sugar. I need to eat."

"Are you sure?"

I swallowed and pushed air from my lungs. "Yes, thank you. I'm quite sure."

"I'll get you some juice."

She hurried off and I looked up, willing myself to calm. It didn't work. Nick was safe wasn't he? *Hit and run. Hit and run.*

The aide returned with a cup of juice, which I sipped and wrestled to keep in my stomach. "Thank you."

"Are you feeling better?"

"Much," I lied. "I'll head back to my son's room now. I have a sandwich in my bag."

"Are you sure?"

"Quite. Thank you for your help."

She looked worried, so I smiled to reassure her. "Really. I'm fine." I stood and stepped towards Nick's room, despite my boneless legs. I went inside, pulled a tissue from the box and removed the photo from my pocket. I wrapped it inside a paper towel and tucked it in the outside pocket of my backpack. Then, I sat. Just as I pulled out my cell phone to dial McGrath, the door creaked open. Dr. Stern strode inside the room. He shook my hand and sat on the side of Nick's hospital bed.

He smiled. "It's all good news, right?"

I struggled for firm ground. "What's your assessment? Prognosis. Treatment."

"Right to the point, aren't you?"

You have no idea.

I shrugged. "I'm anxious to get my boy home and fully recovered."

Doc Stern nodded. "Walking will be a while. Nick has some weakness on his right side, in both his upper and lower extremities. At the point he's released, occupational and physical therapy will be on the treatment plan."

"I've arranged for a leave from my teaching position, so I'll be able to spend plenty of time assisting and exercising him. I'm a master at pushing kids toward independence. Full-time career for me."

"As you know, it's never easy with a family member. It's great that you have the expertise, and Nick can certainly benefit from it, but remember to pace yourself. Don't wear yourself out."

"My boy can test my nerves — even when he's in the best of health."

"The usual course is to schedule therapy three times a week. Clinic works best if you can bring him in, or we can arrange some home sessions if that makes more sense. You'll need a wheelchair for a while. Consider all of that."

It impressed me that Dr. Stern had taken the time to be involved in Nick's treatment plan. Few doctors were aware of much that happened after they released a patient from their care. In my experience, they were barely attentive of other discipline's schedules.

"I'll bring him in, and we'll go from there. It will be best if we both have a reason to get out of the house." *Where would we be safest? At home or the hospital?*

Dr. Stern nodded. "Tomorrow then."

An unexpected panic gripped me. Knots twisted in my stomach. Responsibility for Nick's recovery in the midst of the most gripping crisis I had ever faced? I nodded as reality took hold. "He can come home that soon?"

Stern patted my hand. "All the discharge instructions will be written out. You can make the therapy appointments while you're here today. Set up a schedule that works for your family."

How would I ensure my family's safety much less set

up a schedule? I dialed McGrath. When the call went to voicemail, my heart dropped. I poked my head into the hall. No one. Should I call Ed? What would I say? Someone hurt Nick on purpose. Who? Why? My throat went dry as dust. I paced the room, then redialed McGrath. I left him an urgent message.

"Someone left a photo in Nick's room. It wasn't a random hit and run. It was a direct hit. Please, help me. What if they try again? What if they hurt Lizzie, or Annie, or…" I began to sob. "I don't know what to do."

I checked my watch, hurried into the bathroom, and doused my face with water. There was sufficient time for me to hightail it to the clinics and set up the therapy arrangements. Plus, I could peek inside and make sure Nick was alright. I could order a wheelchair from the home health care store in town. Or not. Nick would walk independently. Soon. If he needed the chair when he returned to school, I'd order it then. In any case, tasks would maintain my functionality. The best defense? A tried and true coping mechanism. *Do it mode.*

I succeeded in locating Nick, and scheduled him for back-to-back appointments with the PT and OT. It meant three trips to the hospital per week, two hours each day. The appointments were midday, so I'd have the luxury of being a mom to all five of my kids for the near future. If I could keep catastrophe at bay, that is. Someone harmed Nick with intent and malice. I was in shock. My worst nightmare became my new reality. I cautioned myself to maintain a grip on rational thought and continued to polish the details of Nick's homecoming. How would I ensure his safety? The safety of all my children?

I made all the arrangements and headed upstairs, struggling for sane thought and for oxygen. Was it the fact that I spoke to Lori and Adrianna that prompted this warning? *We hurt Nick. We're watching you.* I could only hope that my impulsivity hadn't cost me another rung on the ladder out of this mess. Nick's room remained empty, yet panic strangled me. McGrath still hadn't returned my call. Where the hell was he? Lizzie would be in school for two and a half more hours. I phoned the school and informed them that I would pick her up today. What if she were targeted next? She had to be safe at school, didn't she? Unable to sit, I tread the halls. Coffee had been set up in the waiting room. I grabbed a cup—tasteless but hot. The conference room I'd eaten lunch in a few days ago appeared like a sanctuary. Cave-like, it offered me a false but much needed sense of safety and protection. The window overlooked a pleasant courtyard, but rain still hammered outside, and fierce winds whipped branches clear off the trees. I pulled a chair over to the window, sat in the dark, gazed out on the stormy landscape, and took stock.

My greatest fear had been realized. Someone had targeted my kid. Hurt him. McGrath hadn't called me back. Should I call the cops? Marty? Who could I trust in McGrath's absence? I had no idea.

I reminded myself. Life is good. Nick is on the road to recovery. Miracle granted. But even as gratitude filled me, I felt increasingly unsettled. Check that: frightened to death. I missed Jon and our crazy, chaotic life. At the same time, anger gripped me. Why did he leave us? Why did I miss him now? I thought I'd put my mourning to rest. Dealt with. Over. *Just craving a familiar normal, Sam. The predictable good old days.*

My thoughts veered to McGrath. Tears welled. I missed him. I needed him.

Anger didn't suit me. Still, I was pissed at the men in my life. When I needed them most, they eluded me. McGrath's absence was my own fault; I am my own worst enemy. My cell phone vibrated in my pocket. My heart quickened and relief washed over me. McGrath. I pulled it out and read the text message.

"Stay put. Officer Dave is stopping in Lizzie's class.

Casual visit. No alarm necessary. High school officers will look in on the rest of the clan. Where is the photo?"

"In my backpack. Sorry, I touched it. Wrapped it carefully so I didn't get any more fingerprints on it, but probably smudged any prints that were on it."

"No worries. Hold onto it."

"Detective Stevenson was here to interview Nick about the accident. Should I give it to him?"

"No. Give it to me."

Made sense to me. I breathed, my shoulders steadied, and I felt safe. Rescued even. "Thank you," I texted back.

"Everything will be alright. No worries. I'll be in touch."

I settled Nick, left him in Ed's care and headed home. Bone tired, mentally spent, terrorized.

After I kissed the kids and tucked them into bed, I uncorked a bottle of wine and rocked in my wicker chair on the front porch in the midst of a star-studded sky. No one had followed me home. No one had called. No one had left a threatening message. Maybe I was paranoid and the photo was meant to scare the wits out of me and nothing more. Mission accomplished. I was too numb to have the first clue what to do about it, but felt reassured that McGrath was on the case. It was a warning. But of what?

I gazed at the stars and pined for all the men in my life that I'd lost, dreamed of the cigarette I'd never smoke, and wandered inside well after midnight. Bottle empty. Pain diminished. Ready for a good night's sleep. Right after I thanked God for all the good in my life and apologized for whining, and handling crises inappropriately.

CHAPTER NINETEEN

B Y MORNING, THE rain had passed; the clouds lifted to thin white wisps. I spotted McGrath's Jeep in the driveway, and I brewed coffee and delivered him a mug, along with the photograph of Nick, which I had zipped into a plastic bag for safe-keeping."Have you been here all night?"

He rubbed his eyes, yawned, and attempted a weak smile. "Bodyguard duty."

"How can I ever thank you? What about school? Can I allow the kids to go? I'm bringing Nick home today. Tell me what to do."

He laughed and squeezed my arm. "The first order of business is breathing."

I followed directions.

"Send the kids to school. I have to work, but I have friends, guys on the force whom I trust, who will keep watch during the day. Dave will be in Lizzie's building all day with the D.A.R.E. Program and I've asked the others to check in on your kids throughout the day. Marty is on high alert since Nick's accident. He's making it his personal mission to ask around and determine if anyone saw anything the evening of Nick's accident. He thinks maybe someone would rather tell him than the cops. He may be right. It's unusual that no one has reported seeing anything."

"I don't understand why this is happening. Why Nick?"

"Try to calm down. Think. What's your connection?"

"I'm baffled. For the life of me, I can't figure it out."

"Me either. It could be a scare tactic. Could be the Macchione's, could be their extended family. Since the brothers have been indicted, the family may be cleaning house, and eliminating the riff-raff. They don't need anyone else making things difficult for them. Lisa may be part of the purging process. Maybe you're caught in the crossfire. In the meantime, focus on Nick, and I'll take care of the rest."

I couldn't take it all in. None of it made sense. "Considering our last conversation, I want to thank you for being so gracious. Stepping back into my life must be like flying into a bee hive, and I'm the queen bee."

"I hate bees."

"I know you do. I'll try my best to make things right. If I could, I'd offer you a reasonable explanation for my behavior. I'm not sure there is one though, other than fear of happiness."

He glanced at me for a moment, but then turned away. "That's a serious problem, but you're forgiven. Try not to worry, okay? For now, I'm a cop, and you're in need of a cop. The rest will unfold—all in good time."

Time. I had to give him this. I wasn't sure what I could handle. He sounded too wounded to dive back in.

McGrath yawned again, took a long sip of coffee and started up the engine as he glanced at the dashboard clock. "If I hurry, I can squeeze in a couple hours of sleep and a shower. Catch you later?"

I nodded. "Thank you."

He tipped his head, handed me the mug, and backed out of the driveway.

I finger-combed my hair, a last minute thought, as I waved goodbye. After I shipped the kids off to school, I indulged myself with a three mile run, showered and headed to the hospital, ready for this new phase of my life:

Rehabilitation Mom. In your face, oh great intimidators of my family. As far as I was concerned, it was just another Thursday, courtesy of my hero, Detective Jim McGrath.

I walked inside Nick's room and smiled at him. He perched on the edge of the bed and nodded at the door. "Let's go."

"Hospital discharge procedures take a while, Bud. It's hurry-up-and-wait time. We'll be safe dressing you in sweats and eating breakfast, but other than that, we'll have to hunker down, play cards, and exercise patience."

Nick smirked. "Patience?"

"I know, not a strength for either one of us. Just warning you. It'll be a while."

"Is Grandpa coming?" Nick sounded nervous, which made perfect sense. His life had changed; it was no longer business as usual. He'd always been fiercely independent and having his mommy help him button his pants would humiliate him, and make him feel less of a man.

"He'll come whenever we need him. Try not to worry. We'll figure it out. Will can help, and your sisters will shower you with attention. We will all be at your beck and call. I'm worried you'll become a spoiled brat and forget how to do your chores."

He nodded and smiled. "That'll happen."

Three hours later, loaded with a bulging envelope of instructions and Nick's gear, I retrieved the car while the nurse wheeled Nick to the circular drive in front of the hospital. I helped him buckle his seat belt, and we chatted on the drive home.

Nick seemed happy enough, but pensive at the same time.

I patted his knee. "How are you?"

"Dr. Stern said he didn't know when I could go back to school."

I shot him a sideways glance. "Are you worried about getting behind?"

He studied his hands. His coordination was an issue. The reality of his limitations had begun to set in.

"We'll get your work. I'm a teacher, remember? I'll help you stay current. We'll send your homework in with Will, and I can set up an email routine with your instructors. Try not to worry."

"It's not about school, Mom. I miss my friends. And I want to play football."

"Next year, Bud. It's normal to feel anger and apprehension about your situation, but look at the bright side. We can spend quality time together."

"Ugh."

I rested a hand on his shoulder. "I'll try not to be overbearing."

"Give it up, Mom."

Ed strode out of the garage as we pulled in the driveway, a huge smile lit up his face. He'd be a godsend throughout this process.

Between the two of us, we managed to wangle Nick inside and settle him in his favorite new recliner. His weakness primarily affected his right side, making balance difficult. Plus, his muscles had atrophied slightly. With pages of exercises from both the PT and OT to help increase his strength, flexibility, and coordination, we'd get there. Caution remained key. I couldn't overload the poor kid, and my natural tendency was to expect Nick to wear his superhero costume 24/7.

Nick slept while Ed and I set up a schedule. He offered to accompany Nick on one day of therapy appointments each week. I hated to relinquish the chief therapist role, but I recognized how soon Nick and I would tire of each other's company. Ed chose Friday. That worked for me.

"Go, have a life."

He nodded, kissed me on the cheek, and headed out the door.

While Nick slept, I gazed at him. Emotion flooded me.

One lucky girl, I thought. Major crisis averted. I dozed off and didn't wake until the screen door slammed.

Lizzie called out as she shot through the back hall. "I'm home!"

Her shouts roused Nick. He answered with, "Is that my sister?"

Lizzie squealed with delight, raced to him, and climbed in his lap. Nick pointed at the TV remote and Lizzie turned on the set. They snuggled while I sliced apples for their snack.

An hour later, Nick assured me that he and Lizzie could hold down the fort for twenty minutes while I retrieved the older kids from practice, but I allowed my intellect to rule, and made sure that Tom would arrive before I left, and supervise in my absence. Matters were shaping up better than I could have imagined.

By the time we arrived back home, Tom and Mark held court in the family room, performing magic tricks for Lizzie. The smell of pizza filled the air, and a salad sat on the counter. I'd struggled to eat pizza since Jon's death. It had been our Friday night staple and it brought back memories I no longer cared to resurrect. *Thanks, brothers.*

The kids hung on their uncles. Their height made them a human jungle gym, and some traditions die hard around our house. I felt utterly exhausted as I watched them. The letdown after the storm, I realized.

Once their novelty wore off, they helped Nick with his personal needs and Will assisted him to a seat at the table. We set out pizza boxes and let the kids have at it. Tom suggested we give them some time alone with Mark. Evidently, he wanted some time alone with me.

We walked onto the porch and sat, each taking a moment to catch the beauty of the sun streaming through the leaves and listen to the birds.

Tom broke the silence. "You okay?"

After a brief hesitation, I nodded.

"Don't forget. I know you pretty well. I know we don't talk often, but I'm here for you whenever you need me."

"I've got it."

"Sis, lean on me."

"No, I've got it."

CHAPTER TWENTY

IT DIDN'T SURPRISE me when I awakened out of sorts the following morning. I had so much to be grateful for, but I found myself uneasy, still checking out the window, looking over my proverbial shoulder. I grumbled while shuttling the kids off to school, not even dressing until long after they'd left. At ten o'clock, I awakened Nick and tried to establish a bit of routine, assisting him to the bathroom, helping him maintain his balance while brushing his teeth. He'd long since surpassed me in weight and height. Not the easiest of tasks.

Nick cocked his head once I settled him in his chair. "What's wrong, Mom?"

"Nothing," I lied.

"Do you hate being away from work?"

Probably, I thought. I relied on routines. I thought back in time, recalling how grumpy I'd become when I'd had to give up my early morning swims if Jon had a last minute trip.

"Go back to work, Mom. Let Grandpa take care of me."

"Stop being silly. You'll be good as new in no time. It's not work or you that's bothering me."

He persisted. "Then what?"

"Grown-up shit," I mumbled.

His eyes glinted. "Did you just swear?"

I barked out an order. "Time for your exercises."

Not a surprise, but Nick tired quickly. I spent the next hour filling myself in on recent developments in the Macchione case. I constructed a timeline. Just as a precaution, I decided to keep abreast of all news. Just in case.

Two weeks ago, Tony and Vinnie had been indicted on federal charges of corruption, embezzlement, fraud, and extortion. Over forty counts for each brother. Lisa disappeared in conjunction with those charges being filed. News of her disappearance dropped off almost immediately. Too strange.

Then it hit me. Vinnie and Tony had deep ties to the community. Even with the Feds watching them, they considered themselves invincible. The media would be on the take, as well as local law enforcement. They'd cooperate with the guys who paid their freight. Who was looking for Lisa? No one?

The phone rang. My ESP kicked in at the most unexpected times. Lori Woodruff. "Hi, Lori. How are you?"

"Hanging in. It's my only choice. I called to let you know that I retrieved the Brailler from the school, and to thank you."

"You're welcome. I'm glad Adrianna can use it."

"She loves pounding on it. She's picked up a lot watching her classmates, but we still have to practice in secret. Tony refuses to allow her to learn Braille."

"I'm sorry for that. It's horrible that Adrianna has to keep this secret from her father."

"She's grown up keeping secrets. It's the norm for her."

Lori was right. Poor kid. What a lot to shoulder. "If she wants to send me any of her work to check, I'd be happy to look at it. Here's my address." I should have recommended that she show her work to Carol Marsh, but she wouldn't be allowed; Tony forbid it. *Stay out of it, Sam.*

"What a wonderful idea. They are working on letter writing at school. She can write you a letter."

"Great idea!" *Get off the phone. Wrap it up.* "Any word on Lisa?"

"No. It's killing me to sit by and do nothing. I feel so helpless."

"Let the police do their job. I know it's hard to know who to trust at this point, but there are good people on the force. They will find her."

"God, I hope so."

"Me, too, Lori. Me, too."

I ended the call, hoping I hadn't further compromised my family's safety. The call was short, I reminded myself, and even if someone had listened in, nothing of note was said. *Shit.* I suggested a letter. Would someone be watching my mail? I should be locked away. Three minutes later, Di texted and suggested a walk after she arrived home from school. A walk sounded like the best possible medicine for me; a little slice of normal. I texted McGrath. "Is it safe for me to take a walk and leave the kids alone? Will Lizzie and Nick be okay snuggled up in the chair for an hour? McGrath replied with a simple "yes." I should trust him. This nagging feeling kept tugging at my gut. *Move on, Sam. Live your life.*

Nick let out a resounding whoop, "Free time!" He informed me that his buddies were headed to our house after practice. When I returned from our walk, the family room would be stuffed with a bunch of smelly, lanky boys. Delightful.

I hustled into my sweats at 3:30 p.m. Di and I decided to walk through my neighborhood. Not as long a walk as we were usually took, but it met both our schedule needs and our mutual desperation to shed the tension of the last few days.

She pulled into my driveway five minutes later. When I heard her engine shut off, I planted a quick kiss on Nick's cheek, along with instructions that he was to stay put until my return. For all I cared, he and Lizzie could go brain dead watching Japanese animation. Right after they locked the doors and agreed not to answer them.

Di's arms were full of containers of food: lasagna, cookies, and salad for dinner, along with a bottle of wine for me. "Can I say hello to Nick?"

"Look at all of this. You didn't have to do that."

"Did." She smiled and hugged me as I relieved her of her load, and followed me into the house. I stuffed containers into the fridge, and she visited with Nick for a few moments. I rushed her through the conversation and out the door. We took off on our power walk.

"So?" she began, "how are you?"

I nodded. "Surviving."

"We miss you at school. Your sub is excellent, but she isn't you. Jack's walking the halls like a lost puppy."

I laughed. "He is not."

"I'm not just trying to make you feel better, Sam. He really looks lost. You know how much he hates our team of teachers."

That I did. He had nicknamed the other two teachers on our team Grumpy and Weirdo.

"You'll have to keep him happy for both of us. My job is to be with Nick right now."

"How's Detective McGrath?" Leave it to Di to get right to the heart of the matter.

"We're on a little break, but on speaking terms."

"Damn. I knew it. Jack and I were just talking about it today. We figured you'd make some ridiculous decision like that."

"He's busy with a case right now, and I'm busy with Nick. No time to go on a date."

"Now I'm just pissed. You finally find a guy who really loves you, and you erect a privacy fence."

I gripped her arm as she veered into the path of an oncoming teenage driver. "Dangerous neighborhood. Be careful. These kids are speedsters. And they text while driving, remember?"

Di shot me a look after steering herself back to the side of the road. "How are you dealing with that?"

"I wish everybody would quit worrying about me." *I was doing enough hand-wringing for the lot of us.*

"Gone into your shell again, have you?"

"Change the subject, please. Tell me about the boys. How are they managing the new school?"

"We're lucky to live in such a great district. Emilio mentioned that Will is in one of his classes."

Funny, I hadn't considered that. Will, Nick, and Emilio were all freshmen this year.

"Things still settling in for you on the home front?"

She laughed. "The beginning of the year is always a challenge. Exhausting. You know all about it. But the boys are on their best behavior. Ava is the one who kills me. She seems to be adjusting too well. Having a sitter at the house keeps her grounded."

"And you hate it that Ava isn't a mess."

She laughed again. "Sort of."

"I get it."

"Sam." Di halted dead in her tracks and waited for me to do the same. Once I relented and stopped, she gripped my shoulders. "Don't blow it."

I nodded. "I hear you."

"McGrath is a good guy. Let him in."

"If he loves me, he'll wait until my son is well and I'm ready to forge a more permanent relationship."

"Maybe this is about Jon."

Her words pierced like a dagger to the heart. "Jon? That's what you think this is about?"

"You never allowed yourself a chance to properly mourn him."

"What the hell does that mean? I took a full year off after his death before I reached out to McGrath. You don't think that was long enough?"

She didn't back down. "You were preoccupied with

caring for the kids during that year. Keeping everybody intact. Once you accomplished that task, you allowed yourself to be with him, but did you really mourn Jon? Just saying."

Di wasn't privy to my discoveries in Japan. I'd convinced myself that I had mourned Jon while uncovering the details of his death. Had I mourned him? McGrath had been with me then. Did I need to be alone to grieve? Shit, I hate it when people question my motives or my thinking. Especially when I've determined my approach and persuaded myself that I'm done dealing with an issue. Jon. *Finis.*

But he had crept into my thoughts of late. Hell, Nick wasn't the only one who needed therapy.

CHAPTER TWENTY-ONE

NICK AND I survived the following week. Barely. His progress was slow, and he tired quickly. I rented a shower stool and a toilet tube brace, which he hated. He muttered under his breath every time I dropped him off in the bathroom. Swore even. Add the fact that I had to help him into the shower. I tried to respect his privacy, but it wasn't safe for him to step in and out of the shower without support. He insisted I leave the bathroom while he attended to business, but I stood outside with my ear glued to the door, lest he fall and injure himself.

Getting out of the house for his OT and PT appointments proved challenging as well. It took forever to get him ready, then once we arrived at the hospital I had to park the car, trudge a half-mile to the front entrance, fetch a wheelchair, load him into it... It made me think of the parents of my students, who had a lifetime of this ahead of them. A new empathy, now born of experience, dawned within me.

The actual appointments put us at odds, too. Nick didn't want me sitting in, but I required a visual of the exercises so I could be sure we were performing them properly at home. I tried excusing myself now and then, but Nick saw through that.

The good thing? False or not, I felt a modicum of safety. The bad thing? By Friday, we were sick of each other. I opted to order a pizza and pop in a DVD, settled the kids in the family room, and curled up in an overstuffed chair with a good book. I began to relax. My chronic neck ache, from looking over my shoulder 24/7, subsided.

I heard a car enter the driveway. I hopped up and hurried to the window, cell phone poised to call McGrath. Not a Jeep. Not a car I recognized. Fear caused the hairs on the back of my neck to prickle. It was Lori. And Adrianna. They were hauling the Brailler from the car.

I met them at the front door, prepared to turn them away. Why were they here? What did they want? How would I get rid of them?

I opened the door. Lori read the look of surprise on my face. "Sorry, I realize we should have called first, but we were in the neighborhood, and Adrianna has been so anxious to share her work with you."

I scanned the street. It didn't appear they'd been followed.

"Come in, come in." It seemed like the only reasonable course of action.

I lifted the Brailler from Adrianna's arms. It weighed a good fifteen pounds. None of my kids seemed to notice our visitors, so I sat them at the dining room table, and excused myself for a moment. I entered the bathroom and texted McGrath. "Lori and Adrianna showed up at the house. Advice?"

I tapped my foot, flushed the toilet, and turned on the water. *C'mon, McGrath.*

My phone dinged, and the screen lit up. "Hold steady." I nodded at my phone. "Thanks."

I rejoined them and offered them drinks. Adrianna set up the Brailler on the table as Annie wandered in and said hello.

"It's nice to meet you, Annie," Lori said.

"You, too. I'll let you visit, and get back to my movie."

"What are you watching?" Lori asked.

"*Pirates of the Caribbean*. It's a family favorite."

"It's my favorite! Can I join you?" Lori roamed off to watch the movie with the kids. All very out of body. All very *Twilight Zone*.

Adrianna loaded the 11x11 manila paper in the machine and began chatting. "I love this machine. I'm not allowed to use a Brailler at school, but I've still learned a lot. Mom and I practice reading at home when Dad is away, and I'm really smart at figuring things out."

I rested my hand on her shoulder, taken with her determined spirit and her courage in the face of her mother's absence. Teaching was my life's work. It wasn't a job. It was a calling. I seized the moment.

"How many of the contractions do you know?"

Three fingers of each hand settled on the six keys, thumbs poised near the space bar.

Her back straightened with pride. "Quite a few."

I dictated some contractions as a way of checking her skills. Simple words like "for, be, in" which used stand alone letters from the alphabet to take the place of entire words. Adrianna seemed to have mastered them, as well as simple letter combos like "able" and "ing" endings. A sponge, she devoured every new contraction I presented. After thirty minutes of typing we switched to reading, in my estimation the harder skill of the two for a previously sighted person to learn.

I started with simple text, both in order to assess her abilities and afford her some success, so she'd be anxious to learn more.

About fifty minutes into our session, she stopped and rested her hands in her lap.

I was surprised to see her shut down without warning. "Tired?"

After a long moment, she finally spoke. "Can I ask you a question?"

"Sure, sweetie. I love questions."

"You and my mom are good friends, right?"

"I'd like to think so," I answered honestly.

"Does she tell you stuff?"

I let the question sit. "Stuff?"

"Like friends do."

I nodded, caught myself, then answered. "Yes, some."

"She loved you." Adrianna used the past tense.

I narrowed my eyes and waited.

"One time when we were watching that video of you and me, she said she'd told you things she never told anyone."

Like most parents I visited, Lisa shared her grief over Adrianna's disability, her disagreements with Tony over her daughter's education, her worries that she wouldn't be the best parent to Adrianna after having Lauren, her perfect child. All the normal worries and concerns. Lisa touched on her difficulties with Tony, but only with occasional sarcasm. She hinted, but never allowed herself to face her difficulties with him head-on. Guess we had that in common. We both kept our fears and the reality of our lives at bay.

Adrianna grasped my hand. "She said you were trustworthy."

"That's a compliment. Thank you for sharing it with me."

"I trust you, too."

"Thank you." I listened for the kids, for Lori. The hum of the TV echoed in the background.

"I heard my parents fighting the night before my mom went to Grandma's house."

"I'm sorry. I'm sure they didn't mean for you to hear them."

Adrianna had always been a keen listener, not uncommon for the visually impaired.

"Dad told her she'd never see us again."

What? I mentally screamed. "People say things they don't mean when they argue."

"Dad has a temper. A bad one."

I patted her hand. Tears brimmed in her eyes, and she turned to face me. "He told mom he'd kill her if she told."

"Told what, sweetie?"

At that point, Adrianna's tears interfered with fluent speech; I offered her a tissue and waited for her to calm down. "I couldn't hear that whole part, but he was using bad language. Something about Uncle Vincent."

I held my breath. "What are you worried about?"

"I'm afraid I can't remember something. Something important. Something that would make Mom come back."

"Do you think Mom is staying away on purpose because she is scared of Dad?"

"I worry Dad hurt her. I heard a crash, then this big thump. I was too afraid to get out of bed. I pulled the covers over my head and my pillow over my ears, really tight, but now I wish I hadn't done that. Maybe I would have heard something more. Something that would help."

"It's not your responsibility, sweetheart. Let the adults figure it out." I waited a beat before asking, "Have you told anyone else? Aunt Lori?"

She paused and her brow furrowed. "I don't want to get Dad in trouble."

I waited.

"Do you know anything, Mrs. Stitsill?" She gazed at me, and even though I knew she could only see my hazy outline, I understood that it was her way of letting me know she was waiting for an answer. "I know adults don't tell kids all the details. You don't want us to worry."

"I don't know anything more than you do, honey. But if I figure anything out, I'll let you know, alright?"

Secrets are poison. They will eat you alive. I didn't want to tell Adrianna to keep the secret, but I didn't want her to divulge what she had heard either. It could put her in danger. She had shared it with me, maybe that was enough. I stayed quiet about her recollection. It was best.

"Thanks." Adrianna leaned her head on my shoulder and gave me a squeeze. I held her for a long moment, my heart breaking into pieces.

CHAPTER TWENTY-TWO

AFTER THEY LEFT, I texted McGrath to inform him of their departure, double-checked the street for strange or lurking vehicles, and forced air into my lungs. I resumed my position in my favorite chair, snuggled a blanket around me, sipped my wine, and wept. I cried for all the lost children, for all that I'd lost in my lifetime. In those twenty minutes, the losses seemed insurmountable, and for a frightening moment I worried I might not regain my strength.

Enough.

Keeping emotion at bay had been useful in my life. Probably a habit, or maybe even a defense mechanism I'd adopted early. Staying busy, handling current crises rather than unearthing old wounds always made more sense to me. I learned early that the best defense is a good offense. Letting down might engulf me; render me unable to function in my present life. The thought of giving in for more than a few short minutes scared the wits out of me.

I blew my nose, stepped into the bathroom and splashed water on my face, then joined the kids, who had finished their movie and now played a game of Monopoly. Monopoly. Just the game Tony and Vinnie were playing.

A portable walker, folded up against the wall, caught my eye. How had I missed this? Ed had taken Nick to PT and when they arrived home, I was picking up the kids from practice. Nick must have graduated from the parallel bars, or at least his PT had decided it was time to introduce this aid. Nick would be more independent if he made use of it, but I also suspected that outside of the house, he'd hate the idea of the cumbersome device drawing attention to him.

I obsessed about his studies then, and longed to get him back to school. If we could just improve his fine motor skills, I'd feel more confident about his return to classes. As yet, he couldn't fasten his jeans, write with a pencil, or move freely through crowded halls. Wheelchair? His friends would be happy to push him around. But that might create more havoc than his teachers could handle. While I knew what I could manage as a teacher, I taught in a more controlled environment than a high school provided. No, it made more sense to wait a bit longer before I rushed him off to school.

We would hit the books hard next week. It wouldn't be much longer.

The kids remained oblivious to our unexpected visit. I cleaned up the kitchen and spent some time in the laundry room, catching up before the weekend swallowed me whole. I thought about texting Di to see if she wanted to walk in the morning, but remembered our last conversation and decided against it. The thought of her pushing my buttons, bringing up topics I'd sooner avoid, held no appeal. Running a few miles, alone, would fill my exercise routine for a while.

As I lay in bed that night, I pondered calling McGrath to tell him of Adrianna's recollection. It was valuable information, but she hadn't shared any significant details either. I longed to become a cave-dweller, but knew I could not. I jotted everything down, dated it, then phoned him.

His voice sounded drowsy when he picked up.

"Hey," I said. "I'm really sorry to bother you, I can only imagine how exhausted you are, but Adrianna shared a significant recollection with me tonight that you need to be aware of." I recited her memory from my notes.

McGrath came to attention and asked me to repeat the story twice. "Thanks for calling. This could be important. It's certainly something to look at."

"I know."

An awkward silence.

"I guess I'll let you get back to sleep."

"Thanks," he said. "Let me know if anything else comes up, but don't go looking for trouble either. And keep this to yourself."

My nostrils flared with indignation, but I told myself he was just tired, and took a breath before I answered. "I will."

I ended the call, rolled over and fought with my tangled thoughts — why isn't he being friendlier? how can I woo him? will my life ever be normal? — before finally drifting off to sleep.

Lizzie snuck into bed with me sometime during the night, and I awakened to the smell of her clean, silky hair. I snuggled with her for a long moment, then inched out of bed without waking her, donned my running clothes, and slipped out of the house for a three mile run. Early morning dew glistened on the grass, the sun warmed me faster than I would have preferred, and I wound up back at home drenched in sweat. With the house still blessedly quiet, I brewed a pot of coffee and retreated to the front porch.

It seemed odd. Since leaving the photo on Nick's tray, no one had been in touch. None of this made sense.

At loose ends, I longed for what I often complained about. Long days of teaching, car-pooling, laundry, homework. Fact was, I had too much time on my hands, virtually no adult company without my kids present. *Damn.* I missed McGrath.

Lizzie soon joined me on the porch, reminding me that the first Cross County home meet would take place this morning. I hopped up, sprinted inside, and awakened Annie, Marie, and Will. They were all racing in the meet.

Thank God I'd done laundry last night and their uniforms had been washed. And dried.

I debated whether or not to call Ed. Would Nick want to join us? The course was at least a ¼ mile from the parking lot. Could he manage the uneven terrain with his walker? How had this gotten away from me?

By the time I hurried through a shower and dried my hair, Will had matters under control. He'd texted Nick's best buddy, Rob, and asked him to meet us at Salt Park. Nick was awake, dressed, and ready to go.

We veered into the park in the nick of time. Lizzie and I stood near the starting line while Nick and Rob made the rounds with friends. The entire football team flanked the sidelines. Since the girls ran first today, they had good reason.

Annie, my born runner, made the long course look more like a hundred yard dash. She struck an even pace, leading the race throughout, kicking like a sprinter at the end. An easy win. Marie held firm in the middle of the pack. Her chosen sport basketball, she considered Cross County a way to stay in shape in the off-season. More than anything, it seemed both of my girls were more interested in the after-party, where they sipped their sports drinks and young men showered them with attention.

Will ran next, plodding along while Lizzie and I cheered him on. Once he finished, he too joined the throngs of runners and onlookers to socialize. Lizzie headed over to the swings, and I spotted Ed sauntering along the outskirts of the park. I had lifted my head to the sun, hoping to avoid the other parents when I felt a tap on my shoulder.

Marty Jaeger. I took inventory: tall, lean, rugged. My boys' basketball coach, former high school classmate, and volunteer firefighter. Easy smile. Kind of like a cowboy from the Old West.

"Sam. Long time no see."

"Not that long really. By the way, I owe you an apology. You're first on the scene when Nick is hit, and an absolute peach at the hospital, calming me down when I was a basket case. I brushed you off. Sorry."

Marty grinned and waved me off. "No apology necessary."

Last year, I suspected Marty had a crush on me. He responded to the call when our house caught fire, made some lame excuse about having left a shirt there two days later, then we shared a few not so uncomfortable moments over a glass of wine. At the time, I shared that I was with McGrath.

Now, things were different. I was frantic for adult companionship and the kids wouldn't make anything of it. He didn't pose a threat to me or to them. They were used to seeing Coach Marty around. Still, I shouldn't lead him on. *Stop it, Sam. Desperation is unbecoming.*

He pointed to a picnic table under the pavilion where Nick held court. "I see Nick's doing well. Not surprising. That boy of yours has a lot of spunk."

I studied Nick, who was indeed smiling and gesturing as he no doubt told the story of his coma. "Spunk."

"How you doin'?"

"Great," I lied. "Feeling blessed that Nick's on the road to recovery."

"Feel like getting out of the house?"

The twinge of conflict I felt over taking advantage of his kindness melted into the background. "What do you have in mind?"

Marty raised his brows, seemingly surprised that I'd shown interest. "Couple of beers? Downtown? Sit on the sidewalk?"

Sounded like heaven. "When?"

He chuckled. "When we were in high school you used to tell me you needed more notice, but is tonight too soon?"

"Let's not call it a date or anything."

"Suits me. Beers. Not a date."

"I'm not sure if the girls have plans tonight. They

mentioned a party at Coach Jim's to celebrate the start of the season, but the boys' team doesn't have plans. Maybe Will can hold down the fort."

Marty pointed at my bag. "You've got a cell phone. They can call if there's an emergency. Two hours max. O'Callahans?"

"Deal." *What the hell was I doing?*

When I searched the park for the kids, they were headed toward the parking lot. I waved when Lizzie turned around, holding up a finger, letting her know I'd be right there.

"Pick you up? Seven?"

"No, I'll meet you there. Yes, seven works."

I must be certifiable. Avoid McGrath, allow Marty into my life. No threat. Just Marty. Just a friend. Head case. Need to be locked up. Yep, that's me.

Ed waited next to the car after folding up the walker and placing it in the rear of the vehicle. The kids sat loaded inside, anxious to get home, shower, and move on with their day. Ed offered to come by and help out, but I encouraged him to call Helen and live a little. I didn't want him to know I'd made plans with Marty, and I didn't want him to feel responsible for spelling me all the time.

A gleam flashed in his tired eyes. "If you insist."

By the time I reached the restaurant, I had worked myself into a full-on frenzy. Marty had arrived first, and he waved from a sidewalk table as I approached. Nothing like being on display downtown.

I ordered a microbrew and nearly downed it in one gulp. My nerves calmed. This was not a date after all, just a break from full-time mom. Marty eased my angst. He was a great story teller, filling me in on some of the local's antics in his position as volunteer firefighter.

"So, how are things with you and the detective?"

His question surprised me. "Fine, why do you ask?"

"Just sizing up my chances."

I blushed.

Marty laid a hand on my arm. "Joking, Sam. Joking."

I looked into his eyes and saw something else. Not humor, but a bit of sadness and disappointment. I decided to ignore it and offered an explanation for McGrath's absence. "The detective is busy with the Macchione mess."

"You must hear a lot."

"No. He's tight-lipped. But it's all over the news. I can't even name all the counts they're being charged with. I hardly ever see McGrath. When we have time together…"

Marty laughed. "Don't hurt me. I get the picture."

My turn to laugh. *Don't talk about McGrath. Change the subject.* "You're a firefighter. You must hear gossip all the time."

"You're right, I do. And I must admit, I get caught up in it. Politics is all some of the guys talk about. The Macchione deal gives us plenty to banter about. Crazy shit. Embezzlement. Money laundering. Bribery. Predatory lending. Racy texts with their assistants, too."

I shook my head and leaned back in my chair. "Word around is there are bad cops, too."

"I don't know any of them, but my guess is they don't brag about it."

"Mob. Can you believe it? Right in our sleepy little burg. You're lucky you're a firefighter, right? You're out of the fray. Why do they do it?"

"Who? The cops?" he asked.

I nodded.

"Extra pocket change, I guess. Or they owe somebody a favor."

"I can't believe it. In a big city, that's one thing. But Lexington?"

We shared a meal and laughed about the stupid things people do.

I missed McGrath.

CHAPTER TWENTY-THREE

A DEGREE OF calm entered my life, foreign, but welcome. Nick made daily gains, and I suspected it would only be a week more until he'd be back at school and in the thick of things again. As he gained more independence, my responsibilities dwindled, and while he napped that bright September afternoon, I considered a return to work; the thought of normal held tons of appeal. I smiled to myself as I headed out to the mailbox. We had survived this crisis. What a tremendous relief!

Oppressive humidity dampened my back the moment I stepped outside. I paused to pull a weed from the front walk, then looked up. A black Lincoln Town Car was parked on the road, less than a hundred yards from my house. The driver sat inside—window rolled down, engine off, head turned in my direction.

It was a fight or flight moment. My gut told me to run, but if I turned back, it would be too obvious. I continued down the driveway. Goosebumps rose on my arms and my heart clenched inside my chest. *Act nonchalant. Remember to breathe.* I reached the mailbox and grabbed the contents. A miracle. *Take another breath. Check him out.* A mere twenty-five yards from the car, I peered at the driver, desperate to make out his features. I even eked out a smile. He had dark hair, cropped short. A bulky gold chain with a large cross encircled his thick neck, and rested on his black T-shirt. He hid behind aviator sunglasses; his muscled biceps were heavily tattooed. His face reminded me of a cinder block. Hard.

Turn around. Walk back to the house.

I felt his eyes bore into my back as I consciously strolled back up the driveway. *Take a step. Take another.* I willed my flopping feet to make contact with the asphalt. *You're almost there.*

I locked and chained the door as soon as I reentered my home. The mail tumbled from my grasp and fanned out on the hardwood foyer. I slid down the door and wrapped my arms around my legs, a feeble attempt to still my trembling limbs. Somehow, I managed to pull my cell phone from my back pocket, and with shaking fingers, I texted McGrath. If he was in the middle of things, he would be more likely to respond to a text rather than a call. At least I hoped so. "Mob. Watching me. From a car. Across the street."

Hard as I tried, I could not suspend my panic. My gun... I needed to load it and keep it in my purse. As soon as my breathing returned to normal and my legs were functioning again.

I peered at the grandfather clock. Lizzie was due to arrive home in fifty minutes. If I left the house to pick her up from school, it would require leaving Nick home alone. I couldn't risk it. *C'mon, McGrath. Answer me!*

Nick appeared at the top of the steps, and I gathered the mail and stood, hoping he wouldn't question the fact that I was balled up on the floor like a helpless infant.

He clenched the handrails and made his way down the stairs, a slow, laborious process.

I pasted a smile on my face as he met my gaze. "It's a beautiful day. Let's go for a ride and pick up your sister from school."

Nick looked puzzled.

I walked into the kitchen and grabbed my keys from the counter. "The bus is leaving."

He pointed at the dinging clock. "She doesn't get out of school for forty-five minutes. Are you okay? You seem upset."

"I'm fine. We'll drop off the dry cleaning on our way."

Resigned, Nick opened his walker and eased himself into the hall. "You're acting weird."

"Can't help it. I'm a mom."

I turned the key in the ignition, my breath catching in my throat, then eased out of the garage and down the driveway. The Lincoln had vanished. A warning? Mission accomplished.

I phoned the school on my way down the street, alerting them that I would pick up Lizzie—all the while vigilant for the Lincoln. Nothing. Still, my heart rammed against my ribs.

Nick looked over his shoulder into the back seat. "You forgot the cleaning."

I shook my head. "We can sit in the courtyard and enjoy the sunshine."

"Um. It's cloudy, Mom."

"Alright. Enough."

That shut him up.

I cleaned out the glove box and the receipts from the door pocket, then stuffed them into a paper bag while Nick tapped the beat of the radio's songs on the dashboard. I picked up my phone. Still no text back from McGrath. *Shit.* I hadn't pressed SEND. I updated the text, alerting him that I was parked outside the school.

Seconds later my screen lit up. "Officer Dave will walk her out. Sit tight when you get home. Lock ALL doors. STAY INSIDE. Keep the kids with you at all times. UNTIL FURTHER NOTICE."

I nodded. Okay. I had a plan. If I could just will my pulse rate to return to normal. *Settle down, Sam. Get the kids and get home.*

What had McGrath shared with Officer Dave? How

would we do this and not alarm Nick and Lizzie? The bell sounded and kids poured out of the building. Lizzie walked with Dave; she chatted with him, seemingly unfretted by the fact that he accompanied her to the car.

"Hi, Dave."

He passed me a knowing look. Concerned. Caring. "Your daughter is one of the stars of the D.A.R.E. Program. Thought I'd escort her to the car and share the news."

"Thanks." I appreciated him covering for me. "She's a good girl."

I bid him goodbye, and sped for the high school.

Nick looked at me cross-eyed. "Slow down, Mom. You're going to get a speeding ticket."

I blew him off. "Not long until your sibs are done with practice. I say we grab them and drive through Dairy Queen on our way home. It's a good day for a treat."

An hour later, after I double-checked the locks on every single window and chained the doors to my home, I ushered the kids off to complete their homework. I brewed a cup of tea and sat at the kitchen table, holding my head in my hands, missing my beloved Rex, and unable to form a single coherent thought.

Ten feet away, Nick turned on the TV set. A special report filled the screen. "A woman's remains have been discovered near the Salt River in Lexington Heights. Officials fear it may be the body of Lisa Macchione, wife of recently indicted construction owner, Tony Macchione, brother of Mayor Vincent Macchione. Stay tuned for further details."

My heart arrested. Lisa? There was no way. It couldn't be. Three miles from my home? I slipped into the bathroom. It was happening. Again. My head throbbed and my throat burned. I lifted the lid of the toilet and vomited. *I can't do this. Make it stop.*

Lizzie pounded on the bathroom door. "Mom! Mrs. Stewart is here."

Really? Now? "Be right there."

It was as if all the blood had drained out of me. I had no clue why Di decided to stop by, but there was no logical way to dismiss her. I glued a smile on my face and wobbled out the door.

Her arms were loaded down with food.

Nauseous and weak, I could barely speak. "Wow! Thank you." I croaked.

Lisa's face flashed before me. Her sunny smile and optimistic disposition betrayed by intensely brown eyes, ones ridden with deep pain and sadness. Her slender fingers gripped my arm as she thanked me. "I can't tell you how much I appreciate you coming. If only I were half as strong as you..." Her grasp told me she wanted to give me something back. An unspoken bond existed between us; joined by the similar experiences we avoided sharing. Her thick, shiny shoulder length auburn hair, her coordinated outfits, the tantalizing aromas wafting from her kitchen; she created a manageable world for herself, so put together that no one would suspect her life was anything other than ideal....

Di prattled on about Ava and the boys, and whispered about Chris's heightened need for sex in his threatened state. Overnight, Di had become mother extraordinaire. She didn't have time for Chris's neediness, especially when it took the form of demands for daily intercourse. I cautioned her, but knew that I'd felt the same way at one time or another. A man's insecurity could sometimes be cured only through the reassurance of sex. I couldn't help but feel that God had created an awful mess when he'd designed men and women as polar opposites.

I couldn't focus. I couldn't stop thinking of Lisa, or worrying about my children's safety. What the hell was happening? Lisa's dead, desecrated body abandoned in the tall weeds near the riverbank, her little girls, whose beauty mirrored her own, destined to a life carrying this constant loss — a loss which would shape their entire future. I reminded myself that the body might not be Lisa's; she could be in hiding somewhere for a reason I did not yet understand. In my heart, I knew it was her. *Enough.*

As I prepared dinner, I surmised that McGrath would work feverishly into the night, investigating the scene, unearthing leads, interviewing witnesses, anxiously waiting for the coroner to determine the cause of death. I assumed the woman's death to have been a homicide, and although I assumed it was Lisa, a seasoned detective like McGrath wouldn't allow himself to be ruled by suppositions. He'd wait until all the evidence had been gathered and sorted.

My timing? Lousy. I hated the idea of interrupting him. Guilt feasted on my ulterior motives. *You're crazy, Sam. You don't deserve him.* I waited until nearly eleven to place the call.

He answered right away, his voice tired and soft. "Hi," was all he said.

"Busy?" I asked.

"A little." Business-like. Sarcastic.

"Any chance you could stop by? If not tonight, maybe meet for coffee tomorrow? I need... reassurance."

"Reassurance. Humph." A long silence ensued. "I'm headed to the precinct. I can stop by for five minutes. See you in thirty."

I waited by the window, pulling the blinds back every ten seconds or so. My heart was on fire. It was as if I was a character in a romance novel, waiting for my soldier to return from battle. Wanting him. Needing him. I kicked myself. What kind of person was I, placing my own needs and priorities ahead of Lisa's death? McGrath's job?

Get a grip, woman.

I wasn't pulling him away from the case, but offering new evidence. It might help him find Lisa's killer. Plus, I was scared shitless. Maybe the same thug that sat in front of my house earlier that afternoon was responsible for Lisa's death. Maybe we were next! The fact that I desired more than anything to take this man into my bed, strap him to my soul, and let him protect my sorry ass, served only as backdrop to the main event, solving her murder. I stepped into the kitchen and poured two glasses of wine, pausing to light a candle in the family room, and hurried back to the window. He pulled into my driveway on the dot, and I rushed to open the door for him. We paused in the foyer, both awkward, not knowing whether to embrace. I prayed he'd press his lips to mine, fill me with a kiss of deep longing, the kind that spoke volumes. One that said for the moment, he'd forgiven me. That he'd accepted my flimsy apology, and was ready to resume our relationship.

Instead, McGrath shoved his hands deep inside his pockets, impassive.

We walked into the family room, and I handed him a stemmed glass. He set it on the table without drinking.

I searched his sad eyes. "Is it Lisa?"

He nodded.

I knew McGrath. He would feel like he let Lisa down by not finding her earlier, by not being able to prevent her death. "I'm so sorry."

He softened for a moment. A longing in his eyes, an ache. But with a simple blink, he switched back. Cop mode, full speed ahead. "You need *reassurance?*" There was a searing edge to his voice.

I tried to lock his gaze, but he wouldn't look at me, so I pleaded with him. "I feel fractured, like I'm in a million little pieces. I hate to bother you when you're in the middle of this horrible mess, but I'm scared for my family."

"You did the right thing, calling me. I've got men in place to keep an eye on you and the kids, but now I have to get back."

McGrath didn't seem pleased that I had reached out to him or overly sympathetic to my situation. He seemed preoccupied and distant. More than that, he seemed hurt.

I grasped for words..."I love you."

McGrath raised his eyebrows. "You too, kiddo." He patted my knee, stood, brushed off his pant leg, and slowly made his way to the door.

"Can we talk once this is over?"

He nodded and left.

CHAPTER TWENTY-FOUR

I WAS A wreck, a complete and total jumble of emotions for the rest of that long night. After finishing a glass of wine, I wound up where I always do when I need to think — swaying back and forth in the rocking chair on the front porch. Stars sprinkled the moonless sky. The air stuck to my skin at this late September hour, but I savored the peace and quiet at the same time.

How could the world be so still when Lisa was no longer a part of it? How could calm cover the land when her corpse lay atop a slab in the morgue? What would become of Adrianna and Lauren? How on earth would they cope with this loss?

I was getting carried away again. Wallowing. Letting too much in. Time to shield myself; screen myself from living any more horror. If that was possible.

I dove headfirst into thoughts of McGrath. He'd been distracted. That pat on the knee before he left now seemed patronizing. Like a knife puncturing my skin. A sharp and lethal blade. Had it been purposeful? Did he mean something by it? *We were something once, baby, but you blew it.*

My throat clogged with tears. The depth of my feelings for McGrath astounded me. Guess I hadn't allowed myself to face them before. I'd spent a lifetime quelling the murmurings of my heart. Once I allowed him in, I scared myself. And backed away. *Shit.* Di was right. Jack was right. Hell, McGrath was right. I feared the cost of loving and being loved.

Would he come back?

It seemed wrong to worry about my own needs right now.

After a long while, a breeze kicked up, chilling the air just enough to drive me inside. I climbed into bed. The reality of Lisa's murder set in, and I wept for her and her children before I fell into a fitful sleep.

Annie shook me awake at 6:45 a.m. "Mom, you overslept. Get up. Quick."

I'd forgotten to set the alarm. But the older three were up and at 'em, and Lizzie woke easily and I sent her to dress and brush her teeth. I watched them climb on the bus, and directed Annie to text me and let me know they arrived safely at school. She looked at me like I'd grown antlers, but agreed to humor me. A woman was just found dead in the park nearest our home. It sort of made sense. I put Lizzie on the bus myself, daring anyone to pull onto my street and stalk me.

Hectic mornings like this led to discombobulated days, which was how the bulk of the next six hours unfolded. Nick, who'd been a trooper since his arrival home, awakened in a foul mood, surly as an angry bear.

"I'm not going to PT or OT today," he announced.

I leaned him forward in bed and placed his walker adjacent to where he sat. "Not a choice."

"I mean it, Mom. No dice."

"Are you sick?"

"Yep. Sick of going. Not going back. It's not helping. I still can't walk. I still can't write or play the guitar. What's the point?"

I pasted a bright smile on my face. "It's natural to feel discouraged when therapy isn't progressing as quickly as you'd like, but those feelings usually crop up when a breakthrough is right around the corner."

"You can drop the cheerleader act, Mom."

Dreadful day, here we come. I needed time to grieve for Lisa, and I wanted to spend time lost in thoughts of McGrath. *How could I win him back?* I felt exhausted by Nick's challenge. I hesitated, not quite sure if I felt up to the task of dragging him out of bed or propping him up, literally and emotionally, throughout the day. Maybe we both required a few more hours of sleep. In light of his mood and the time, I hesitated. What would a couple more hours in bed cost?

"Go back to sleep. I'll be back in an hour or two, and I'll expect you to have a new attitude by then. I'll finish the laundry or entertain myself in some other fascinating fashion while you transform yourself."

I shuttled folded laundry into drawers, swept the kitchen floor and dusted. I added a shower to my regimen, steeling myself for the chance that his mood had not improved with the added sleep.

The door to his room stood ajar. I peered inside. He'd managed to flip his legs over the side of the bed. I stood in the doorway. "Good morning," I said. "You seem happier."

"Stop making a big deal about everything, would you?"

I weighed my options. He'd never get better if we started skipping therapy sessions. I marched inside his room, pilfered a pair of sweats, underwear, socks, and a t-shirt from his drawer and tossed them at him.

"Get dressed." I walked out and shut the door with a click.

When I knocked on Nick's door fifteen minutes later, he didn't answer. Unease gripped me. I knocked again. He'd been awake five minutes ago. Rather than wait, I threw the door open. He lie in bed. Seizing.

I grabbed my cell from my pocket and dialed 911. Somehow the words found their way out of my mouth. "Son. Seizing. Thirteen years old. Recent closed head injury." Recited my address.

I rushed to Nick's side. Soothing him came naturally.

"It's okay, Bud. EMS is on their way. Hang in there,

sweetie. It's gonna be okay."

He shook so hard, his bed rattled. His eyes rolled back in his head. Paralyzed with fear, I continued talking to myself as much as to Nick. "They'll be right here. Stay with me. You're going to be fine." *Where are you, God? Need you. Now, please.*

I kept an eye on the time. The doctors would want to know how long the seizure had lasted. *Forever.* After three interminable minutes, his body finally calmed. I continued speaking to him in reassuring murmurs. "You're going to be okay. Help is on the way." The doorbell rang two minutes later. Thankfully, we lived close to town.

I opened the door, quickly ushering the paramedics inside. "He's at the head of the stairs. A quick right when you reach the top."

I waited for them to pass and hastily followed behind. By the time they arrived at Nick's side, attached a blood pressure cuff to his arm and took his vitals, he was coming around. Groggy and disoriented, he appeared frightened. I hurried to the foot of his bed, hoping to calm him with my words. "You had a seizure, Bud."

His eyes pleaded with me.

One of the paramedics asked Nick his name. He answered correctly. They asked him his age and where he went to school. Again, Nick gave the right responses.

Thank you, God.

Even though Nick had weathered the storm, the paramedics insisted on a ride to the hospital. Nick argued, adamant that he didn't need to see a doctor. I phoned Ed, filled him in, and he agreed to meet us at the ER.

I rode in the back of the ambulance with my boy, now dazed from the medication they administered to keep him from seizing again.

A chill ran through me. White noise echoed in my ears. My cell vibrated in my pocket. I rifled it out and read the screen. McGrath. *Not now. Later.*

CHAPTER TWENTY-FIVE

I'M NOT SURE if good things come in threes, but bad things certainly do. One, Lisa's murder. Two, McGrath's pat on the knee. Three, Nick's seizure. God must have read my mind, because that seemed to be enough for twenty-four hours. There weren't enough hours left for much more.

Nick remained seizure-free for the rest of the day. We'd be allowed to head home by evening if that continued. Ed, rock that he is, held me together until it was time for the kids to be picked up from practice, then headed off to take care of pressing grandchildren matters.

"I'll order pizza." He kissed my cheek and hurried out the door.

The attending neurologist wrote Nick a script for increased Phenobarbital. With another EEG scheduled for the following week, we'd be good to go once he awakened.

Nick slept for another hour, then woke and flashed me a crooked grin. "Told you I didn't want to go to therapy today."

"Nice." I poked his ribs and told him he'd be fine to finish the assigned paper for his freshman composition class. It was to be a memoir, and he'd told me he'd decided to write about his coma. I hadn't yet been allowed to read any of the piece. Nick had demanded use of a new dictation application to assist him with his writing assignments. His recitations were then transcribed into words on the page. I'd used the app several times with my learning disabled students. It didn't perform perfectly, but close enough, and Nick deserved privacy in reliving his experience through his writing.

After he and all the other kids fell asleep that night, I peeked.

It was hot that day, and when I woke up that morning, I already dripped sweat. A day like any other, birds sang outside my window, streams of sunlight flooded the loft where my brother and I slept, and fluffy clouds dotted the sky. Little did I know it was the day that would change my life forever.

My grandmother had prepared a man-sized breakfast. Bacon, eggs, homemade hash browns, and jelly jars filled to the brim with orange juice. My brother and sisters and I ate like we always did when we spent time at the cottage. We licked our plates clean. Outdoor air does that to a person.

After racing to put on our swimsuits, we joined our grandfather for a morning of fishing.

Life on the beach was easy and we spent our days filled with a false sense of security. Nothing could go wrong in a place as beautiful as this, where the fish jumped over the waves while we rowed onto the middle of the lake, baited our hooks, and basked in the warm rays, lolling in the boat, waiting for that first tug on our lines.

We'd caught a boat load of perch that morning. My baby sister, Lizzie, delighted that, for the first time, she'd matched my catch. After we made our way back to shore, we spent a lazy hour scaling and filleting the yellow flesh. My grandparents fried them in a light batter. I swear, I can still taste them.

From the sandy beach, I heard the car's tires crunch on the gravel driveway. My mom's friend had driven her up north. When she joined us on the beach, I read her eyes. Mom and I are like that. We have all kinds of conversations that don't include words.

I kicked a rock. Like that helped. Then I comforted my mom. I couldn't imagine what it was like for her. Not only did she have us kids to worry about, but she'd just lost her husband, and the man who turned out to be the best dad she could ever have found for us.

Then, I felt sad and selfish. I worried about what would happen to us. Kids at school who had lost a parent seemed lost. I didn't want to feel lost or alone. That's when I leaned my head on my mom's shoulder. I looked at her again. I knew there was something more.

Somehow, our dog had died, too. My dad had loved that dog as much a guy could love any living thing. And Rex had loved him in the same way. I guessed it was fitting that the two of them were joined forever in heaven.

That day, I vowed to make the most of myself. Live life like each day mattered. I vowed to make sure my mom, my sisters and my brother never felt lost or lonely. To always let them know that dad was still with us… through each other.

My mom always tells me there are reasons for everything, even if we don't understand them at the time. I'm still working on the reason. I sure miss my dad. And Rex.

Word after profound word, Nick dredged up feelings in me that I'd locked up tight. There still, but unattended. I'd not allowed myself the time to think much about the day I told the kids about Jon's death, or his memorial, or the loss. Even now, I preferred not to go there. Instead, I chose to swell with pride over the fine young man my son was becoming, despite the aftereffects of his brain injury, the residual obstacles involving his motor skills. What were the lessons I learned from Jon's death? I taught my kids that things happen for a reason, as Nick reminded me, but I'd yet to figure out any reason other than it had allowed McGrath into my life, and that I'd begun to trust enough to love again. I better not blow it.

I unlocked my phone and listened to McGrath's voicemail which I had ignored earlier. I'd told myself I was too busy with Nick's crisis to take his call. While that was true, I'd still taken my time getting to his message. His words sounded scripted, like when he first called me to ask questions about how well I knew my husband and described the woman who once thought I was married to her husband. All cop. The sand, spilling through the hour glass, sifted too fast. I dialed McGrath well after midnight.

"I'm so sorry," I said.

"What's wrong?"

My long choking sobs filling the line. "Nick had a seizure. I'm crashing and burning." Goosebumps rose on my flesh, even as I wrapped a blanket around my shoulders and flicked on the gas fireplace.

"Tell me." His voice softened. He sounded like my friend, rather than my foe.

I regained my footing, apologized again, and begged his forgiveness. "I'm an idiot. I pull away from you when I need you most. I can't help it. One of my damned frailties. I want you back in my life. I need you."

He sighed. Then he laughed. "Woman, you're a hot mess."

After a welcome sigh of relief, I chuckled. From now on I needed to be on my best behavior. One of those deals I made with God that I was sure to muck up in the next five minutes.

"Good point. My bones ache for you."

"Not just your female parts, huh?"

"There's that."

I wished like hell he could have thrown the bubble light on top of his vehicle and headed to my place.

Even though it wasn't yet Christmas, visions of McGrath danced in my head all night. *Holy hot McGrath.*

CHAPTER TWENTY-SIX

I MUDDLED THROUGH the next day. McGrath indicated it might take up to three days for specific details about the investigation into Lisa's murder to be released to the press. I didn't bother to call him with questions the following evening. Instead, I focused on my children, offering them an evening of popcorn and a slideshow of our digital family albums. I often did this when the kids were younger and Jon traveled out of town on business. In light of Nick's recent essay, the timing seemed right. Seeing photos of Jon made all of us feel more connected to him.

I set up the TV so we could watch the show on the large widescreen. We nestled on the floor in front of the couch with overstuffed pillows and light blankets. I turned on the set and the slides passed over the screen.

"I remember that," Lizzie squealed. It was a shot of Jon, holding her in the palm of his hand when she was three years old, lifting her up over his head like a prized trophy. I hugged her close.

There were photos of trips to the cottage, some of Jon when he was Will's age. The resemblance startled me. Even Marie seemed flabbergasted and asked if she looked like her dad.

I looked from one child to the next.

"You all look like him," I joked. It was true. They all

carried a part of Jon with them, whether it was in the form of expressions he used, his angular nose, the square set of his jaw, or the cadence of his voice when they spoke.

Memories bubbled up like the fizz in the orange soda they drank. Pictures of Rex devouring Jon's breakfast on the counter, photos of the kids diving off Jon's shoulders, fishing in the lake, eating mounds of barbecued chicken at the cottage. All good. We shed a few tears, but I sensed a good deal of healing took place, too. They'd never forget their dad. I'd never allow that to happen.

I shuffled them off to bed by eleven, and then turned on the late night news. Lisa's photo crossed the screen and I kicked up the volume. I'd known and respected Lisa, and the reality of her death crept through me like a toxic tide. My heart ached for Lauren and Adrianna. Their asshole, crook of a father made their loss that much worse. I hoped and prayed their spunk and determination would see them through this unimaginable time. My kids and I had just revisited our loss. It would never go away, but so far, I liked to pretend that we were weathering it, and within our little cocoon, we were doing alright. I also prayed the loving and steady guidance of their Aunt Lori would stabilize their already shaken lives. They were destined to grow up orphans.

I collapsed into bed around one in the morning, only to be awakened by the vibration of my cell phone at 2:12 a.m. Since I'd been sleeping fitfully, rousing myself proved easy. I rolled over and picked up my phone, narrowing my eyes to read the screen. McGrath.

I slid the 'on' button and answered.

"Hi," he said. "You awake?"

"Sort of. I've been dozing. Too much on my mind to sleep."

"Can I come over?"

I sat up and switched on the bedside lamp. "What's wrong?"

"Just want to talk."

"I'll be waiting."

I shuffled into some sweats and pulled back my hair. It would take him about thirty minutes to make the drive, so I poured myself a short glass of wine, and set out a glass for him.

His car pulled into the driveway a short time later, and I met him at the door. He looked exhausted — dark circles rimmed his eyes, a thick five o'clock shadow curtained his cheeks, and a rumpled dress shirt hung from his slumped shoulders. I offered a sympathetic smile as I let him inside. He leaned toward me and I offered him my cheek, but he turned my face to his and kissed me full on the mouth instead. My hunger for him didn't surprise me. It was his hunger for me that rattled me. In a good way. I wrapped my arms around him after that kiss and buried my face in the curve of his neck. I inhaled the last hint of his spicy scent, at once feeling centered and as if I'd finally arrived back home. "God, I've missed you," I murmured.

He stuck his nose in my hair and inhaled deeply. "Me, too."

I led him inside, poured him some wine, and joined him on the sofa in the family room. I lit a candle on the table and turned to face him. In the dim candlelight, his eyes looked flat — all the sparkle had been extinguished. I'd never seen him like this.

"You look awful. Long day?"

He scrubbed his face with his hand and locked eyes with me. "The worst. I wanted to tell you before you heard it on the news. Details about Lisa… this was a gruesome murder. I've seen a lot in my career, but it's always the women and children that get to me."

I nodded, grasping his hand and easing my fingertips along the soft hairs of his arm as a sign of support, waiting patiently for him to get to the heart of the matter.

His voice wavered. "There were signs of a struggle."

I teared up, thinking of Lisa's last moments lived in fear and absolute terror.

"Her eyes were gouged out before she was shot. It was an execution style murder. Personal." His voice was devoid of emotion. Flat, like his eyes.

I gasped and began to shake. The air went cold in an instant.

"There were defensive wounds on her hands, fingers and arms. She tried to protect herself during the assault. Obviously, her attacker overcame her."

"But if she put up a fight, there could be DNA under her fingernails."

McGrath shook his head. "Nancy Drew."

I ignored him. "If you could see that she struggled, when was she killed? Recently, right? That means she's been alive. She's been somewhere since she disappeared. How long had she been dead when her body was discovered?"

"Probably six to eight hours."

"You saw her body?"

McGrath closed his eyes and inhaled sharply. "Yes."

My stomach turned. If McGrath had let me help, maybe we could have saved her. But no, he insisted on leaving me out of it. Who knows what he knew and when he knew it? Where had he been looking for her? If he had shared the details with me, maybe *I* could have saved her. I should have probed more. Insisted that he allow me to lend a hand. If I'd gotten involved, I could have…

My thoughts were beyond ridiculous. Beyond irrational. Maybe the shock… of Nick's accident, of Lisa's death… was taking its toll. If I'd gotten involved… I could have gotten myself… KILLED! My turn for a head shake, a feeble attempt to will my brain to make some sense of the facts. Not that it mattered now, but I couldn't help asking the questions, "We have to find out where she was all this time. Was she hiding and her killer found her? Had she been kidnapped?"

"Working on it."

I arched a brow. "I'm sick to my stomach right now, but I also have a theory."

McGrath narrowed his eyes at me. "Go for it."

"You said it was personal. Eyes are a big deal here. Tony hated Adrianna's vision impairment. More important than that, he blamed her vision problems on Lisa. He could never accept that something in his DNA had caused this. The blow to his ego at having a less than perfect child enraged him. It didn't fit his image. Drawing attention to Adrianna by allowing her to receive special education services irked the hell out of him, too. He became explosive during meetings at school. Whenever talk of Adrianna learning Braille came up, he'd lose it and insist that she not be taught Braille. Pound his fist on the table. Scream and shout at us. Agreeing to teach Adrianna Braille was like giving in, he'd say."

McGrath nodded, his wheels spinning.

"When I met with Adrianna's current teacher, Carol Marsh, at that picnic a couple of weeks ago, she mentioned that Tony caused a huge scene at Adrianna's IEP meeting last spring."

McGrath looked confused.

"Individualized Educational Planning Meeting. It's where we discuss services for a child's impairment."

He nodded.

"Tony could never accept that Adrianna would lose her vision entirely, or that teaching her Braille was a way of readying her for that eventuality."

"You think Tony killed her."

"Yes. It'll be easy to prove, because she should have his DNA under her fingertips. It's a slam dunk."

McGrath turned my hand over in his and etched a figure eight onto my palm. "Her body was cleaned up."

"What?"

"She was doused in bleach."

I covered my face with my hands. "That's... that's... horrific! What kind of person...?"

"A last ditch effort to destroy evidence."

"But you said she had defensive wounds, so you could see bruising and cuts?"

"Yes."

"Even if he cleaned her up, it's hard to clean under someone's nails. He would have had to have had a tool to scrape under her nails."

"You're right, Sam, but his people are professionals. They do this for a living. Although the fact that she still had hands may mean it was not, in fact, a professional job. I just don't want you to get your hopes up. It's not as simple as you think."

"It *was* him," I raised my voice, then looked toward the staircase and hushed. I didn't want to wake my children. "Don't you see?" I whispered.

"I don't disagree with you, but it leads me to believe that he didn't plan this. He killed her in the heat of the moment. This was a brutal crime. It's as if he realized what he'd done in the aftermath. It's not unusual for a predator to come to his senses after the deed is done and try to erase all evidence of his involvement. It doesn't have to make sense to us. It just needed to make sense to him at the time."

"I always thought of Tony as the type to hire someone to do his dirty work."

McGrath nodded. "That's the word on the street. In this case, *if* he did this, I'm afraid his wrath got the better of him. He came to his senses much too late."

"But why now? Why would he kill her after they'd been married for so long? He's had affairs. It's not like was committed to their relationship. I don't get it."

"She left him."

"Yes, but she came back. I would've guessed he'd have been happy about that. Even if he didn't want to be married to her and slept around on her throughout their marriage, he liked to maintain appearances. And he craved control over everyone in his life." I paused for a long moment, feeling bile fill my throat. "We're missing something."

McGrath shook his head. He sipped his wine, then sank back against the couch. "Yes, but I'm too tired to think straight."

I rested my hand on his thigh and leaned my head on his shoulder. He put his arm around me and squeezed. I listened as he inhaled, then let out a ragged breath.

"I've got to get home and get some rest." McGrath glanced at the staircase. "Besides, the kids will be up soon."

I turned to the kitchen clock. "It's four in the morning. We're safe for a couple of hours."

He leaned his head back and drifted off.

I replayed the three years I spent in the Macchione home. Pored over every conversation Lisa and I had, peered through my mind's eyes in fits and starts. I finally landed on a buried memory.

The call came midway through my visit. Lisa answered the phone, then handed it to me. Wanda, the program secretary, informed me that my next home visit had canceled. Lisa overheard my conversation. She whispered, "Stay for coffee." I looked outside. Blinding snow pelted the windows as it blew and drifted in the howling winds. I glanced at the muted television and read the warning – EMERGENCY ALERT: STAY OFF THE ROADS. I nodded at Lisa and told Wanda that I was staying put until my next appointment. Lisa gathered Adrianna in her arms and put her down for a nap. Lauren had spent the night at Lori's so it was just the two of us. We sat in her cozy kitchen – she filled delicate china cups with rich freshly-brewed coffee, and warm homemade apple pastries lined our plates. A private coffee klatch.

Lisa looked down at the table. I sensed it was serious. "You divorced your first husband?"

"Yes." Dizziness engulfed me. In a flash, I was back in my old bedroom – three years before I'd met Lisa; Annie was three, Nick, an infant. My ex stumbled up the stairs, mumbling expletives. I feigned sleep, but he accosted me anyway. Leaving my body was

old hat by then; I simply thought about my plan as he was driving himself into me. I must have said something without realizing it, because the next thing I knew, his hand hit my face. Hard.

"There is only one way you will leave this house... in a zip-up bag."

I began to shake at the memory. I couldn't even raise my coffee cup to my lips.

"Are you alright?" Lisa asked.

"I'm trying to be. I thought I'd put this in the past."

Lisa placed a gentle hand on my arm. "I'm sorry, Sam. I didn't mean to resurrect old wounds."

I nodded, steadying myself by holding onto the edge of the table and breathing.

When I looked up, Lisa locked my gaze. "Can I ask you something?"

After a long moment, I was able to respond. "Sure."

"How did you get away?"

I recited the story, sounding like a weather reporter rather than a real person with real emotions. But the more I spoke, the more unfiltered I became.

"It took forever to hatch a plan. Almost a year, I think. It seems like a lifetime ago." I wanted a cigarette. Had I really lived that life?

I chuckled. "It's not funny. I don't know why I'm laughing, but I remember the feelings... the constant fear, the knot that took permanent residence in my stomach. And then, even after I left him..." Tears welled in my eyes, and I swallowed over the lump in my throat. "I couldn't rest. What if he found me? What if he decided to kill me and the kids?"

When I looked up at Lisa, she held me in her tender gaze. We shared a mutual unspoken understanding. I knew why she asked the question. She knew I knew.

"How did you hatch the plan?"

"Once I gathered the courage to leave, I drafted a detailed plan. I stashed every nickel I could over those long months. Besides cash, I needed a job, a place to live, a sitter for my kids. I wanted to be far *enough away and in a place where I knew no one, so he wouldn't find me through a friend. I discovered Lexington in my job search. I had always wanted to work in an Early Intervention program, and they were hiring for the following school year. I fulfilled all the required qualifications, and drove here for an interview, planning the appointment for the middle of the day so I had time to drive, interview, and return home without my ex putting together the facts. After I got the job, I searched for housing. It was the scariest thing I'd ever done. I was embarrassed, ashamed, lost, and alone. I didn't want to tell another living soul my story. Why had I picked an abusive man for my husband, for the father of my children? Why didn't I leave him when he was jailed for leaving the scene of an accident when he rolled his truck, drunk and carrying a loaded gun?" I shook my head, still horrified at the life I'd chosen.*

"I wasn't able to find a house to rent, a place with a backyard for my children, so I signed a six-month lease for an apartment. Not the life I had imagined for me or for my children. That's not important, though. What's important is that I survived. I packed the car when my ex was at work. Just the essentials. Nothing more. Once he passed out that night, I lifted my sleeping children from their beds." Tears streamed down my face. I was no longer able to keep emotion at bay. "I kissed each one of them as I placed them in their car seats, praying over and over again that he would remain in his alcohol induced coma long enough for my kids and me to escape."

"Would you have done anything differently?"

I shook my head. "It was the best decision I ever made."

"Did he find you?"

I nodded, another memory smacking me in the face, and swallowed the bile that rose in my throat. "One night, once the kids and I had moved to our house in town, about seven months after I'd left, he knocked on my door in the middle of the night. He was drunk, of course, and cursing. I knew who it was before I reached the door. The kids were asleep, but if he kept it up, they wouldn't be for long. It was an impossible situation. Open the door and I could be dead. Don't open the door, and have my children screaming and crying in fear of their own father."

"What did you do?"

"I called the cops."

"And?"

"They came and took him away. They locked him up, not because he disturbed me, but because he assaulted an officer in my front yard." I shivered at the memory. "I had already filed for divorce at that point and we were five months away from a final decree. Thankfully, when the time came, I didn't have to appear in court. As far as I know, he never came back. For all I know, he could have drunk himself to death by now."

"What about the kids? Did they ask for him? Did they miss him?"

"It hasn't been easy, but now that they are a little older, and now that they have Jon, they are happy and well-adjusted. It helped that they were so young, I think, at least that's what I tell myself, and when they've had questions, I've answer them honestly. Their dad was not a good father or husband. I did what I thought best, for our happiness and our safety."

Lisa nodded, and I guessed she was putting the pieces of her life together in a new and profound way.

I shuddered reliving the memory. How *had* I lived through that?

More importantly though, had Lisa shared my story with Tony? Had she tried to do the same?

I leaned my head on a sleeping McGrath's shoulder. It was more than my brain could process.

* * *

I woke with a jerk. Six bells chimed on the grandfather clock in the entryway. "McGrath," I ordered, shaking his shoulder. "Wake up. The kids will be up soon."

He woke with a start. "I fell asleep."

"No shit, Sherlock." I grabbed his shoes and dragged

him to his feet. "C'mon, I'm not ready for the kids to see you here. You're a mess."

He balanced on one foot like a flailing child as he attempted to put on his shoes while hustling to the hallway. "Great, now I'm being kicked out because I look like crap."

I planted a firm kiss onto his mouth. "I love you."

He grinned, patted my derriere, and slipped his tongue between my lips. "I love you, too. We have to stop meeting like this."

I shut the door and curved around just in time to see a sleepy-eyed Lizzie on the steps. "Who was that?" she asked. "I heard a man's voice."

"Grandpa came by to drop off some coffee." My empty hands were a dead give-away, but Lizzie was too groggy to notice. "Now come here and give your mommy a morning kiss." I stretched out my arms and she tumbled into them. I picked her up and carried her to the couch, shielding her eyes to the two empty wine goblets on the table in front of her.

God help me.

CHAPTER TWENTY-SEVEN

IT TOOK EVERY ounce of strength I possessed to get the kids out the door. My head felt like a thousand jackhammers had taken up residence, and the empty wine glass on the kitchen counter didn't justify the pain.

Where had Lisa been for the past two weeks? I picked up the phone to call her sister, hesitated, and then wondered why. While I mulled over my uncertainty, I took note of the dirty dishes in the sink. Somehow, I managed to rinse them and stash them into the overloaded dishwasher, before I sank down on the sofa with a tub-like mug of coffee.

Today, Ed would accompany Nick to his therapy appointments. I glanced at the clock. Within the hour, he needed to be awake and in the shower. I still had time to phone Lori and express my condolences. I picked up the phone and dialed. Lisa's very distraught sister answered my call.

"Sam?" Her voice caught.

"I'm so sorry, Lori. Is there anything I can do?"

After a long silence, she spoke. "I'd love to talk if you have some time, but not on the phone. Could we meet somewhere? The mall, perhaps?"

Had she gone mad? The mall?

"I guess so." The list of possible reasons for her request exploded in my already pained head. Did she not want us to be seen? Followed? Meeting in a public place wouldn't allow us much privacy, but it would provide us with a modicum of safety.

I sensed the urgency in her voice, so I offered an immediate plan. "I'm available later today. Say, two o'clock?"

"Two o'clock at the Lexington Mall. Let's meet by the fountain."

After I agreed and signed off, I hurried into the shower. Should I text McGrath? As I stepped out, I heard the plunk of a guitar coming from Nick's room. The chord sounded cacophonous, as if Nick had tried to strum a chord and missed. I waited. The fact that he attempted to play his six-string? A hopeful sign. I listened for more music, prayed for a melodic sound. Again, I heard a failed attempt. Nick needed a victory here. *C'mon Lord.*

I held my breath for a long moment. Silence. I told myself to get busy drying my hair, allow matters to unfold as they may, but my curiosity got the better of me. I simply draped a towel around my body and stood motionless, poised for a miracle. Nothing.

Had he simply stopped playing? Maybe Nick heard the water shut off from the shower. Maybe he hadn't wanted me to hear his feeble attempts to play. The sound of a creaking bed emanated from his room. I assured myself he'd moved onto another activity and flicked on the blow dryer. The steady hum of the dryer lulled me into a false sense of security, and I became distracted by the task at hand. Several minutes later, I heard a huge crash above the motor's drone. I tossed my hairbrush and blow dryer on the counter, threw on my robe, and ran to Nick's room. I hovered outside his door and knocked.

"Nick?"

"What?" he howled.

I opened the door and took in the scene. The usual pile of dirty clothes sat in the center of the floor, stray crumb-filled bowls, empty drinking glasses and school papers lay strewn about. I searched for the sound of the crash. Finally, my eyes settled on Nick's guitar, smashed to smithereens at the foot of his bed. He must have mustered enough strength to lift it over his head and heave it into the bed frame. It looked as if he'd successfully hit his target. His precious Gibson Blues King was thoroughly and utterly destroyed.

I fought tears as I stepped over the mounds of clothes toward him, then sat on the side of his bed and gathered his large frame into my arms.

"It's okay," I hushed. "It's going to be alright."

"Stop lying to me!" Nick shouted. "Stop pretending."

"You're going to get better," I promised. "You're not a patient person, and your injury requires time to heal."

"Ever since Dad died, nothing's been right." His locked eyes with mine, imploring me to understand, to rescue him from his demons. His uncooperative body.

I glanced at Jon's photo, which sat proudly displayed on Nick's desk. It occurred to me that his desktop was the only area in the entire room that was free from clutter. The half-opened blinds created slats of light on Jon's face. I could have sworn he watched us now. In that instant, I understood Nick with a depth I hadn't allowed myself in some time. Nick and I were cut from the same cloth. He didn't have the time or the energy for patience. He needed his body to work so that he could move on with his life. Not tomorrow, or next week, or next month, but today. He needed to keep busy, distract himself from his grief and pain. Sitting around waiting to heal didn't suit him.

I held a weeping Nick in my arms as a tear spilled down my cheek. "I know, honey. I know."

I joined Nick in his moment, and let myself feel his pain as well as my own. He was thirteen years old. He'd lost his biological father when he was two, the man who'd been his real dad when he was twelve, his prized dog, and his grandmother six months later. A short year after that, he'd sustained a life-threatening, closed head injury. In this moment, I recognized that he couldn't begin to understand or appreciate that he'd been given a gift when he'd awakened from that coma. Life didn't seem hopeful for him right now. I hated that I couldn't fix this for him. *Dammit, Jon. Where are you when I need you?*

I held him close and stroked his back for a few moments, then tipped his chin up toward mine and planted a kiss on his freckled forehead.

"Dammit," he whispered.

"What?"

"I broke my guitar." He shook his head and swore under his breath. "SHIT. SHIT. SHIT!"

I took his right hand in mine and stroked his fingers, then placed his left hand on top of his right and performed the same ritual again. "These fingers will strum the most beautiful music one day. Your soul demands it. Your body isn't collaborating with your brain right now, but it will."

"You're full of shit, Mom."

I smiled. "I know."

Nick rested his head on my shoulder and sighed. "That's what I love about you."

"What you're not going to love is paying for a new guitar…"

* * *

Once Ed and I loaded Nick into the car and they drove down the street, I ran back inside, gathered my phone, purse, and keys, and hustled out to my car. I sped off to meet Lori at the mall. As I drove, I considered the questionable decisions I'd made in the past with regard to my safety, and dialed McGrath. The call went directly to voicemail, so I left him a quick message, informing him of my meeting with Lori, along with the time and place. He'd probably have advised me not to meet her, but that ship had already left port, so

I shrugged my shoulders and told myself that at least I'd
tried to reach him. The mall had to be safe, didn't it?

I checked my rearview mirror like a vigilant fugitive,
touched my hand to my fluttering stomach, and noticed
beads of sweat forming on my forehead. Overreacting, of
course. We were meeting in a public place. It didn't appear
that I'd been followed. As I pulled into the lot, I decided to
park as close to the mall entrance as possible. I also kept my
keys threaded between my fingers in case of an unforeseen
emergency.

Luckily, I located a parking spot within sprinting
distance of the main entry, and verified that I'd locked the
car doors before doing a perimeter search for unsavory
thugs. *Isn't paranoia grand?*

My watch read 1:55 p.m. Five minutes to reach the
fountain. I entered the concourse, searching for Lori. No
sign of her. I ordered an iced coffee from Starbucks, dropped
into a chair at an out of the way table, and took a breath. My
shoulders ached and my respiration felt shallow.

I glanced at my watch. Two o'clock on the dot. I scoured
the area for Lori.

*Calm down, idiot. She'll be here when she gets here. Her sister
just died, and she's probably juggling two distraught little girls
and a scary brother-in-law.*

I tried to distract myself by people-watching. As much
as that usually amused me, I couldn't focus. Neither the
leftover hippies in their Birkenstocks nor the obese women
in their stretched out Mickey Mouse t-shirts and bullet-
proof polyester leggings kept my attention today.

What would Lori tell me? Had she known Lisa had
been hiding? Kidnapped? Had she been sworn to secrecy?
By Lisa? Or someone else? I couldn't imagine Lisa running
away and not informing Lori of her whereabouts. Unless
she'd been concerned about putting Lori or the kids in
harm's way. *You did the same thing, Sam. Remember?*

The hair on my arms stood at attention. Ten past two.

Still no sign of Lori. I played with the plastic lid on my coffee cup. Sucked on an ice cube. Pulled out my phone and checked it. No calls. No messages. I parked my cell front and center before me, so I could watch the screen.

I tried to think logically. In one hour I needed to arrive home. It took me thirty minutes to drive home in rush hour traffic, which started about three o'clock in our territory. I had thirty minutes more. If Lori didn't show up, we could set up an alternative time. I stared at my cell. *What the hell's wrong with me?* I picked it up and dialed Lori.

Straight to her voicemail. My breathing halted. What if something had happened to her? I opted not to leave a message. Instead, I ended the call and phoned McGrath, telling myself to be rational when he answered. But he didn't answer. I left him a simple message. "Lori is late for our meeting. Trying not to worry. Or totally freak out. Call me."

Why was I so panicked? I'd run late before. I scanned the shoppers. No Lori. I'm not sure how I knew, but I felt certain she wouldn't make our meeting. Had she simply decided not to come? Or was she in danger?

I waited five minutes longer than I should have, then determined no one was following me, hurried out to my car, and high-tailed it home.

CHAPTER TWENTY-EIGHT

I DESPISE LAST minute glitches. Broken dates leave me disgruntled and disappointed. Quite frankly, I have a difficult time getting past it. My admission of this weakness doesn't come easily. If I'd confessed to my lack of flexibility years ago, perhaps Jon wouldn't have been gone so much. Maybe he would have recognized that I was lonely. The fact of the matter was, I'd never be entirely sure if Jon had betrayed our vows. When I'd visited Japan, all indications pointed to his faithfulness, but could I ever know that with certainty? It's not like I could depend on his killer to tell me the truth.

Why on God's green earth is this bothering me now?

It's the downward spiral. All because Lori missed our appointment. Silly. Stupid. The weight of the last few hours caught up with me. I felt exhausted. And why the hell hadn't McGrath called me back? More important than my selfish thoughts, where was Lori and why had she missed our appointment? Was she dead? Had she met the same uncertain fate as her sister? Should I drive to her house?

Why am I carrying on like the world is hunky-dunky when I've lost a friend, am being followed, and my kid was the victim of a targeted hit and run? Denial—a familiar and welcome friend.

I eased down the street and spotted Lizzie's school bus

just ahead. Annie, Marie, and Will would be at Cross County practice till five. I stopped the required distance from the bus stop and waited for my teensy little girl to bound down the steps. She wore her usual smile, hair disheveled and clothing askew. My rainbow child had had a great day.

I looked just ahead to see Ed's car in the driveway. I pasted a smile on my face and unlocked the passenger door of the car. Lizzie plopped into the seat and leaned over for a kiss.

In less than thirty seconds we were home. I spotted Nick seated on the front porch. He waved and smiled. Unusual, if you considered the morning we'd experience.

I squinted. No sign of a walker or a cane.

Lizzie sprinted inside for a snack. I stepped outside and walked around to the porch. I approached slowly, not wanting to appear overly anxious.

"What's up?" I asked.

"Baby steps," Nick said, repeating the words he'd heard me utter on a regular basis the past few weeks. He stood steadily without help and began to walk towards me. I rushed to him, wrapping my arms around him.

"You're amazing. I'm so very proud of you." I fought back tears, knowing that I'd risk pushing Nick over the edge if I acted like his mother.

"Your high school son will attend his Freshman year after all."

"Will can help with anything you need," I agreed, "and I'll email your teachers and ask them to supply you with notes from the lectures. You won't need to worry about writing right away. They'll accommodate your disability. You can use the dictation application for any assignments in the meantime."

"Mom." Nick narrowed his eyes with a perturbed glare. "I'm not disabled."

I nodded. "Right."

"I'm perfectly capable of speaking. I can let them know

what I can and cannot do. Geez."

"Sorry." I dipped my head like a naughty puppy. "It's hard for me to turn it off."

Nick shook his head. "You're annoying."

"This calls for a celebratory beer," I said, hoping to distract him.

"Get me one, too," he said.

"In about eight years." I laughed and headed inside. Ed and Lizzie huddled on the sofa in the family room, engrossed in a chapter book, and the air was rich with the aroma of homemade spaghetti sauce. The concoction's gentle bubbling on the stove reminded me of the good in my life. So much to be grateful for. Why the hell was I involved in solving Lisa's murder? I had a perfectly fine life. Busy. Worthwhile.

Who the hell was I kidding? I dug to the bottom of my purse and blind-searched for my cell phone. Sure enough, McGrath had returned my call. He hadn't left a message. The way I saw it, that meant one of two things. He didn't have any news to report, or he had news to report that he couldn't or wouldn't leave in a voicemail. Then again, I hadn't left him a message other than to tell him that Lori had been late for our meeting. He didn't yet know she hadn't shown up at all. What did I expect, he had ESP? A sign of my growing insanity. I popped my beer and Nick's soda as I reminded myself I had more significant issues to attend to right now, gathered up the drinks, and stepped back onto the porch.

Nick shot me a serious frown, then smiled. "I see you changed your mind and brought me a beer after all."

I handed him the can of soda. "Nice."

His frown returned after he drained half the soda.

"What's wrong?" I asked.

He pointed to a Crown Victoria parked roadside to the south of our home, almost a football field away. "See that car?"

It required great effort to keep my voice level. My heart raced like a horse breaking out of the gate. "The Carter's grandparents have a big car like that."

"Cops drive Crown Vics, Mom."

"And you know this, how?"

Nick continued to study the car, ever watchful boy that he is. "I've been watching a lot of television."

I narrowed my eyes, trying to see if anyone occupied the vehicle. Like a cop. Or a thug. "Maybe you should be a cop when you grow up."

"Like your boyfriend?" Nick congratulated himself on his joke by laughing.

I glared at him. "Very funny."

He laughed harder. The familiar cackle he used whenever he knew he'd hit a solid chord. We continued to peek out from between the changing leaves. Fairly hidden, we could spy without notice. Maybe the driver thought we couldn't see him. Entirely possible. *Go ahead, Sam, fantasize.*

"Maybe it's a car from a funeral home," Nick said.

"Or the FBI," I joked, trying to lighten my rising fear.

"I mean it, Mom. Call your boyfriend. It's too weird."

Nick's sixth sense kicked in, just like mine, and while I had cause for alarm, he had no real reason for the hair to stand up on his neck.

"Do you really find it that odd?" I asked.

"I know I haven't been out much lately, and I know I've watched too many true crime shows, but as long as we've lived here, I've never seen a car like that parked on the road. I notice cars, Mom. It's one of the things Dad and I had in common."

I nodded as I patted his hand. Jon had taught Nick tons about automobiles. They'd often discussed makes and models over dinner, or while tossing the football in the front yard.

"The model was discontinued this year," he said, reminding me that he'd kept up with his hobby. "It was the only rear-wheeled vehicle built in North America to be used as a taxi, in fleets and for police cars."

I leaned forward to obtain a better view. The thick shroud of leaves made it difficult to discern much in the way of detail. "Can you see inside? I can't." I narrowed my eyes to slits, but still couldn't determine if there was an occupant in the car.

"I feel like running down there and checking it out. If someone's casing out the Carter's place, I'll scare them off." Nick clenched his fists, readying for a fight I wouldn't allow him to pursue.

I shook my head. He'd just walked unaided for the first time today. He couldn't dash down the street and tackle a bad guy. "You're just nervous because the car's black. You're overreacting."

"Right, Mom, because I'm always the one on the verge of hysteria in this family."

He had me there. I was dying to run inside and call or at least text McGrath. I excused myself.

A sardonic smile curved on his lips. "You're going to call him, aren't you?"

I peered at him. "Listen, Buster, you're starting to fray my nerves. Yes, I'm going to call Detective McGrath, but not because you're freaking out about a strange vehicle. He phoned earlier, and I need to return his call."

"Don't leave me out here by myself," Nick warned. "Someone could snatch me."

Mid-stride, I stopped. Nick had a very valid point. I sank back into my chair.

"What's wrong?" he asked. "You look like you've seen a ghost."

My throat was dry as sand. I tried to speak, but I couldn't. Finally, the lies came. "I just remembered that Detective McGrath has an important meeting. Plus, it's time for me to pick up your brother and sisters from Cross Country practice. Care to join me?"

"Only if we can circle the court on our way out and see if there's someone inside that Crown Vic. Case out the situation," Nick teased.

"Deal."

I didn't dare leave Nick alone on the porch. I ordered him up and inside the house. He complied, showing off his newly acquired ambulatory skills. I smiled, my heart warming with his victory. He was one of my most precious gifts.

We made it inside just as Ed started the water for pasta and pulled a baguette from its paper sleeve.

I grabbed my purse and keys. "Nick and I are headed to pick up the kids." I closed my eyes and nodded in Ed's direction. "We have so much to be thankful for."

"Hence, the spaghetti and meatballs." Ed flashed a huge grin at Lizzie whose head bobbed like one of those dashboard dolls. "C'mon, Lizzie," he said. "Help me set the table."

I yelled as Nick and I met in the garage, "Be right back." It startled me that Nick was walking so well, with solid balance and even a glimpse of the old cadence to his steps.

We slammed our car doors in unison, and I backed out of the garage.

"Drive slow," Nick ordered.

I inched the car along the street, and asked him to feign looking out the window for a lost pet. I needn't have asked. He'd already poised himself on the edge of the seat, just like he used to do when our beloved Rex had taken off in search of his dad and we had to hunt him down.

Not a single sound between us. Not a solitary word, not a breath.

"It's a guy. He's sitting in the driver's seat," Nick said, "staring at his phone."

"Did he look up at you?"

"No. Too preoccupied."

I held my breath. "Do you recognize him?"

Nick narrowed his eyes, looking confused. "He looks like a guy from out of a Mafia movie."

I laughed to break the tension. "I'll tell Detective McGrath that he has some serious competition when I talk to him."

"Mom." Nick sounded exasperated. "I'm serious. The guy looks scary."

"Too many cop shows," I reminded him. "We're not going to scare your siblings with any dinner talk of our investigation. Our findings remain between us. I promise to keep you posted after I speak with Detective McGrath." Then, I laughed.

"You mean your boyfriend."

I slugged Nick in his good arm.

CHAPTER TWENTY-NINE

IT KILLED ME to wait until the kids were sound asleep to phone McGrath. I snuck into the bathroom right before dinner and texted him that I'd speak with him about eleven o'clock that night. Had he checked on Lori? Did he know anything more about Lisa's death or her husband's arrest? From past cases with McGrath, I understood that he'd be exquisitely careful in pursuing an arrest. He wanted to assure the charges would stick, and he'd call it right.

I tucked the kids into bed about ten o'clock and padded downstairs to finish washing the pots and pans. I toweled off the pasta kettle and fought not to bang it against the metal drawer of the stove as I put it away. Although I was tempted to call McGrath now that the kids were upstairs, I suspected that as soon as I placed the call, one of them would show up and overhear me.

In the quieting house, I recited a silent prayer, thanking God for Nick's recent gains, for my blessed family, children and Ed alike, then put thoughts of them aside and shifted to crime mode. It's called compartmentalization. I couldn't quell my mounting anxiety, so I slipped upstairs with my cell phone in hand, donned my nightgown, crawled under the covers, propped myself up on my pillow, and turned on the TV. It hummed softly in the background when I dialed McGrath.

He picked up on the first ring. "Sorry we keep missing each other. You okay?"

"Trying to be." I shared Nick's progress first, then went on to tell him about Lori. "Have you checked her home? I tried her cell when she didn't show up at the mall, but the call went directly to voicemail. It doesn't make sense."

"She didn't show at all?" McGrath sounded worried.

"No. Then Nick and I were hanging out on the porch and he noticed a Crown Vic parked alongside the street. Just like the other day, but a little further down the street."

"Macchione's guy maybe?"

I whispered, nervously fingering the edge of my sheet. "Exactly what I'm thinking. Nick and I used the time retrieving the other kids from practice as an opportunity to check out the car. He was my lookout. There was an occupant, driver's side, involved with his phone. Nick said the guy looked like a Mafia guy from TV. When we arrived home, the car had disappeared."

"I wonder if it's the same guy from the other day."

My head sank back against my pillow. Why hadn't I checked out the guy for myself? I might have recognized him. "I'm an idiot. I didn't even glance at the guy."

"Don't worry about it," McGrath said. "Is Nick bothered?"

It touched me that McGrath was concerned about Nick's reaction. "I'd like to think he's forgotten about it already, but I'm sure he'll tell his friends once he's back at school. I made him promise not to mention it to his siblings. That means it'll be out on the wavelengths before too long. But worried? I'm not sure."

"Not much will come of it from that end, I suspect. I'd really like to come and stake out your place, make sure all of you are safe."

"What about Lori? Aren't you worried about her?"

"Sure," he answered. "More about you, though."

"Do you think these guys are looking for Lori? Waiting

around here to see if she shows up?"

"It's possible. But now that Lisa's body was discovered, I'm not sure why. Maybe they think she knows something."

"What would she know that would make a difference?"

"We can only speculate at this point. Their ties run deep. My concern is yours and the kids' safety. Maybe we should get you out of town."

"I'm not a part of it. I don't understand why Nick was hit or why goons are sitting on my street. I haven't done anything. We aren't leaving. I've just gotten my kid home. Things are just settling down. Plus, if it is the Macchione's, they can find me anywhere. I'm staying put."

"I know you need to stay home. I'm punchy and grasping for a logical solution when there isn't one. It could be Lori they're after, it could even be me."

"You?"

"I'm looking into some things internally. As I mentioned, we suspect local law enforcement connections. The more I ask around, the more people clam up. It won't be long until this is wrapped up though. Evidence is mounting against Tony and other members of the local family. I expect arrests soon. I'd tell you more, but you don't need to know."

"Right. I'm busy having a normal life."

"Exactly."

I gazed at the painted swirls on the ceiling, bathed in the shadows from the television screen. "I miss you."

I heard him breathe. Sounded a little heavy to me. "Me, too," he said after a long moment.

I imagined snuggling under the covers with my own hunky detective. Him nipping at my neck, caressing my breasts with his gentle fingertips. A shiver ran down my spine. I rolled onto my side and forced my breath to return to normal. "We're getting distracted."

"Tell me about it."

"Will you check on Lori?"

"Right now." He cleared his throat.

"I guess that means I have to hang up."

"I'll be in touch," he promised.

I eased the phone under my pillow and snuggled down into the mattress. My eyes felt heavy. I just drifted off when I heard a soft knock on the front door, which was directly beneath my bedroom. I peered at the dial on my clock. Eleven twenty-five. My stomach knotted. I talked myself down. The door was bolted and locked. Every night. The windows on the first floor, too. And I had a peep hole in the front door. I clutched my cell phone, slipped out of bed and into my robe, and crept downstairs.

On tiptoe, I peeked through the hole. Lori. Her eyes danced furtively. She wore black. To conceal herself? I inched the chain off the door and opened it, wrapping my robe tighter around me.

I leaned out to see past her shoulder. I didn't spot a vehicle either on the street or in my driveway. I looked back at Lori. The porch light illuminated her sorrowful gaze. I also noticed the large overnight bag that weighed down her shoulder. She certainly couldn't spend the night here.

I drew her inside quickly and flicked off the light. The less attention on the street the better. She looked broken; my heart went out to her.

"It cooled off a lot tonight. Are you cold?" I shivered, amazed at what I said in the way of a greeting. "Let me brew you a cup of tea."

I guided her down the hall and into the kitchen. I pulled out a chair and sat her down. She still hadn't uttered a sound, clearly shell-shocked and numb. I turned on the light above the stove, grabbed a mug from the cupboard, filled it with water from the tap, and warmed it in the microwave while I retrieved a tea bag from the pantry.

The rhythmic ticking of the grandfather clock seemed magnified, somehow suspending time. In the soft darkness, Lori's gaze remained glued to the floor.

I steeped her tea bag, then held out the cup, encouraging

her to take a sip. I sat down next to her and took her hand in mine. Watchful. Waiting. "It's going to be alright," I said. "Everything will work out."

She nodded. Tears began to streak her cheeks. "I know you're right. It just doesn't feel like that right now."

"Can you tell me what happened?"

She stayed quiet for several minutes. Finally, she looked up at me. "He was there. When I went to leave and meet you at the mall. Just sitting there in his fancy car. Daring me to leave the house."

I wondered if the same Crown Victoria had graced her neighborhood, then wound up in mine. "Who?"

She grimaced. "One of Tony's minions. I've met him before. His name is Mario. He used to be Tony's driver. Imagine. This squat creepy Italian with a crooked nose and door-defying shoulders."

"So he's a wide-body?"

Lori looked confused.

My sense of humor doesn't work with everyone. "Tell me the whole story," I encouraged.

"I've spent a fair amount of my adult life avoiding the Macchione's. In fact, when Lisa decided to marry Tony, both my parents and I fought with her. For weeks."

I nodded. Step one of active listening.

Lori's eyes brimmed with tears. "It's been an absolute nightmare from the very start. I loved my sister... but marrying Tony sealed her fate. She was destined for an unhappy life from the moment she met him. Even if I tried harder, I couldn't have helped her or prevented any of this... I can't believe she's dead."

I squeezed her hand as she sobbed. "I am so sorry you lost her, Lori."

After a full five minutes, she choked out, "More th..an an..y..thing, I want... T..ony to... pay."

This could be the break McGrath needed, interviewing Lori, free of any pressure from the Macchione clan. On the other hand, I could ask a few questions.

"Where was Lisa for the past two weeks?"

"She refused to say. She only told me she was leaving and that she'd be back for the girls before too long. I pleaded with her… it was too dangerous. She was on her way to my house for the girls… with Tony's connections… it was only a matter of time before…"

"She was on her way to your house?"

"The night of her murder. She texted me and asked me to have the girls at my place. I did. But she never showed up." Lori broke down again.

"How did you get here?" I asked. "Does anyone know you're here? Your husband?"

"I left the house through the backyard, walked several blocks on the side streets, then called a cab. My husband travels for business. I asked him to stay home for a few days after the news of Lisa's death, but the autopsy will delay the funeral and he needed to get back on the road. I'm sure he thinks I'm at home."

"Where is he now?"

"California. He's due back in five days."

Five days? Sounded like *her* husband was a prize, too. I don't like thinking ill of the dead, but my Jon had skirted some important events in our life in the name of his career. I guessed my experience wasn't unique. Men got distracted. They sometimes devoted their souls to their careers, not their marriages. Her sister just died! You'd think he could have waited until after the funeral. I feared for Lori. Being alone for that length of time could prove risky. She was vulnerable. And someone wanted to mess with her.   I turned to her and whispered, "What about the girls? Where are they?"

"With Tony," she said, a deep sorrow in her voice. "He picked them up after Lisa's body was discovered."

"Are you in danger?"

"Tony suspects I know something. Or, by the sheer fact

that I'm related to Lisa, he feels I should be eliminated. He has nothing to lose now. Lisa's dead. He's going to prison. Why not get his pound of flesh while he can?"

"When did she decide to leave? And why on earth did she return to Tony in the first place? Wouldn't it have been safer for her to make her escape from your house?"

Lori shook her head. "I'm not sure how straight she was thinking. She'd been formulating her breakaway for years. In fact, I stopped believing she would ever leave. How long does it take to summon the courage to walk out?" Lori cocked her head at me, sizing me up. I waited for her to continue. "You were an inspiration to her. She said you faced a similar situation and demonstrated strength and determination in the face of insurmountable odds."

I knew all about taking forever to muster courage, hedging forever when make a life-changing decision. And Lisa had far more demons to face than I ever did. Then again, maybe not. I'd been lucky. I'd survived. It would be a challenge for me to hold onto this lesson, but I recognized its importance.

I nodded, closed my eyes, and wondered if I hadn't shared my past with Lisa, would any of this have happened? Again, I was assigning responsibility and blame in a place it did not belong. I was not in charge of the world. I was only in charge of me. And my family. Why did I feel so guilty?

This entire situation was far more than I bargained for, and I struggled to remain calm. "I'm hoping the authorities are closing in on him. In fact, I have a detective friend who's on the case. He's trustworthy. Would you be willing to speak with him? You may be able to offer valuable information that would help put Tony away." I paused for a long moment. "Do you know *anything*?"

"I spoke with the police after Lisa's disappearance, but shared the bare minimum. I didn't want to jeopardize her welfare. Trust me, Tony has guys on the force who do his dirty work. Besides, Tony didn't commit the murder. He most certainly is responsible, but well-protected by his brother... by the family."

These theories were Lori's, not based in fact, but mere suppositions. McGrath must be closer to the truth. He had to be. "Who would he have put in charge? Would it have been Mario?"

"I have no idea. Like I said, I've tried my damndest to stay away from that side of the family. I spent time with Lisa and the girls at my home, or at our parent's home. We weren't welcome at Lisa's when Tony was around. He knew we disapproved of him and the way he treated her. It made things harder for her to have us visit. He'd beat her and claim she'd lied to us and was trying to make him look bad. We kept a safe distance, for our own good, but mostly for hers." Lori paused to swallow some tea.

The poor woman was a wreck. I closed my eyes, trying to block out the terror Lisa must have endured. And the shame, and the guilt. As I suspected, Tony was far worse in private than he'd appeared when I'd made home visits to instruct Adrianna. I narrowed my eyes, trying to recall bruises, some signs I had missed. "She never told me. I knew Tony was verbally abusive, but I didn't know he beat her. I'm so sorry I didn't do more to help her when I was there."

"She wouldn't have wanted you to know. Plus, he hit her where it didn't show. The back of the head, her arms, her legs. He threatened her and claimed the police wouldn't believe her if she reported him. He said she'd never see her children again."

"He terrorized her into submission."

Lori nodded, regret filling her eyes.

"My friend will figure it out. His name is Jim McGrath. Please let me call him."

Lori fingered the handle of the mug. "It has something to do with Adrianna. Tony's allowed me to have the girls since Lisa's disappearance. But I can see it in his eyes. It pisses him off just to look at her. The depth of his anger doesn't make sense. She's his child! His defenseless child!"

"He blamed Lisa for Adrianna's vision impairment, and from all indications, he's a narcissist, plain and simple."

Lori's back straightened. "If I'm being stalked, are you?"

Her question caught me off guard. "Why would you think that?" My heart clenched inside my chest. Did Lori know something more? Suddenly, none of this made sense. Both Lori and I were being watched? By whom? Why? Tony must know that the authorities were closing in on him. He wouldn't make any stupid moves now, would he? What was my connection to all this?

I shuddered. The urge to shepherd Lori out of my home overwhelmed me. I glanced sideways at the clock. Midnight. I'd placed my cell phone in the pocket of my robe on my way to answer the door, hadn't I? I patted it to reassure myself, and excused myself for a moment.

I ducked inside the first floor bathroom to text McGrath. "Lisa Woodruff here. Arrived 11:25. Claims she's being stalked. Intimidated. Maybe followed. Safe for now. No cars outside." I flushed the toilet and washed my hands.

On my way out of the bathroom, I turned away from the kitchen and stepped into the study where I peeled back the curtains and searched the street for unusual vehicles. I could see little beyond the path directly in front of my home through the cloud cover, darkness, and heavy foliage. It appeared that we weren't being watched.

Lori sat right where I had left her. She appeared more sullen than ever. Defeated even.

I touched her shoulder. "None of this makes sense. Please let me ask Detective McGrath to join us. He'll ensure your safety for the meantime."

Her voice came back flat. "I told you. Tony and the mayor have cops on their payroll. I can't risk it."

"Detective McGrath is not on the take. I'd bet my life on it. Please."

"I can't." Lori stood, visibly trembling. "I should go."

"No. Spend the night here. You can sleep in my daughter's room. Just let me run upstairs and move her into my bed." I eased Lori back into her chair and nodded. She returned my nod.

"Be right back."

I whispered to Lizzie as I picked her up. "Sleep with me." She tucked a drowsy head into my shoulder and offered a half-smile. I settled her in my bed before I hurried back to Lori, helping her up the stairs while I carried her bag. Lead heavy, I wondered what on earth she had packed inside. Then again, did I really want to know? I was in over my head. Way over. *Holy Crap. What had I done inviting this woman to spend the night?*

I placed the bag at the foot of the bed in Lizzie's room. Lori sank onto the edge of the bed. "Thank you," she muttered.

"I know it all seems like too much to bear right now, but I'm hoping that the worst is over. Tony's going to be locked up soon. You'll be able to raise the girls. The Feds will put away both the mayor and his brother. They'll clean up the city. The Macchione's clan will be exiled and they will have to scrounge around for some other town to corrupt."

Lori's voice remained flat. "You really believe that?"

I nodded, mustering all the sincerity I could manage. *Fairy tale.*

She looked disappointed. "I thought you were smarter than that."

I froze. Why was I letting this woman stay in my home? What the hell was I thinking? "Get some rest." I stood and left the room.

I ducked into my closet to phone McGrath.

He picked up on the first ring. "What the hell is going on?"

"Lori claims one of Tony's men is following her. Stalked her even as she was about to leave to meet me earlier today.

She's not sure why, but I think Adrianna might be the link. Plus, Tony may think Lisa's decision to leave him came at my suggestion. I shared some things with her years ago..."

"Sam, don't draw conclusions. None of this is your fault... I'm parked outside your house. Let me in."

"I can't. I just settled Lori in Lizzie's room. Nick's already suspicious. And tomorrow is his first day of school. I can explain Lori's presence, but if the kids see you here, it will conjure up all kinds of drama and anxiety. Let's keep things low key. I can't imagine why anyone would follow either Lori or me. Lori thinks Tony is on a rampage to take out everyone who has ever set up a roadblock but... it's preposterous. Absolute insanity. Are you any closer to arresting Tony? And what's going on with the Mayor? Why is it taking so long to get these crooks off the street?"

"You know the answer, Sam. The wheels of justice grind slowly for a reason. If we're going to solve Lisa's murder, we need substantial evidence. Otherwise, Tony gets away with slaughtering his wife. That won't serve anyone well. Not Lori and not Lisa's children."

"This is bigger than both of us. That's what you're saying."

McGrath sighed. "At least. I'm parked right outside. I'll be here until the kids leave for school in the morning and Lori is safely out of your home. It makes no sense for her to have arrived at your house at this time of night. What in hell is her motive?"

"Good point. Why here? She's sure there are cops in bed with the Macchione's. I'm guessing, but it seems that the story of leaving my abusive ex stuck with Lisa. She shared it with Lori, and that brought her to me. Maybe it's her need for closure. I have no idea." I paused and took a very deep breath. "Even after all I've been through I can't believe stuff like this really happens."

"Sam, you know it does. I understand you are horrified by the notion, but with the Macchione's at the helm, it's a given. Listen, it's late. Try to get some rest. Once you send Nick off to school, call me. If anything comes up after I leave in the morning, call me. I promise I'll pick up."

"I'm tired," I admitted, "but I'm not sure I can sleep."

"Fantasize about me. That will help. And remember, I love you."

"I love you, too. Let's not be stupid ever again."

"Deal," he said.

CHAPTER THIRTY

IT IS A mother's nature to sleep light, to remain alert, even in her dreams. The fact that I housed a virtual stranger that night, the fact that Lizzie slept by my side, all elbows and knees, the fact that although I should have been able to give in to exhaustion knowing that McGrath was parked outside my home to protect my family, I remained in the heightened state of awareness that allows long moments of drowsing. Only drowsing.

I believe I nodded off just minutes before I shot out of bed, having heard something alarming, although I couldn't say what. A pop? Screeching tires? The whine of a car's engine? Was that what I heard? As I peeled back the drapes, a car sped away.

Adrenalin kicked in. I threw on my robe, darted to Jon's closet, turned on the light, grabbed his gun from the case, loaded it, and ran down the stairs. The door remained locked. I inched back the chain and unbolted the door, opened it, and scanned the landscape. McGrath's car was still parked on the street. All was quiet. I should have felt safe, relieved even, but I didn't. My antenna told me something was wrong. Very wrong.

I flicked on the porch light, alerting him, and sprinted to his car, calling his name, gripping the gun, my fingers poised to aim and fire.

"McGrath? Are you there?"

He must have seen me running towards him. He was on the lookout, right?

No response. Had he nodded off? Didn't seem possible. The sound. It had been so loud.

The light cast eerie shadows in the dim moonlight. Panic gripped me. Where was he? Why wasn't he answering me?

I peered through the passenger window. His head rested against the steering wheel at an odd, uncomfortable angle. I tugged on the door handle. Locked. I called his name. "McGrath." Louder. "Jim. I'm here. Let me in."

My heart rammed against my ribs. *No. Not McGrath.*

I rushed to the driver's door. The window was shattered, glass shards crunched beneath my feet; I reached inside, searching for the door lock.

"McGrath! Wake up!"

The latch popped beneath my fingers. I pulled open the door, rested my hand on his shoulder, told myself to remain calm. *It will be alright. It has to be.*

I needed a phone. *Shit.* I reached inside McGrath's pocket. No dice. He probably put it in the console. *Shit.* I climbed in beside him, reached over him, rolled the smart switch in my hands. The overhead light snapped on. Blood. Lots of blood. I ran my hand over his head, pulled it back to look. More blood. *Look again, Sam. Closer.* With gentle fingers, I probed. Abraded skin around a hole. On the left. At the back of his head. A knot clogged my throat and I fought back tears. *Keep it together, Sam. Act now. Panic later.*

"Stay with me, McGrath. Do you hear me?"

I slid off my robe and pressed it to his head wound the best I could. Phone. I needed a phone. There. In the coin tray.

I pressed the numbers.

"911. What is your emergency?" A sweet, saving voice.

"A police officer's been shot. Send an ambulance. 8765 Foxcroft. Hurry."

"I'm sending an ambulance now, ma'am. Can you tell me what happened?"

"I don't know. His name is Jim McGrath. You have to hurry."

"The ambulance is on its way. Where are you now?"

I couldn't breathe. I couldn't speak. Frozen. Paralyzed.

"Ma'am?"

I opened my mouth, but the words wouldn't come. Someone shot McGrath!

"Does he have a pulse?"

I grappled for his wrist. Fumbling. Shirt sleeve. *Damn it!*

The words came. "No. I don't know. I don't think so. I can't..." *Oh my God, no! This can't be happening!*

"Calm down, ma'am. Try again. Feel for a pulse."

I unbuttoned his cuff, placed my fingers against his wrist. Prayed. Concentrated. Prayed. Concentrated. "I feel it! I feel it! He's alive!"

"Good job. Now tell me your name."

"Samantha. Samantha Stitsill," I choked out. "I hear them. I hear the ambulance. It's coming."

Flashing lights. Screaming sirens. I ran my hand over McGrath's head. Another wound. Front left.

"McGrath, stay with me. Help is almost here." *Oh, God, please! Hurry!*

"Tell me what happened, ma'am."

"I don't know. I was in the house. Asleep. I heard a noise. A car. Speeding away. I ran outside." My hand rested on McGrath's shoulder. "I can't talk to you. I have to be with him."

"McGrath. You're going to be okay. Please. Don't leave me!"

Paramedics bounded from the ambulance. Medics swarmed us, barking orders, and ripping open their duffle bags. Stethoscopes, oxygen masks, IV bags, paddles. A magnetic force Velcroed me to McGrath, but I had to step away.

I backed down from the vehicle, offering them access to McGrath and giving way to my tears. Two uniformed officers approached from behind. They flanked my sides, each gripping an arm. I didn't resist. Nor did I stop willing McGrath to stay alive. I prayed as hard as I have ever prayed in my life.

Marty Jaeger stepped from his F150, sizing up the situation. He approached me, but the officers told him to step back.

"It's McGrath," I choked.

"Hey," he said to the patrolman. "She's good. She's a teacher. And a widow with a bunch of kids inside. I coach her sons. She and Detective McGrath are friends."

The officer scrutinized me as he asked, "What was Detective McGrath doing here?"

I double-clutched. "You'll have to ask him. He'd want to be the one to tell you."

Marty leaned forward. "What can I do, Sam?"

My teeth chattered uncontrollably and even though my arms were wrapped tight around my middle, I shook like I'd been tossed in a meat locker. "Check on him. Make sure he's okay. Tell him I love him. Tell him he has to make it. Call Ed. Ed Stitsill. His number is in my phone. My phone. Where is my phone? I must have left it inside... on my nightstand. Lizzie's in my bed."

Marty glanced at me. "For God's sake, Wilson," he boomed at the officer, "let her get something to wear. The woman's in shock."

Officer Wilson squared his shoulders. "Can't ... procedure. If you want to get her something, go ahead."

Marty locked eyes with me. "Sam?"

Tears obstructed my vision. I didn't care about clothes. I cared about McGrath. "The back of the bathroom door. My sweats."

Marty checked with Wilson. "That okay?"

Wilson nodded. "Go ahead."

A female officer approached me. "Spread your legs," she said. "And raise your arms to your shoulders."

I remained as cooperative as I could, fixing my eyes on my beloved McGrath, watching as the paramedics placed an oxygen mask over his face, and started the IV. *Don't leave me. Stay alive. Dying is not an option. Do you hear me?*

Marty attempted to hand me my sweatshirt, but an officer intervened, summoning an evidence technician.

Marty waited as a tech arrived at my side. "Ed's on his way."

I watched a member of the forensics team bag my hands, inserting them into a liquid, rinsing them, and then pouring the liquid into a small bottle and labeling it. Unreal.

The officer handed me my sweatshirt.

"Thank you." I zipped the heavy shirt, my eyes still locked on McGrath. I asked Marty, "Please. Can you check on him?"

Marty nodded.

"Tell him I love him."

Marty sprinted toward the ambulance, a mere fifteen feet from where I remained locked in the officer's grasp. Through the flashing lights, it seemed as if McGrath's eyelids fluttered while Marty spoke to him, and although I couldn't read Marty's lips, I noticed McGrath's hand move as he was loaded inside the ambulance.

I closed my eyes. *Thank you, God.*

Marty jogged back over to me and smiled. "He gave you the thumbs up. The guy must love you, too."

Through tears, I attempted to return his smile as the ambulance rolled away. My throat constricted. I could barely breathe. Marty wanted to comfort me, but he knew to let the police do their job.

I swallowed hard, then looked at the officers who continued to clasp my arms. "What's the next step?" The sooner I did what they wanted, the sooner I could race to the hospital, to McGrath's side.

"We have to take you to the station," Officer Wilson explained. "The forensic team is working. Once they've done their job here, we'll head over there, ma'am."

The team began to secure the scene. How could this be happening? My kids were still inside. How could they not have awakened to the screaming emergency vehicles? What about Lori? How would I explain her presence in my home? To the cops? To the kids? And how could I communicate with Marty free and clear of the cops?

Marty read the worry on my face. He consoled me. "It's okay, Sam. I'll wait here with the kids. When Ed arrives, I'll head over to the station. Meet you there?"

I mouthed a *thank you*.

The officers led me to their unit. The scene seemed surreal. Crime scene tape lay stretched around the perimeter of my home. As they stuffed me in the cruiser, I sank into the back seat, and wept for my children. What the hell had become of us? Whose life was I living?

* * *

As long as I had lived in our small town, I had never stepped inside the local police precinct. Until two years ago, I had been a rule follower for my entire life. I chastised myself for straying in the least from what I had been raised to consider right, honest, and true. I beat myself up for leaving a light on when I exited a room, for arriving less than ten minutes early for an appointment, for not returning a parent's phone call on the same day I received it.

I suppose that's why I felt completely turned inside out when I was dragged inside the police post and treated like a common criminal. In my pajamas and a sweatshirt, no less. A fair chunk of my taxes had gone to building this new precinct, but I never had a desire to step through its doors. Oddly enough, I soon felt another feeling, fairly new, settle over me. Fury. I understood the cops were just doing their job, but quite frankly, I didn't have time to indulge them. My place was with McGrath. Not out in public in my jammies.

After being fingerprinted, the officers led me inside an interrogation room. Small. Plain walls. Tiny desk. Two metal folding chairs. Freezing cold. Two way mirror. I shook my head in disbelief. In all honesty, I could have been here before, and justifiably so. I'd killed a man on my basement stairs. In self-defense, true, but how had I wound up here now and not then? It hit me like a cleaver, right between the eyes. *Stay focused, Sam. On McGrath.*

When Detective Rooney entered the room and introduced himself, I shook his hand and asked, "May I please have some clothing? I'll be better able to speak with you then."

Rooney stretched out his left arm, a brown shopping bag laced between his fingers and thumb. "Your father-in-law sent these along with Firefighter Jaeger. A female officer will assist you to the restroom. After you dress, we'll meet back here. I'm sorry for the inconvenience. Marty explained who you are. Please understand we are bound by procedure. Once we're finished here, I'll have someone drive you to the hospital."

I fought to maintain control. I didn't want to cry again, but I felt so thankful in that moment. Someone had their wits about them.

The female officer who guarded me at my home appeared in the doorway. She accompanied me to the restroom, where I changed into the clothing Ed sent along with Marty. After escorting me back into the interrogation room, the woman offered me a seat and some black coffee. My shivering eased, and I glanced at the wall clock. 2 a.m. If I finished answering questions, hopefully within the hour, I could hustle to the hospital, check on McGrath, and still arrive home in time to hand Nick off to his first day back at school.

I tossed my business as usual thinking off as shock

induced, fully aware of my feeble grip on sanity. Little could be done to repair it. At least, not now. Priority one? Get the hell out of the police station. Priority two? Get to the hospital. Priority three? Get McGrath healthy and permanently secured in my arms. Priority four? Take care of my kids.

It's how I handle crises. Make a list. Set up a schedule. Get it done. But this time, it didn't sound manageable. Jack was right, I couldn't keep this up. I was headed for a padded cell, and there was no one to rescue me. I swallowed the bile which rose in my throat and laid my head on the table in front of me. Tears flowed across my face, and I gulped air, unable to inhale enough oxygen.

I'd deal with the issues at hand, have Marty drive me to the hospital, and go from there. If I could just lift my head from the table.

Detective Rooney returned to the room. "Are you alright?"

I couldn't move. I tried, but nothing happened. My head felt like it had been bashed in by a ball peen hammer. It took a full sixty seconds before I finally raised it. It throbbed and felt as if it were about to explode. I finally nodded.

He assumed the seat across from me, leaning forward in a friendly manner. "First of all, I'd like to express my sympathy."

It was as if I'd been gutted and stuffed. Immediately, I began to tremble. "Is it McGrath?"

"Sorry," he said. "I didn't mean to alarm you. As far as we know, Detective McGrath is holding his own. I understand your shock and grief at his being shot. Finding his shooter will be our top priority."

I nodded, relief washing over me.

"If you could just share the events from your perspective, please."

I explained what I could without incriminating Lori or McGrath. "Detective McGrath and I have a personal relationship. It is his place to explain why he decided to park outside my home last night. I spoke with him shortly after midnight, I believe, then drifted off to sleep. I'm not sure what time I heard the gunshot. It took a second to register the sound, but as soon as I did, I grabbed my gun, and ran outside."

He leaned forward, like I'd just delivered him a case of his favorite beer. "You have a gun?"

"Personal protection for my family. My husband's gun before his death. Mine since then," I said matter of factly. "I probably set it down in McGrath's vehicle, or dropped it on the ground. I have no idea."

Rooney nodded as he jotted down a note.

I explained how I had discovered McGrath, called 911.

"There will be a thorough investigation. Of course, we will speak to Detective McGrath when he's able. Do you have any idea who the shooter could have been?"

I paused, but only for a moment. "He's been investigating Lisa Macchione's death, so I would look at the Macchione family if I were you." *Safe territory.*

Rooney arched an eyebrow, then narrowed his eyes at me and nodded. "I know what Jim was working on. Can't be too careful with that family. Did he share any recent developments with you?"

"No," I lied. "But it's all over the news. Lisa's death. Her husband and the mayor's indictment. I wouldn't put anything past those guys." We shared a look. The unspoken words said volumes.

"We're finished here for now." Rooney accompanied me to the front desk where I spotted Marty at the counter chatting with the desk officer. He turned to face me.

"Ready?"

I simply nodded, and refocused on getting to the hospital as quickly as possible.

We climbed into Marty's F150 and sped off to University Hospital. Once we reached the information desk, we were informed that McGrath had been taken into surgery, where doctors were attempting to remove the bullet lodged in his brain. *In his brain.* My knees went weak. The second wound I'd found was superficial, a grazing bullet. It would be hours before we knew anything certain. I asked Marty if he had my cell phone. He handed to me. I phoned home and spoke to Ed.

It was 4:32 a.m. Ed sounded as awake as I felt. He assured me that he would ready the kids for school. He also told me that the crime scene had been mostly tidied up, and that little evidence of what had occurred appeared outside my home would remain by the time the kids went outside. Blessedly, the kids had slept through the entire event, and Ed made no mention of Lori's presence. I explained her friendship, and that she had arrived at my place late last night after a squabble with a family member. He took me at my word, and said he would manage that, too. Told me to focus solely on McGrath's health. He had me covered.

I paced the halls for the first hour of McGrath's surgery, then entered the surgical waiting lounge and took a seat in a corner of the room. I held my head in my hands, turned the pages of a magazine without a single image registering in my mind, and finally leaned back and closed my eyes, unable to form one coherent thought. I murmured prayers for the next hour; it was all I could think to do. I stood up and carved a path on the carpet. I drank sludge out of cardboard cups, and felt my limbs go numb from exhaustion. It was all surreal. I'd just left here with Nick a short time ago, and now I was begging God to spare McGrath? Impossible. Whose life was this? It couldn't be mine. Make it stop. Please.

Who shot him? Why? Once McGrath's health returned — I refused to believe in anything short of a complete and full recovery — I vowed to never let go of him. Perhaps a leash. Not realistic, but my promise nonetheless.

At 7 a.m., a surgeon entered the room and called my name. "It will be touch and go for the next twenty-four hours. We were able to remove the bullet, but injuries such as Detective McGrath's are uncertain in terms of long term effects. He'll remain under care in the ICU — full-time, round-the-clock care, and under police protection."

"May I see him?"

The surgeon looked to the accompanying officer, waiting at a safe distance with Marty, who had kept vigil with me all night. The officer placed a call, then nodded his assent.

CHAPTER THIRTY-ONE

I STEPPED INTO the recovery room where a nurse guided me to McGrath. A uniformed officer, stationed by his bedside, nodded and allowed me to approach him. Tears filled my eyes. He looked so helpless. Unfamiliar even. Gray. Bandaged. Tubes and masks, all delivering needed fluids and oxygen, added to my panic, but I attempted to reassure myself that he received the best possible care, especially as an officer of the law.

I leaned over and whispered into his ear. "I love you. I'm never letting you out of my sight again. You hear me?" I squeezed his arm and planted a firm kiss onto his stubbled face.

I looked up as a nurse assessed his vital signs. "When will he wake up?"

"It could be a while. If you want to sit in the waiting room, I'll be out to get you as soon as he comes around."

I took her at her word, taking solace in the fact that she'd said *when* he comes around rather than *if* he comes around. Marty and I walked back to the surgical lounge. I sank into a chair, propped up my feet, and closed my eyes. Several hours later, that same nurse shook me awake and told me McGrath had roused from the anesthetic. I flew from my chair and followed her into his private room, passing the officer now stationed outside his door.

I smoothed the hair on McGrath's arm. "I'm here."

He opened his eyes. *Thank God.* Relief swept over me like warm rays from the sun. He attempted a smile, which I returned.

"Can I help you?" he asked.

"It's me. Sam."

He studied my face. "Sorry, can't place you."

"It's the anesthetic and the shock," I assured him.

He didn't look convinced.

"You were shot. Do you remember?"

McGrath winced as he attempted to shake his head.

"Don't worry. It'll all come back to you once you've rested."

He looked confused. Perplexed about where he was, who I was. I tried again. "I'm your woman." I smiled.

"Then I must have very good taste," he said before closing his eyes and drifting off.

I rolled out the tension in my shoulders and rubbed my throbbing temples, then forced myself to walk to the nurse's station. When she looked up at me, all I could say was, "He doesn't remember me."

She patted my arm. "Not to worry. We see a lot of this with this particular type of general anesthetic. Allow twenty-four hours for the drug to leave his system. You're very lucky. This man has an angel watching over him. It's a wonder he survived the shooting, and a miracle that the doctors were able to remove the bullet without damage to his brain. He's going to be fine."

I nodded, still unsure. My trust in the medical profession, as well as the rest of the world, had been tested more often than I dared think about. As much as I wanted to believe her, I would wait and see for myself.

"Why don't you go home and get some rest?" she suggested. "Leave your cell number at the desk. We'll be happy to call you if anything changes."

I checked my watch. 9:30 a.m. Ed had most likely gotten

the kids off to school, somehow managed Lori, and traveled back home. To be sure, I phoned him. He sounded drowsy when he picked up.

"How's Jim?" he asked.

"Holding his own. How are things at home?"

"Smooth sailing. Your friend must have vacated sometime after you went to bed. There were no signs of a visitor in Lizzie's room."

"Odd." I turned back to last night, before McGrath's shooting. "I'll call her later. She probably made up with her family and decided to return home."

"These things happen," Ed responded.

"You sound tired."

"I'm home now," he replied. "Just about to catch some shut-eye."

"I can't thank you enough for your help. Did Nick get off okay?"

"He was concerned about you. Mumbled something about the Mafia. But he made it out the door. I think he actually felt good about his return to normal."

I stayed silent for a long moment, mulling over how all this affected Nick and the rest of my family. I had no idea.

Ed interrupted my thoughts. "Sam, you aren't in any danger, are you?"

I summoned a laugh from some deep pretending place, hoping to dispel his worry. "Of course not." I stopped myself. *Enough Wonder Woman.* I let silence fill the line.

Ed broke the quiet a full thirty seconds later. "Sam?"

"I'm not sure, but there's a distinct possibility McGrath's shooting is related to a case he's working on. It involves the Macchione family, and it's got more arms than an octopus. I'm more frightened than I've ever been in my life. I have no idea where to turn or who to turn to, or how to handle a situation of this magnitude." I paused another moment. Should I tell Ed more? Yes. He was all I had. "Before his shooting, McGrath warned me… trust no one. I want a simple, boring life…" Tears flowed freely down my cheeks.

"You are to stay at the hospital with Jim until further notice. He has a police guard, doesn't he?"

"Yes."

"I know you want to handle things at home with the kids, but let me. We will move forward with this plan until further notice. I'm not asking you, Sam, I'm telling you."

"We can trust Officer Dave at the school. McGrath had him keeping an eye on Lizzie, and there were police officers checking on the older kids at the high school."

"If that's what he told you, honey, it's already in place and you need to trust it. Let the authorities take it from here. You hear me?"

"I don't know what I'd do without you."

"My pleasure." He signed off.

I weighed my options. I heard what Ed said, but in reality, I couldn't hide out for the rest of my life. As long as the kids were safe, I was safe, too. At least that's what I convinced myself. Living in fear didn't suit me. It made the most sense for me to go home for a couple of hours. I needed to check and see if Lori had left me a note, get a few hours of sleep, and return to the hospital to check on McGrath again before the kids arrived home from school and practice. I needed to see my home was still intact.

I didn't spot Marty in the surgical lounge, so I rode the elevator downstairs and found him sitting in the cafeteria, drinking coffee. He stood when he spotted me. "You okay?"

"More than that," I admitted. "McGrath is going to be okay. Mind delivering me home?"

"My pleasure." He took my arm and guided me through the building, and then out to the parking garage.

Thirty minutes later, I entered my home. I kicked off my shoes and looked around. Everything appeared normal, save the fact that the sink had been emptied of dishes and the interior of my home had been tidied up. Ed's doing, no doubt. I walked upstairs to Lizzie's room. The bed had been made, all signs of Lori's visit erased. I stepped into my bedroom to search the nightstand and the bathroom counter for a note. *Could she really have left without a trace?*

Lori must have heard the gunshot, panicked, and fled. In her shoes, I'd have done the same. Was she the intended target? For now, any concerns over her abrupt departure slid to the bottom of my priority list. McGrath held the top spot, my children the second. After that, I didn't possess the time or energy to think about much else. Plus, my certainty over whom I could trust had dwindled to an all time low. Who had been working with McGrath on Lisa's murder? I had no idea, nor did I understand who he trusted within the FBI's investigation into the Macchione's illicit dealings in the city.

Even though brilliant sunshine spilled into my room, I felt chilled. I threw on my thickest sweats and fell into bed for a fitful three hours of sleep. I tossed and turned, picking up my cell phone, confirming that I hadn't missed a message from the hospital amidst my worry about McGrath's amnesia.

I finally gave up on getting any serious rest, plodded into the bathroom, stripped down, and stepped into a hot shower. I missed Rex. I didn't feel safe enough to journey through my neighborhood by myself. If he were still alive, I'd have snapped on his leash and gone for a run. I needed to seek out protection through the authorities. Could I trust anyone enough to explain recent events? Not likely. I seemed destined to watch my back. Every waking moment. The nighttime moments, too. I couldn't live like this. It was neither reasonable nor desirable.

I longed to sit on my front porch with a tall mug of coffee and attempt to relax, but that didn't feel safe either. *I needed McGrath more than ever.* I loaded the washer, brushed on some make-up, grabbed some chicken from the freezer for dinner, jumped into the van, and headed back to the hospital. With cops stationed outside the door of McGrath's room, it seemed like the safest place to be.

"I'm Samantha Stitsill." I presented my driver's license to the officer stationed outside McGrath's room. I recognized him from earlier that morning. He checked my ID against his list and gave me the go-ahead. I introduced myself.

"Do you know Detective McGrath?"

He shook his head. "Not personally, ma'am. I've met him once or twice. He's got a great reputation, though. I'm really sorry about this."

"Thank you. How's he doing?"

"Far as I know, he's been sleeping. Nurses have been in and out, but nothing out of the ordinary."

"Has he had other visitors?"

"The chief of police from Lexington was here earlier, but as far as I know, Detective McGrath slept through his visit."

"Any word on finding Detective McGrath's assailant?"

"No, ma'am. Not as far as I know."

When I entered McGrath's room, a stiff wave of exhaustion swept over me. He looked weak and small. His shaved head bandaged, the wraps hid the road map of stitches from his surgery, and his face looked thin and drawn. Didn't seem possible that this strapping man could ever appear diminished, and I cautioned myself that the presence of the tubes and monitors along with the cannula seated in his nose caused me to feel so uneasy. It had not been all that long since I sat in this same hospital complex with Nick, so I reasoned more than one issue prompted me to feel overwhelmed. In that moment, I felt insignificant, alone, and a whole lot queasy.

I cranked open the blinds, hoping an infusion of sunlight would lift my spirits. I had three missions. Help McGrath wake up, remember me, remember himself. The pressure to pull him back from the abyss hit me full force. While I recognized the anesthetic wouldn't be out of his system yet, I longed to have him whole again. *Pronto.*

I leaned over and kissed his cheek, praying I'd be able

to accomplish reversing the roles of Snow White and the handsome prince, and that the sheer brush of my lips on his stubbled cheek would awaken his memory.

His eyelids fluttered.

"Good morning," I said, even though it was early afternoon.

He blinked, locked eyes with me, and looked confused.

"Hello," he said.

I smiled, fighting back tears. He didn't know me.

"You may still be under the effects of the anesthesia. I'm Sam. You and I are friends."

"I'm sorry. I'm having difficulty remembering things. What happened?"

I breathed a sigh of relief. The McGrath I knew and loved was still in there. Inquisitive, searching. "You're a police detective. You were parked outside my home because you were concerned about my safety, and you were shot."

He nodded slightly, squinting in search of a memory, trying to make some sense of things.

I plodded on. "I live in a small town, Lexington Heights, about thirty minutes from where you live in Lexington. I've been to your home. You have a man cave on the river. Overstuffed furniture, hand-carved ducks on your mantle. Very comfortable."

I dug out my phone and showed him a photo of his deck and the river below. "Once I was canoeing the river with a friend. We tipped our boat and you witnessed the entire event from your deck. You hurried down to the riverbank, like a knight in shining armor, and offered to help." *Please remember.*

McGrath shook his head and winced.

"Are you in pain?"

"Killer headache."

I rested my hand on his arm in a gesture of comfort. "I'll check with the nurse and see if it's time for more medication."

He shook his head. Winced again. "No meds."

I laughed, pleased that his personality hadn't changed.

He looked at me quizzically. "I'm funny?"

"You have a great sense of humor. It's one of my favorite things about you. That and the fact that, other than the occasional glass of beer or wine, you're not into drugs of any kind. You tough out aches and pains."

"Good to know."

"You're also a fan of food. Grilling is your preferred food preparation method. You're quite the cook."

He half-smiled. "You're making me hungry."

"You're on a liquid diet for twenty-four hours after your surgery. How about some ice chips?"

"No, tell me more about myself instead."

"Hmm..." I paused to think. Did he want to know his history? Where he lived and worked? Or the more personal details? What I thought about him? What I loved about him? I wanted to tell him that he was the sexiest man I'd ever met, and that he had a way of making my blood simmer to a rolling boil whenever he looked at me, but it seemed too soon to jump into that. "What would you like to know?"

"Do I have a family?"

"You were married once, a long time ago. You don't have any children, and you've been estranged from your birth family for most of your adult life. I'm not entirely sure of the details. It's a subject you've avoided."

He narrowed his eyes at me. "What about you?"

"I'm a widow with five children, ranging in age from ten to almost sixteen."

"You were busy for a while. What is that? A kid a year?"

"My husband and I each had two kids when we married. Then, we decided to have one more. Jon's been gone for two years now, so my life is busy with my children."

A flicker of recognition crossed his face.

"What?"

"I just had a flash. Freckle-faced kid. Red headed. He

yours?"

I grinned. "Nick."

"Nick," he repeated. "What's he like?"

I smiled. "He knows me like the back of his hand. He's almost fourteen. A freshman in high school. He has a great sense of humor, like you, and his first love is the guitar."

"Sounds like a great kid."

"He is."

The room fell quiet but for the ticking of the wall clock, and the intermittent beeping of a monitor. Then the whoosh of the blood pressure machine kicking on and off as it monitored his vitals.

I held McGrath's hand as he drifted off to sleep.

CHAPTER THIRTY-TWO

I INSISTED ON meeting with McGrath's neuro-logist, Dr. Evans, in order to understand the implications of his memory loss, and the prognosis. "Sometimes it's the trauma of the event," Evans explained. "It will most likely be a gradual recovery. He may remember his life in a linear pattern, but it will probably be more segmented than that; it will come to him in bits and pieces and in random order. Eventually, he will integrate the memories. Surprisingly, his short term memory seems mostly unaffected. That's a good sign."

"How long will recovery take?"

"In my experience, there is no rule, but several months of recovery can be expected."

"What can I do to help him?"

"We will have him see a speech therapist. He will be taught memory techniques and you can help trigger memories through the methods they share with you both. In the meantime, Detective McGrath will benefit from plenty of rest. Keep his stress to a minimum and encourage him not to become disheartened if his memories are disjointed, or if he doesn't progress as quickly as he would like."

I nodded. There was nothing more to be done.

* * *

The next week seemed interminable. Between the kids and spending every kid-less minute parked at McGrath's bedside, I lost sight of time and space. His memory hadn't returned, but he had established his road to physical recovery, and he seemed content with my company. Trusting even.

Nick returned to school — full steam ahead. He spent his after school hours on the cross country track, encouraging his teammates although he was far from able to participate.

Still no word from Lori Woodruff, but that was the least of my worries. I assumed she and the girls were safe and sound since I hadn't heard otherwise. As I sat at McGrath's bedside that afternoon, I flipped on the TV. A Special Report flashed on the screen. Mayor Macchione had been killed in a scuffle with his brother, Tony. "Oh My God!"

I turned up the volume as the reporter repeated the news. Mayor Macchione DEAD. Anthony Macchione taken into custody. I listened for news about the family. Nothing.

McGrath, propped in the recliner, opened his eyes to the sound of the report, and his eyes narrowed. "What's that?"

"It has to do with the case you were working on when you were shot." I explained the details to him, reminded him of Lisa Macchione's death, and shared finally that we had been working together somewhat, based on my association with the family through my teaching of the Macchione's visually impaired daughter.

He reached out to brush his fingertips across my arm. "Sounds like we're quite a team."

I smiled. He felt connected to me. Headway.

"We are," I agreed. "It won't be long until you remember. You're going to be laid up for a while, but the surgeon has suggested your release. I think the department felt they could better protect you here, but with the news of the mayor's death and Tony's incarceration, you may not require a 24-hour police watch. This new development may tip the scales."

He seemed oblivious to the details of the case. Any time I ventured into career territory, he ignored me and pouted. "I've been after them to release me for days. I'm ready to go home."

"I have an idea. Would you consider coming to my place, instead? That way, I can keep a close eye on you. I'm not sure the doctor or the department feels secure about letting you return home without a caretaker."

"Shit," he muttered.

"What, you don't like the idea of moving in with me and my five children? Think of it this way, it'll be educational." I thought about suggesting that I'd be available to deliver sponge baths, but...

He grinned. "What are my other options?"

"Hire a health care worker to move in with you. Your physical condition is fairly stable, but with your lack of memory, no one feels confident that you're ready to be on your own."

"I just want to get the hell out of here."

"See? You're sounding like your old self."

"Could you take me home?"

I patted his hand. "I can't move in with you, if that's what you're suggesting. Don't worry. We'll figure it out."

"I'm antsy," he confided. "I need my memory back. I know that you and I are friends. At least, I trust it. When guys from the force stop by, I don't feel the same sense of calm that I feel with you. In fact, I feel like I'm not measuring up. I see the pity on their faces. I need to be on my own. Get my life back. Maybe if I went home, it would help jar my memory."

I laughed and shook my head. "Take a deep breath. Your memory will return, but you can't force it. Patience."

He grimaced, stood, and stepped inside the bathroom. "Apparently, I'm not a patient person." He closed the door behind him.

I'd seen him like this before, when angry at me for

shutting him out of my life. He needed time to assimilate what had happened. A lot like my Nick, I realized, his stubbornness would be soon be overridden by his desire to feel close to someone. I planted myself first on his list of supporters in hopes it would allow him to reach out to me.

When he stepped back into the room, he locked eyes with me. "What's your place like?"

I smiled. "How about this? We convince the surgeon and the department to spring you. You come home with me, and then during the day, when my children are at school, we can spend some time at your place. That way, you can begin to reestablish your roots, yet you won't have to completely fend for yourself. Think of it as a gradual reentry."

In the meantime, I hoped that the Macchione disaster would close in on itself, and McGrath and I would no longer be in danger. With the mayor dead and Tony behind bars, I couldn't imagine anyone would give a hoot about either McGrath or me. *A girl can dream, right?*

"Deal," he said, smacking his hands on his knees. "Now, let's get me sprung."

"Settle down, Detective. It may be a while. I'll visit the nurse's desk and put in your request, but try to exercise a tad of tolerance. Nothing happens quickly in the medical world, nor in the world of law enforcement. This decision will require the input of both, and your health and safety come first, so just hold your horses."

I kissed his cheek, the first time since he'd been fully awake. I cautioned myself that it wasn't proper for me to insert myself into his life in the same fashion I had previously assumed. In all fairness to him and to myself, I wanted him to remember us before I dove into bed with him again.

His hands came up around my face. His fingers gently pressed my cheeks as he drew me into him and parted my lips with his tongue. I couldn't help myself. I fell onto his lap and wrapped my arms around his shoulders.

"We've done this before," he said, sounding a tad

bemused when he finally came up for air.

"Once or twice," I teased, barely able to keep my wits about me. I hadn't realized how much I'd missed *us*. There were so many things to consider. Should I allow a physical relationship? McGrath had no memory of me yet. It seemed wrong to forge ahead with that when he had so much recovery in front of him. On the other hand, a bit of foreplay might trigger his memory. "Maybe this is the true path to re-discovery."

"Works for me."

I pushed myself up. "We'll decide later. Right now, I'm going to see if I can arrange your discharge." I left a gaping McGrath in my wake.

Finally, after lots of prodding and convincing, both the hospital and the department agreed that he could be discharged to my care. They insisted he wait overnight, so that they could set up psychotherapy and occupational therapy appointments, and plan for police protection after they assured themselves that the Mayor's death and Tony's arrest allowed a measure of safety for McGrath that he hadn't been afforded before.

Time allowed me the opportunity to ease my kids into the idea, change the sheets, and run the vacuum. Not a heck of a lot of time, but flexibility is my middle name.

I returned home at four o'clock, met Lizzie at the bus, and strolled down the street with her. "How's your friend, Mom?"

"Well enough to come home from the hospital."

"That's great. Is he going to need help?"

"Yes, he is, and we're just the family he needs. He'll be staying with us for a while until he's ready to go home."

She bumped me and giggled. "Does this mean I get to sleep with you?"

I grinned. "Not a hardship for me."

"You love snuggling with your little girl." Her smile spoke volumes.

We entered the house. I served her favorite snack before we jumped in the van and ventured out to pick up the kids from practice. She divulged all to the older kids once they loaded inside the van.

"Mom's boyfriend is moving in."

Nick broke out a little ditty. "Mom and the Detective, sitting in a tree…"

I hushed him. "This is serious. The poor man doesn't remember much about his life. We're guessing it has to do with his injury, but he's going to need gentle introductions back into reality. It's our job to be patient and kind. No teasing. He has no memory of… his relationship with us."

"He doesn't remember that he's your boyfriend?" Nick again.

I glared at him via my rearview mirror. "No. And it's not your job to jog his memory in that regard. Understood?"

Annie snickered. "Sure, Mom."

Good God, I needed reinforcements. "I'm serious, you guys. The man doesn't have children. He requires quiet, not commotion. I'm counting on all of you to be on your best behavior. Lizzie will move in with me, and Detective McGrath will occupy her room. Got it?"

Nick chuckled. "Whatever you say, Mom."

"I'm glad we've cleared that up."

* * *

I guided McGrath inside Lizzie's room and set his plastic bag of valuables on the bed. "I apologize for the princess-themed bedroom. We'll go to your place after you've taken your required nap."

He inventoried the pink and purple walls, the plastic glow-in-the-dark stars on the ceiling, the polka-dotted bean bag chair in the corner, then he plopped down on the slim twin bed.

"Care to join me?"

Nice to know his testosterone levels remained intact. "Don't tempt me. Knowing my kids, they've placed hidden cameras throughout the house. Trust me, we can't be too careful." I kissed his cheek, turned on my heel, and closed the bedroom door behind me.

Once McGrath awakened, he joined me in the kitchen. I served him a steaming mug of coffee and sat down beside him.

"I have a few questions," I said.

His gaze became intent. He'd woken up a different man. Now, he seemed like a cop again. Getting him out of the hospital? A good idea. I thought better of my decided course of action, and veered left.

"How about we head to your place? We can gather some clothes and essentials, then sit out on your deck for a while and watch the river go by."

"I can't wait."

"Your memory will begin to return. Gradually. It's what the doctor said, and I've Googled it. The most likely scenario is that you will begin to recall past events, then eventually catch up to present day. Granted, it's not a guarantee, but I'm thinking some time in a familiar environment can't hurt."

"Google. You like to Google things. Somehow, that seems familiar."

"See? You're making progress already. You'll be back to normal in no time."

I snagged a baseball cap from the boy's closet so McGrath could cover his wound. We loaded into the van twenty minutes later, right after I placed a turkey sandwich in front of him. I stopped off at the police station first, leaving him to play with the car radio while I picked up my gun. Recovered after the shooting, I hadn't taken the time yet to retrieve it. I stuffed it in the bottom of my oversized handbag, the same one that contained ammunition.

I fully expected a tussle over the recovery of my weapon,

but it appeared I was expected at the station. My attorney neighbor, Stewart James, had indicated he would call ahead for me. He had. I rejoined McGrath in the van, passed him a smile, and headed for his place.

I checked on him as I drove, glancing at him now and then, trying to be casual, yet size up how he was doing. His elbow rested on the door, hand cupped on his chin, eyes gazing out the window. I considered asking him if he recognized anything, thought better of it, and hummed along to the tune playing on the radio. McGrath seemed pensive as his gaze shifted out the windshield. He leaned forward and let his eyes travel from one side of the road to the other.

"I got nothing," he said.

"Stop trying to force it. You're a driven man, and I respect you for your tenacity, but anytime anyone tries to force something, it won't work. Human nature. You'll get all balled up and your brain won't be able to function."

McGrath adjusted his cap, sank back in the passenger seat and closed his eyes.

"Good boy."

He reached over and rested his hand on my thigh. I patted it, then returned my hand to the steering wheel.

"Five more minutes, and you'll be home." I smiled at him, but his eyes were still closed. "Deep breath might help."

McGrath inhaled sharply, held it, then exhaled slowly.

A few minutes later, I pulled into his driveway. His grass had been mowed. His mail had been neatly stacked on the dining room table. I considered asking him who had a key, besides me, but would he be able to tell me? Probably not. Maybe a neighbor. Maybe someone from the force. I should know this. *Later.* The house smelled a bit musty; it had been closed up too long. I opened windows and turned on fans — to air out the place and make it feel homier. Then, I retrieved a couple of glasses from the cupboard, filled them with ice water, and called to McGrath, who had gone into his bedroom to search out some clothing to bring back to my place.

"McGrath," I shouted. "Join me on the deck?"

"Coming."

I beat him outside and swept up the pine cones, needles, and debris which had collected in his absence. By the time he joined me, I had cleared the deck. I pulled two chairs to the railing, facing them toward the river. We had spent evenings here before, and I hoped the familiarity and the soothing sounds of the river burbling below us would relax him.

He smiled as he stepped outside, then looked sad. "This is a really nice place."

"Remember my advice," I coached. "Don't force it."

"It's weird." He sat in the chair beside me, inched it over closer to mine, and grasped my hand. "It's comfortable here. Not familiar exactly, but easy."

I nodded. "It's an easy place. You've done a great job here. You're handy with wood. You built this deck, and you carved the ducks on your mantle."

We both went quiet and breathed in the beauty of our surroundings. Squirrels chattered in the pines that enshrouded his property, water burbled over the rocks, and patches of sunlight splashed on the deck and landscape before us, reflecting off the meandering water below. I spotted a canoe with two women passengers and recalled again that moment when Di and I had spilled our boat, then gripped McGrath's hand a little more tightly.

He leaned over and kissed my cheek. "I feel better. Honest. It's too strange. I'm past ready to get back to normal, just don't know what normal is."

"I think this. You're still the guy you've always been. Much hunch is that instinct will play a powerful role here. Up for trying a little experiment with me?"

"Game." His eyes sparkled like I hadn't seen them in far

too long.

I smiled back at him and noticed that his dimples had filled in some since he'd been eating better.

"Okay, here's the plan. I'll ask you a question, and you answer it. Don't spend time thinking or wondering, just say the first thing that comes to mind."

He inched even closer, like a kid anxious to climb in the front seat of a roller coaster. "Deal."

"The mayor of a mid-sized city and his brother are indicted on charges of corruption, embezzlement, fraud, and extortion. They have well-known and well-established Mafia ties. The brother's wife goes missing and is found dead a few weeks later..."

McGrath grew excited, as if the coaster were just rounding the first curve. "I just had a flashback. You. Me. Gun range."

"Yes! You taught me how to shoot a gun."

"When?"

I locked eyes with him, not wanting to miss any clue on which I could build. "A couple of years ago."

"We've known each other for a while, then?"

I nodded.

"What was the status of our relationship before my injury?"

I grinned. "Let's worry about that later. You were talking about the gun range..."

"I'm a good shot, aren't I?"

"I can't say I'm the best judge of your marksmanship skills, but yes, I believe so." *Good sign. Ego returning.*

"Okay." He nodded, seemingly satisfied with his newly discovered memory. "Go on. The mayor, his brother, the wife."

"I have good reason to believe that the wife was killed by her husband. Truth is, I knew that family a long time ago." I continued to explain my relationship to the Macchione's visually impaired daughter and Lori's presence at my home the night he was shot. Basically, I recited the Reader's Digest version of recent events.

McGrath seemed enraptured by my story, forgetting what I'd told him about it two days prior, and intent on hearing my every word. "Somehow, you, me, and Lori seem to hold the key. Or we have at least irked someone."

I laced my fingers with his. "Just what I'm thinking. But even more than that, I believe that Adrianna is the lock that needs opening. She knows something. I spent time with her after her mother's disappearance, and she shared that she had heard her parents' arguing the night before her mother went missing. I've spent time poring over it, and I've decided that she's too frightened to tell. Now that her father's been arrested for killing the mayor, maybe she will feel safe enough to talk to me. That might lead us to your shooter."

"I'm on leave. But I agree with you."

"Another question."

"Shoot," he said, his eyes alight with humor.

"No funny business. My real question is this. Why would someone target you? And who?"

"Somebody's worried that I know something." I recognized the expression that I'd seen hundreds of times before when we were working a case together. He turned cop on me, right then and there.

My lips curved into a wide smile.

"What?" he asked.

"Nothing. Continue."

"Whoever shot me considers me a threat. If I've been working this case, then I must have been close to solving it."

"Or," I added, "Lori Woodruff's decision to visit my home drew the attention there, and you just happened to be in the wrong place at the wrong time."

McGrath narrowed his eyes, as if remembering. "Somehow, that makes sense."

Several long silent moments passed between us.

"You once kept case files here. Do you think it's possible that you did with this case as well?"

Lost in thought, McGrath ignored me. "Where's Lori?"

"No idea. I haven't heard from her since the shooting. I'll phone her cell."

I retreated inside and dug my cell phone out from my handbag, loading my gun in the process. Seemed like a thing to do.

I dialed and waited. The call went directly to her voicemail. I left a short message. "Hi Lori, it's Samantha Stitsill. I haven't heard from you in a while. Just wondering how you're doing."

I rejoined McGrath on the deck. His elbows rested on his knees, his face nested between his fisted hands.

"No answer."

"Tell me about the shooting." He peered at me, apparently trying to make sense of the chronology.

I shared all that I remembered.

"Lori probably heard the shot. If she feared for her life, she most likely fled. Unless she shot me!"

"She didn't. I heard a car speed away, and she didn't have a car. A taxi dropped her off." I thought about it for a few minutes. "I can't imagine where she went. I'll drive to her home, knock on the door, and see what I can find out." I worried I might be stretching my safety quotient a tad by connecting with her, but the more I turned it over in my mind, the more convinced I was that Lori was not involved in McGrath's shooting. She was as much a victim of the Macchione's as the rest of us.

"I'll come with you."

I gazed at the river, catching a shard of sunshine as it moved over the rocks below, and thought it through. "You can't. The department will have my hide if I involve you in the case while you're still recovering. Remember? You're on an official leave."

His sneaky grin said it all. "We're just visiting a friend."

"We'll get in a bushel of trouble if anyone finds out."

"I'm physically able. My memory may not be fully restored, but I feel great."

"Sure you do. Still, if anything were to happen to you on my watch, I'd never forgive myself."

McGrath became agitated. "They didn't return my service revolver, did they?"

"Let's go for a drive."

CHAPTER THIRTY-THREE

W E PARKED IN front of Lori Woodruff's home. A well-manicured landscape greeted us; rows of rosebushes in full-bloom along the perimeter of the walkway. Birdsong filled the surrounding trees, reflecting a calmness which I couldn't force myself to embrace. McGrath followed me up the path as I cased the house and then glanced back at the street to make sure we weren't being watched.

I climbed the stairs to the porch and rang the bell near the oversized oak door. After several long minutes, the locked tumbled on the other side of the entry. Adrianna opened the door. Hammer, the missing German Shepherd, stood at her side.

"Adrianna, honey. It's me, Mrs. Stitsill."

"I know." She looked at me with blank eyes. "I smell your perfume."

"My friend… Mr. McGrath is with me. Is Aunt Lori home?"

She stood back. "Yes. Come in."

I stayed put. "Why don't you let her know I'm here? I didn't call ahead. I don't want to interrupt her."

"She's upstairs packing. It's okay."

Packing. I stepped inside. McGrath followed and closed the door behind him. "Are you going on a trip?" There were already four suitcases, two laundry baskets, and three oversized boxes in the hallway.

Adrianna smiled sadly. "Just to my grandma's house."

Didn't look like a simple visit to Grandma's.

Lauren filed in behind her, looking puzzled.

"Hi, Lauren. I'm Mrs. Stitsill. I used to come to your house and teach your little sister when she was a baby. Do you remember?"

"Sort of," Lauren said. Her dark eyes spoke of her sadness and hesitancy in the face of her recent loss. I remembered her as a timid little girl. While she'd grown into a teenager, her personality didn't appear to have changed. She had to be fourteen now. I guessed that she understood far more than Adrianna about her mom, her dad, and the fact that their lives had been completely toppled by their own father. She shrank into the hallway as I spoke.

"I'm so sorry about your mom."

Adrianna threw her arms around my waist. "Maybe it's a mistake."

"Oh, sweetie, I wish it was." I held her as she cried, and watched Lauren disappear upstairs.

My gut told me that Adrianna knew far more than she had shared. Could I get her alone? Could I gently jostle her memory? I needed to do so quickly, before she left town and buried the memories deeper inside.

I heard footsteps and looked up to see Lori descending the stairs. Pale and drawn, almost lifeless, she warily approached us.

"How can I help you?" Her voice flat, it appeared she had no desire to let me back into her life. Maybe she felt threatened. Not by me, per se, but by the situation. If Tony had been arrested, was there any possibility he would have posted bail and been released? Was Lori worried about his minions? Now that she appeared to have the girls in her custody, would she be safer or in more danger? Was that why she seemed reticent to speak with me?

It seemed essential that I strike the right chord. I

introduced McGrath as a friend and then said, "Please accept my condolences. Your family has been through so much, and you seemed... so distraught the last time I saw you. I needed to see with my own eyes that you were okay."

Short. Simple. Sweet.

I tried to talk around Adrianna, but at the same time leave Lori an opening, if she wanted one. Two weeks ago, she had turned to me for help. At the time, she'd chosen to seek me out, rather than share her grief with her husband or a close friend. What had changed?

"We're headed off to my mother's shortly. I'm anxious to get on the road."

"How long will you be away?"

"I'm not sure."

I saw no sign of her husband. Was she leaving her life behind? "Can we help you? Fix the girls a snack?"

Adrianna turned toward her aunt. "Please, Auntie, please. I haven't had a Braille lesson in forever. Can I show Mrs. Stitsill what I've been practicing?"

Lori softened. "Of course. You and Mrs. Stitsill can work at the kitchen table while Lauren helps me finish packing." To me she said, "While the girls put their belongings in the car, we can talk about... Adrianna's progress."

I nodded.

Once Lori returned to packing, Adrianna said, "I'll get the Brailler."

I sent McGrath to the living room and advised him to look for clues. Specifically, where was Lori headed and for how long?

I met Adrianna in the kitchen where she sat at attention, her chair pulled up to the table, hands suspended as if she were ready to play her Brailler like a musician poised to play a concert piano.

As I gazed at this beautiful child, I momentarily forgot my mission. I shook my head and reminded myself that I had limited time to accomplish my task. I pulled the cumbersome

Brailler from its case and situated it in front of Adrianna, handing her a sheet of paper to insert into the machine. She expertly handled the job, feeling her way to the paper guide. Her vision seemed even worse today, most likely due to the recent stresses on her life. Yet, she remained a trooper, holding on with both hands to what life still had to offer her.

We spent a few minutes reviewing contractions. Bright as a diamond, she remembered everything. I mapped out a few new contractions for her, then dictated two paragraphs for her to type. She paused to recall a few of the finger formations required for use of the combinations, and then plunked out the entire passage within minutes.

I smiled and rested my hand on her shoulder. "You're a master."

She smiled at me, clearly proud of her intelligence and her ability. "Really?"

"You've always been an impressive young woman."

"Thanks." Then, without another word, she began to press the keys of the Brailler. She turned my way once, about ten minutes in. "I've been writing a story in my head. I'm putting it on paper for you."

I wondered if it were really that simple.

"You can read it later," she said, "after I leave for my grandma's. Hopefully, I'll remember all of the words and the contractions."

"Don't worry. Spell out words you're unsure of, or ask me. I'm sitting right here, you know."

She typed furiously, not stopping to ask questions, and breathing hard, as if she were running a race. I rested my hand on her back as a source of strength. One courageous little girl.

Ten minutes later, she lifted her hands from the Brailler with flourish, like she'd played the last note of a sonata. "Finished. I don't think I've left out anything."

I smiled at her and applauded her efforts. "We'll call this Chapter One."

Adrianna had filled two sheets of paper, which I quickly tucked inside my bag while she heaved the Brailler back inside its case and latched the cover into place.

I glanced over my shoulder, feeling a presence, and saw McGrath leaning against the doorway. He smiled at me, nodding.

I gave Adrianna a quick hug, then told her that she could keep my Brailler while she visited with her grandmother. "That way, if you want to begin the next chapter, you'll have everything you need." I excused myself, dashed out to my car for my school bag, and returned to her side with a new sheaf of paper. "There's enough in this pack for you to write an entire novel."

"How many sheets?"

"One hundred! Now, find your Aunt Lori for me, so I can tell her goodbye."

Adrianna headed toward the stairs, calling for her aunt.

McGrath and I faced each other in the kitchen, too afraid to speak.

Lori entered the room a few moments later, clearly frazzled, but less guarded and not as distant. "I'm sorry I wasn't more cordial when you arrived. Some days, I can barely put one foot in front of the other."

I knew all about that. "You've been through so much. I'm not going to ask why you left my house so abruptly that night. I'm trusting you had a very good reason."

Lori glanced at McGrath, then back at me.

"May I speak freely?" she asked.

"Yes."

Lori diverted her attention to the staircase, making sure her nieces remained well out of earshot. "Tony is getting what he deserves. They caught him red-handed after he killed his brother, and I can only hope that while he's behind bars, the authorities can put enough evidence together to convict him of my sister's murder, as well. The guy's been bad news from the get-go."

"Don't forget he still faces embezzlement and corruption charges," I said.

Despite his amnesia, McGrath's cop mode clicked in. "There's little chance he'll see the light of day again. In the meantime, you need to establish guardianship of your nieces with the court. Under the circumstances, you won't have any difficulty securing custody, if that's what you intend to do."

"I was never able to have any children of my own," Lori said. "My nieces are my life now that Lisa is gone. I can't think of a better way to remain close to her than having her girls with me."

"Don't stay away too long," I advised. "I know you and the girls need time and space to heal, but they have a great deal of support here in the schools and the community. Don't try to handle everything yourself."

"I'm not sure," Lori said thoughtfully. "I hear what you're saying, but for the girls to be put through the exposure of the media coverage of their father's trial, especially after losing their mother, a permanent vacation seems like a great idea to me."

I thought about her life and how she'd described her husband, who spent more time traveling for business than he did at home with her. I'd lived a life like that myself. If I had the chance to do it all again, would I have done it differently? *Oh yeah.*

This opportunity could change the course of Lori's life. Far be it from me to change her mind.

I gave her a gentle hug and wished her well. "Please let me know if there's anything I can do to help. You have my number."

Lori nodded and whispered a "thank you" as Lauren and Adrianna entered the room.

"Ready girls?" she asked.

They chorused, "Yes! Let's go!"

Adrianna approached me for a hug. She wrapped her

arms around my waist, pressed her head to my chest and held on for a long moment. "I love you."

I fought back tears as I hugged her. "I love you, too, sweetie. Keep up with your story."

She nodded, and I smoothed her hair with my fingers. I couldn't look at McGrath for fear I'd break down. I quickly gathered my bag and purse.

"Off you go," I said. "Give me a call when you get back, Lori."

She simply nodded. We made our way to the front door, let ourselves out, and drove the thirty minutes home in silence. Just as we were rounding the corner into my neighborhood, McGrath cleared his throat and spoke. "You okay?"

"No," I said, "but I will be."

I stood at a crossroads. I couldn't really involve him in anything more pertaining to the Macchione case. Why had I allowed him to accompany me to Lori's? While it was a positive sign that he slipped into cop mode at Lori's house, I recognized that if I included him in my thoughts and suppositions, I'd be placing his career in jeopardy, tempting him to plummet back into the case before he was truly healed and ready. The poor man had amnesia. He'd been assigned a medical and professional leave of absence. Would I ever learn to think before acting? *Probably not.*

I glanced at the clock. The school bus would arrive any minute. With luck, I could hurry McGrath upstairs and settle him before Lizzie's arrival. She could munch on a snack and begin her homework while I started dinner. In forty-five minutes, we needed to pick up the kids from Cross Country practice.

I helped McGrath carry his belongings to Lizzie's room. He looked beat, so I suggested a nap. He didn't put up a fight. Meeting my crew in his memoryless state might cause the poor man to add a panic anxiety disorder to his list of problems.

"We'll be gentle," I assured him.

Two hours later, the kids were home, showered, and relatively quiet. They helped set the table and tackled their homework without too much prodding. I left them to finish their studies while I went upstairs to awaken McGrath and allow him time enough to shower before dinner. He gazed at me sleepily, reaching out and drawing me to him.

"I don't remember this," he said. "But I'd sure like to."

I planted a kiss on his lips and instructed him that he had thirty minutes to get himself showered and dressed for dinner.

I didn't have time for my nerves to overpower me. Way too busy. Still, worry zipped through me like an electric current. I shifted Nick into Jon's old spot at the kitchen table and asked McGrath to assume Nick's seat. We gathered together for a chicken dinner with baked potatoes and steamed broccoli. The same old crap, as Nick called it.

We made small talk about the kids' school day, and they included McGrath by asking him if he was any good with numbers. After establishing his algebra and geometry talents—they quizzed him on theorems and algebraic expressions—I left him at the table with the kids. I cleared away the dishes and they retrieved textbooks. Picking his brain would prove a much wiser decision than picking mine—even with his memory loss.

CHAPTER THIRTY-FOUR

I CLIMBED INTO bed a little past midnight. Lizzie snored at my side and I suspected McGrath, after his first 'family' evening, had drifted off as well. I flipped on my bedside lamp, remembering in the first truly thoughtful moments I had all day, the Braille pages that Adrianna had written. I retrieved them from my bag and read them. Her story proved simple yet succinct.

THE LAST NIGHT
I awoke to the sound of hushed voices, growing louder as I became more awake. My mom and dad fought a lot, but this fight was different. Like, really serious. I lay in bed, scared, frozen in place, torn between wanting to know what was happening and being too afraid to move.
"She's your child." I heard my mother say.
"Is that why my brother can't stop looking at her? Looking at you?" My father's voice rose. As tempted as I was to hide my head under my pillow, I did not. I listened.
"It was over a long time ago." My mother tried to reassure him.
"You could have told me. We could have undone this before it ever happened."

My mother continued. "I don't believe in abortion."

"But you lied to me." My father said. "He lied to me. Did you think I was stupid? That I wouldn't figure it out?"

"I don't know." My mother shouted, and I could tell she was crying. "I told you I'm sorry. I'm here. I'm doing what you want. What more must I do to prove to you that I love you and I want our family to stay together?"

"You left me!" he yelled. "That woman, the teacher, she planted the seed, didn't she?"

"Mrs. Stitsill had nothing to do with this. Yes, she left her husband after years of abuse. Yes, she spoke to me about it. But I'm back and I intend to stay. We deserve a second chance."

"Not good enough. You and Vinnie don't deserve my love. Adrianna does, but you haven't made it easy for that little girl. You've bastardized her from the very start. Her blindness was no accident. It's God's way of letting you know what a horror you are! A slut!" (I'm not sure if I spelled those words right, and I don't know for sure what they mean).

I heard a crash. Then, a thud. No more talking. Just silence. I lay in bed, listening. Waiting for my mother to come into my room and check on me just like she did after every fight she had with my dad. But she never came.

I never saw her again.

Lisa's face flashed before me. The look in her eyes the day I told her about leaving my ex. While I wasn't explicit, I warned her. In so many words, I told her my story. Leaving a control freak with an ego the size of Texas would cost her dearly, and the price could be her life. Once Tony learned that his brother had fathered Adrianna, once he felt the weight of Lisa's betrayal... there's no way to get away from a man intent on killing you, intent on revenge. In the end, she didn't stand a chance.

"There's only one way you will leave this house... in a zip-up bag." My ex's words echoed in my head, and I shivered with a bone-deep chill.

I could have shown McGrath the story, but I didn't. Instead, I delivered it to my lawyer neighbor, Stewart, after I walked the kids to the bus stop the following morning. McGrath must have still been asleep, because he hadn't ventured out of Lizzie's room yet. Stewart assured me that he'd transport the document to the proper authorities, and assured me that I had nothing to worry about. Through his connections at the federal level, he had kept abreast of the Macchione case all along, and guaranteed me that Tony no longer posed a threat to anyone.

"Did you watch the news this morning?"

"No. Why?"

Stewart gripped my arm. "Oh, you don't know. They've arrested Marty Jaeger. He's a suspect in both McGrath's shooting and your son's hit and run. I thought that's why you stopped by."

I couldn't catch my breath. Marty? He was my friend. He was in my home after McGrath's shooting... with my kids. He spent hours at my side. He was a respected member of our community. A firefighter. A coach. There must be some mistake. "Are they sure?"

"According to my contacts, Marty came to Detective McGrath's attention just before he was shot. After the shooting, Marty's bank account grew exponentially, with no logical explanation. It's a slam dunk. They've tied him to the family."

"But why?"

"Word on the street is a gambling problem. Guess he owed the family money. And anyone with a brain in their head could see he was sweet on you."

"Help me understand, Stewart. Why target Nick? I won't rest until I know my family is safe."

"I asked the same question. Nick's the new man of the house. The mob decided to hit him as a warning to try to get you to back off."

"Back off from what? What did I do?"

"Sam, you've been mixed up in some heavy duty stuff since the Rosie Stitsill cash. When you gave me that money for the boys two years ago, I did some research. You were in over your head with that woman. Her husband, that Jon Stitsill character, had connections to the mob and God only knows who else. Once you get in the mob's way, it's hard to get out, sometimes impossible."

I looked at him, disbelieving.

"I notice things, Sam. I'm a lawyer, and I work with the cops every day. I don't know all you did or how deep in you were, but I know that you got the Macchione's attention. They don't like attention.

"Count your lucky stars that Marty and the Macchione brothers are done in this town. There is no chance they will risk anything more, especially now that Vincent is dead and Tony is behind bars. They've been pulling the strings in this city for far too long. They are done."

I bid Stewart good day and stood on the curb, fighting to remain upright. Marty. So close I had never suspected. So close I couldn't believe it.

Once I summoned the strength to walk across the street, I took in my home—its tulip and cherry trees, the squirrels skittering up their bark, my wraparound porch, the sunlight streaming through the leaves. For now, I wouldn't think about the horror Marty wreaked on my family. For now, I would hide in the safety of McGrath's arms. I walked inside, climbed the stairs and crawled into bed with him.

We had a lot of catching up to do.

CPSIA information can be obtained at www.ICGtesting.com
Printed in the USA
LVOW11s1326030214

372093LV00001B/1/P